ENIGMA

ALSO BY TONYA KUPER

ANOMALY

ENIGMA

TONYA KUPER

Entangled Publishing, LLC
2614 South Timberline Road
Suite 109
Fort Collins, CO 80525

Entangled Teen is an imprint of Entangled Publishing, LLC.

Visit our website at www.entangledpublishing.com.

Edited by Kate Brauning
Cover design by Amber Shah and
L.J. Anderson Mayhem Cover Creations
Interior design by Toni Kerr

ISBN 978-1-63375-005-0
Ebook ISBN 978-1-63375-006-7

Manufactured in the United States of America

First Edition July 2017

10 9 8 7 6 5 4 3 2 1

For Fletcher and Sullivan, my loves,
&
Mom

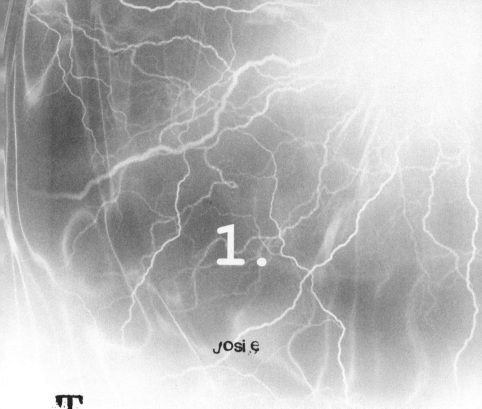

1.

JOSIE

Three days ago, I killed someone. Every time I close my eyes, I see his body convulse as the bolt of lightning I Pushed struck his body. I still see Santos's face contorted in pain before he sinks under the surface of the water.

I opened my eyes after brushing my hair and swept my toiletries off the faux-marble counter into my backpack. Stepping out of the bathroom, I scanned the rest of the room for my belongings. My blue bra lay on the floor where I'd dropped it the night before, next to the paisley bedding. It had been beyond embarrassing shimmying that thing off under my shirt when I was right next to my hottie bedmate.

I plopped my backpack on the bed and grabbed my bra. It was still dangling from my hand when the door leading to the parking lot swung open and Reid smiled at me from the threshold. Perfect. Of course he walked in at this exact moment.

My face flushed with heat. I scrambled to stuff my garment into my bag, but the clasp hooked on one of my bracelets. Trying to work the clasp off my bracelet took way more effort and time than it should have. The stupid thing was stuck. I peeked up to Reid to see if he was still looking at me. Wrinkles formed at the corners of his eyes as he coughed into his hand. He looked over his shoulder as he pretended to hack up a lung to camouflage a laugh.

My cheeks had to be as bright as a red shirt from *Star Trek*, like the red of imminent death.

Sharing the motel room with Reid, my trainer, was convenient and safer. But him being my kind-of-sort-of-boyfriend also meant I was hyperaware of personal stuff, like how much time I spent showering or Reid catching me staring at him constantly. I mean, we shared a bed and were definitely into each other, but he'd never seen my bra before—on or off.

He'd now witnessed me wrestle with my undergarment—and lose. Which was both slightly embarrassing as his trainee and absolutely mortifying as his kind-of-girlfriend.

Reid looked at me, his brows pulling up in sympathy. He crossed the tiny motel room in three strides and stopped beside me. His warm hand touched my wrist as he studied the clasp and he gently unhooked it from my bracelet. He caught my lacy bra before it fell to the bed.

Reid Wentworth was touching my bra, and my boobs weren't even in it. What were the odds of that?

He'd worked my bra better than I had. How had he gotten his bra-handling knowledge? The thought made me break into a full-body sweat.

Reid turned to face me. "I just turned in the room key. Cohen, my contact from the Hub, called while you were in the shower. The Hub gave us the green light to a safe house outside Flagstaff. We gotta pack ASAP and get on the road. They want us there before nightfall."

I sat on the bed. "I'll be ready in three minutes. I think I'll miss this room, though." We'd only spent one night, but something about it felt more secure than our two previous stops.

My bra was still in his hands. I yanked it from him. "Thank you."

"I'll help you with your bra anytime. Just say the word." He winked.

I wanted to hide.

"Wait." He pulled his duffle to the bed. "You'll miss the mustiness of a seventies motel in need of a major facelift?"

With the bra safely tucked away, I bent to lace up my boots. "I know, it's weird, but I like this place."

He walked into the bathroom and came out with his toiletries. "You like the wood paneling, the shaggy Muppet carpet, and an air conditioner that's louder than my bike?"

I peeked toward the rattling air unit. Despite the jolting noise, the curtains floated gracefully above the machine like paisley ghosts.

The room seemed more hidden than the other places

we'd stayed, nestled in the woods somewhere in New Mexico. We drove rural highways instead of interstates all the way from Florida to stay under the radar, but I still felt exposed, afraid someone would see us. Now the mountains and trees gave me a sense of coverage, of safety.

I tied up my other boot. "Yeah, it's old, but I like it."

Hiding, tucked away in a dark room, I could almost pretend I hadn't murdered another human being. Being around people reminded me I was dangerous, that I could be an incomprehensible monster. Maybe I was keeping others safe if I was hidden.

A loud, deep buzz sounded, drilling into the recent memory of gunfire and weapons, of people dying. My heart paused and I dropped to the floor, kneeling behind the bed.

Reid strode to the bedside table where his phone buzzed, but his wide eyes watched me, worry etched on his face.

Duh. Way to jump to conclusions. *Chill out, Josie.* I forced myself to stand.

The phone buzzed again, vibrating against the wood and reverberating in my bones. I blinked and jerked, an involuntary flinch.

It's just his phone. Get a grip.

But a buzz meant someone was contacting Reid, contacting us. Any communication was bad news at this point.

Reid stepped to me hesitantly, as if he were approaching a skittish stray dog. Understanding flashed across his face. "That will probably happen for a while. But it will get better." He touched my hand for a moment, but it was enough to remind me that we were safe. For now. I relaxed my posture as I exhaled.

At my side, he positioned the phone so we could both read the screen.

I stared at the contact information, a line of pound signs. The meaning of the symbols finally registered. The number was restricted and blocked. I read the first line of the message.

This is Meg.

My body was numb. I couldn't feel my fingers or toes. They didn't exist—or if they did, I couldn't control them. I reread the three words.

My mom. I wasn't sure I wanted to read on. Not just because I didn't want bad news, but I didn't want bad news that had anything to do with my family.

Reid bumped his shoulder to mine. "I didn't think we'd hear from your mother this soon after her last message." His voice was quiet.

It had been three days since I'd seen her face on her video message. Three days ago seemed like forever, yet it didn't.

The phone buzzed again, making me jump, waking my body from a fear-induced paralysis.

Eli and I are redirecting to the Hub. 3 Founders need to be present to make executive decisions for the entirety of the Resistance. If the need arises, I have to be present. We should be there tomorrow. The Council is unaware there is a mole within the Hub. Use caution.

Hearing from my family made my heart burst with

sweet relief because it was confirmation they were still alive and well. But fear squashed the celebration, turning my blood to cement.

I needed a minute to think. I couldn't let my family go to the Hub with no way to protect themselves. I shoved the phone out of my line of sight, toward Reid. Instead of moving, he caught my hand and whisked me around to face him. "Josie, I know that look." He let my hand fall. "If I take you to the Hub instead of the safe house, not only will I be disobeying direct orders, but it could get both of us, and possibly others, killed. You'd be giving the mole what he wants—you."

He was right. The mole wanted *me*. And the best way to get to me was through what I cared about most. My family.

I took a step away from Reid, and the back of my legs hit the bed. I sank down onto the mattress.

My mouth opened, but I couldn't put two words together. My thoughts jumped from the mole, to my family, to the Consortium.

Reid stepped in front of me, his sober expression replaced with brows arched in concern. "Josie, I understand how you must be feeling—more than you know. But I'm supposed to keep you safe."

I shoved myself off the bed. My knees buckled immediately and I rocked onto my heels, falling back to the mattress. Frustration clamped down on my emotions and I was ready scream. I couldn't look at Reid, but I held a palm up as I stared at the phone still in his hand.

He gave me his phone, the text message already pulled

up on the screen. Then he sat next to me, making the bed dip under his weight. I read the message again.

What were my choices? If I went to the Hub, the biggest community of the Resistance, I'd be trapping myself with someone who wanted me dead. If I went into hiding with Reid, I'd still be hunted by the Consortium, plus separated from my family. Neither option was a vacation.

The muscles in Reid's jaw flexed as his gaze traveled over my face. "I know your family means everything to you. Eli shouldn't have to be involved in this."

That was the part I couldn't take. I let my head drop into my hands, slumping between my knees. The smell of bleach from the linens was almost comforting.

I couldn't wrap my head around the fact that Eli, my nine-year-old brother—the only sibling I had left, one of the people I cared about most in this world—would be staying in the same compound as the mole, as the person who helped Santos try to kill me. Swallowing the ache in my throat and the sting in my sinuses, I willed away my tears.

"Josie." There was a desperation in Reid's voice.

I slowly sat upright and lifted my eyes to meet Reid's.

Reid looked toward the window. "The Consortium wants all Anomalies dead because we're too dangerous. Since you're on your way to being the most powerful Anomaly on the planet, you aren't just the target—you are the freaking bulls-eye."

I wasn't what mattered. Eli would be in danger. I was the only one who could protect him. I was the only one who could protect a lot of people.

My family seemed to be under attack. My older brother had died after allegedly being contacted by the Consortium, my dad was supposedly undercover at Science Industries in L.A., the Consortium's headquarters, assassins had attempted to kill me, and my mother had taken drastic measures to keep her family safe for years. Being two of the Founders of the Resistance, in direct opposition to Schrodinger's Consortium, my parents were automatically on a kill list. Us two older kids were, too. Eli wouldn't be exempted. Logically, I had every reason to fear for my little brother's life. The cute dude wouldn't even develop Oculi abilities for over seven years, but that wouldn't stop the Consortium from taking him out. Santos's infiltration and betrayal was proof that the Consortium saw my family as a threat and would take whatever steps needed to eliminate us.

Reid stood and crossed the small room to shut off the air unit. A whole new world of muted sounds came to life. A mourning dove cooed nearby, two housekeepers spoke in hushed tones outside as they pushed a cleaning cart on the cracked sidewalk, and a truck rumbled in the distance. There were spaces in the new quiet, spaces with virtually no sound but plenty of room for thought.

If it was important to the Consortium to destroy my family, we couldn't discount any action or effort when it came to them. Right now, plans involving my family were being changed. If they were at the Hub, it was reasonable to assume I would want to be with them. Someone could be using my mom and brother as decoys, as a way to me. My family was bait. Despite the tranquility of our little hiding place, fury simmered in my stomach.

I shoved off the bed again and stepped to Reid's side, making him look at me. His eyes fluttered shut. "I wish I could just take you away from all this." His dark lashes fanned upward as he opened his eyes. "But this is your decision."

His compassion for me meant more than I would be able to convey to him. If this were a normal life and we were normal people, his care for me would've been all I needed. But our world was anything but normal. My safety didn't matter, no matter how much he cared about me. My priority was keeping my family and others safe. If that put me in harm's way, so be it. "You and I are more powerful than the mole and we'll out number him. Statistics are in our favor. And he doesn't get to use my family as bait."

Reid shook his head and something flickered in his eyes. He tugged me against him, my chest colliding against his. My fingers dug into him, pulling him closer.

Terror trickled through my nervous system, seeping through every inch of me, infusing my body. "I need to go to the Hub," I whispered. It wasn't a want, it was a need. I needed to keep my family safe. And in doing that, I'd be facing my own mortality. But what scared me more was facing their mortality, Eli's mortality. I'd already lost one brother.

Standing in front of the lone motel room window, our bodies bathed in rays of morning sunshine, to anyone watching, we would have looked like we were glowing from within, like superheroes. But superheroes wouldn't let fear cripple them like this.

Reid let his forehead rest against mine and closed his eyes. "I don't like this idea for a lot of reasons. But I know that's selfish." Blue eyes stared into mine. A sadness masked his face that I didn't understand.

"Sorry," I whispered.

He pressed his lips into a tight line. "Let's go." He squeezed me then turned to finish packing.

"How are we going to identify the mole?"

He zipped his duffle bag. "I have no idea, Josie."

I plucked my phone from the bedside table, the varnish of the dark wood worn along the edges. His Adam's apple bobbed as he swallowed. "You need to know something. *We* have to be different in the Hub." He shook his head. "We can't, uh," his voice scratched. "We can't do this in *there*."

"What?" I let my gaze drop to the ground.

"Josie." I couldn't look at him until I was sure the sting in my eyes had dissipated. "Josie, look at me."

That was my luck. My first boyfriend ever broke up with me on my birthday, then my long-time crush ended anything between us before we even had a chance. Two guys ditching me in under two weeks. That had to be some kind of record. For losers.

The shabby motel floor creaked under our feet as Reid dropped his bag, stepped in front of me. "We have to play by the rules in the Hub, and I'm someone who trains others to *follow* the rules. One of the rules? No trainer-trainee relationships. A romantic relationship between trainers and trainees clouds the trainer's judgment. So we can't do this." He motioned between us.

Understanding why didn't make the rejection any less painful.

Reid dipped his head, his dark hair falling forward, leaving an inch between our noses. "Make no mistake, I love what we have." The deep line between his brows reappeared. "But going into the Hub means putting the mission before us. And I'm all for it. We don't want anyone, including the mole, to know how we feel about each other. It could be used against us. Also, if the right people found out, there would be consequences. I would be stripped of my trainer privileges and thrown out of the Hub, and you would be thrown out, as well. At this point, we need to be in the Hub and take advantage of my position if we want to catch the mole and figure out what is going on. We can't be anything more than friends for now. No one will report us outside the Hub, but inside? In front of the Council? That's a different story. At least until the Council deems you no longer a trainee, which is unlikely—at least for a while. If we continue on to Flagstaff, we won't have to hide our relationship."

We'd have to give up what we'd just gained. I understood the rule, the trainer couldn't have his judgment compromised by getting involved with a trainee. This wasn't a typical teenage crush, though. What we had wasn't just a two-week whirlwind romance; this was a lifetime of growing together. I'd known him for as long as I could remember. He was my older brother's best friend.

I couldn't move. I'd lost my family, my friends, my home. I'd naively thought maybe I could have the one guy who understood what I'd lost and understood me.

A weird pressure bloomed in my chest, but I had to ignore it. I had to move and focus before tears fell and I became a puddle on the floor. Besides, we needed to get on the road.

My feet didn't want to budge, I didn't want to make this choice. But I had to. I backed away from Reid. "Come on." Stepping to the bed, I flung my backpack over my shoulder. "We have to catch a mole. Before he kills my family. Or me."

Reid snagged his duffle, his face drawn in worry, and opened the heavy door, squinting into the bright morning light. Neither of us spoke as we secured our bags and our helmets, and I climbed on the bike behind Reid. I forced myself to move as though nothing was different, touching Reid when I had to without reservation. But everything was different.

Reid turned the key, revved the throttle, and the engine roared to life under us. Turning his head over his shoulder, his pale irises met mine. "Last chance. Left to Flagstaff or right to the Hub?"

My chest felt restricted, like I was wearing what I imagined a corset would feel like, and I couldn't pull in a full breath. Left to be with Reid, but not my family. Right to protect my family, sacrificing a romantic relationship with Reid. The invisible corset wrenched tighter. "Right." I gripped his waist, anticipating the turn.

He didn't reply, but he moved his hand on top of mine for a second to squeeze it. Bits of asphalt spat away from the tires as we headed north toward the Hub in the Rockies. The wind whipped through my hair, a flame of red twisting behind me from under my helmet.

In *Star Wars* terms, I was Luke Skywalker and the Consortium was my own version of the Empire who wanted to wipe out all Jedi. We were off to join the Rebels—the Resistance in the Hub.

The white line on the road trailed alongside the motorcycle, as if it were holding our hands, guiding us. There was something comforting about that white line. Even if it had to break, it came back. That's what Reid had been for me the last couple of weeks—my anchor.

I tightened my hold around Reid's waist, pressing my body against his back. The warmth of his leather jacket on my stomach combated the cool breeze that had picked up the higher we climbed into the mountains as our journey stretched late into the day.

An hour ago, he'd said we'd arrive at the Hub soon. I hoped for my numb butt's sake it was sooner rather than later. Despite the peacefulness in watching the highway disappear in the mirror, the growl and *whoosh* of each semi passing us in the opposite direction made me flinch. With each flinch, I was taken back to the moment I Pushed the lightning that killed Santos. My mind was stuck, replaying the image over and over. The white light had temporarily blinded me as it streaked down the oil-slicked sky to Santos. His body had convulsed, his face contorted in horror.

No matter what I had done the last few days, how often Reid had made me laugh, or how much we'd kissed late at night, guilt and shame had weaseled into my thoughts. The guilt-shame of taking Santos's life wasn't letting up. In fact, it was getting worse.

We rounded a bend in the road and my chest twisted as if someone were ringing me out like a wet towel. My left lung ached like nothing I'd felt before. Was it my lung, though? Or was it my heart?

Was this what it was like as Santos drowned? Had his lungs hurt and was his heart on the verge of explosion? Another picture of Santos coming after me on the beach, a sick and menacing smile on his lips, flickered in my mind.

Another eighteen-wheeler passed and the lightning flashed in my mind again. When the face came into focus, though, it wasn't Santos—it was Eli.

Fear seized me, and I beat both hands on Reid. That's when I noticed my hands were shaking, and my heart rate matched the rhythm of the shaking, fast and sporadic. Frantic.

"Josie?" he yelled over his shoulder. I couldn't manage words, I just beat my right fist into his back, holding on for dear life with my left arm, hooking it around his middle.

Reid slowed around the next curve then pulled off the road at a scenic lookout. I jumped off the bike before it came to a complete stop, flinging my helmet off of my head. The gravel crunched under my boots as I ran to the edge of the lookout. Leaning over the railing, bracing myself on my forearms, I hung my head as I concentrated on deep inhales and slow exhales.

Reid's feet crushed the gravel as he sprinted to me. "Josie?" His voice was a higher pitch than I'd heard before, and it cracked at the end of my name.

His warm hand landed gently on my back. "What's wrong?"

I shook my head, unable to answer.

Santos was a traitor. Santos tried to kill me. I will not be the reason Eli dies.

A panic attack over Santos and this mole and imagining myself killing my little brother. At least that's what I thought it was. I just needed the feeling to pass.

I held up a finger, inhaling through my nose to the count of four and exhaling through my mouth to slow my breath and pulse. Eli and I often used the breathing during tae kwon do and sometimes after for guided stretching and meditation.

Santos was a traitor. Santos tried to kill me. I will not be the reason Eli dies.

I wiped the perspiration on my forehead away with the back of my hand. Reid didn't force me to speak, but patiently stood behind me, his hand still on my back.

I eventually straightened, letting out a long, pain-free sigh. Finally, I could breathe.

"Santos?" he whispered. I nodded and my heart squeezed again just hearing his name, but not as severely this time.

Reid's hand slowly roamed up to my shoulder. "Are you okay?" That was a loaded question.

No, I wasn't okay, but he already knew that. He'd held me every night when I woke screaming from nightmares. He'd listened as I rehashed the Consortium's attack on the rooftop after the serum hand off to the vice president. He'd watched me grow up with my family and knew they were everything to me.

I touched my fingertips to his hand gripping my

shoulder. I wanted to throw my arms around him and burrow my head into the crevice of his neck, the place I fit perfectly. I wanted to breathe in the smell of him, a clean, musky scent, and feel his warmth around me. Instead, I pulled my fingers away and nodded. "I'll be fine." The words came out quieter than I intended.

I finally raised my eyes to take in our view. A blanket of evergreens covered the mountains surrounding us. "This puts Endor to shame." I wished it were Endor. No one would be hunting me there.

Crickets had begun their evening song, serenading us, filling in the silence. Moving forward, I leaned against the aluminum guard rail, the metal cool on my upper thighs through my jeans. I kicked a spray of gravel, rocks assaulting plants on the way down the side of the mountain into the gorge.

Reid stepped beside me, his presence simultaneously calming because he had been my support since this whole mess started weeks ago, yet jarring because he couldn't play the same role anymore. I cleared my throat. "This is beautiful."

His eyes focused on the mountains in front of us. "This is home," he said.

"Welcome home." I guessed this was my home now. Temporarily. Indefinitely. I didn't know.

I stared at the place where the mountaintops kissed the watercolor sky. Pink cotton-candy clouds battled shadows gobbling up the mountains. The sharp smell of pine reminded me of family camping trips—my brother Nick and I racing through the woods and stony creek beds.

The scent made me want to run, faster than I had ever before. Run to Mom and Eli in the Hub and find the mole.

Running to them also meant losing my relationship with Reid. As much as I wanted to get to the Hub for them, part of me didn't. Reid was my older brother's friend who I'd secretly had a thing for since I was little. He was the one person I'd always wanted. How was I just supposed to turn off those feelings?

Reid turned to face me, his hand reaching for mine, but he allowed it to drop before he touched me. He was afraid to get close. He was putting space between us to keep me safe.

I had to let him go. An invisible pain spread through me. I was a piece of glass struck by a hammer. A spiderweb of cracks hid under my skin. I hadn't thought being safe could hurt more than being in danger.

I closed the space between us, his face only inches from mine. His eyes shut for a moment as he sighed. "Josie." The word was drawn out and whispered.

I traced his jawline with my forefinger. I had to get close. I needed it. I needed him. I shifted my weight forward to rise up on my toes, to touch my lips to his, but then I stopped.

I couldn't kiss him when I couldn't have him. I backed away, instantly feeling chilly.

A crease formed between his eyes. "We probably need to get going."

This was it. We were done.

I turned to his motorcycle, but a Jeep had replaced Reid's bike. Two weeks ago that would've freaked me the hell out, but not anymore. Reid had Retracted his bike and Pushed a Jeep. He used his Oculi abilities to manifest the vehicles, to observe reality. I opened the door of the Jeep and slid into the seat, limp and numb, sadness weighing me down. I stared out the windshield, focused on the mountain across the valley, but I wasn't really seeing it. In my peripheral, Reid scooted behind the wheel and sat unmoving for several seconds. He hit the steering wheel with the palm of his hand, making me jump in my seat.

Reid turned toward me, his gaze intense. He swiftly slid his hand behind my neck and pulled me to him.

His lips crashed to mine and pressed my mouth open. The warmth of his hand cupping my face and the grip on my waist, as if I'd disappear, fused me back together, making me whole again. My fingers twisted in his hair, pulling him closer. When his tongue swept over mine, my soul ignited. Reid was the human form of helium, making me weightless, letting me soar. We kissed until we were both breathless.

I let my hands slip down to his chest, his heart thumping against my palms. "Reid," I whispered.

His mouth hovered inches from mine. "*That* is how I feel about you," he said, his breath tickling my lips. "I can't do it. I can't be without you. We're stronger together."

I inhaled deep, thinking maybe I would fly away from the brief high of overwhelming joy. "I need you."

He rested his forehead to mine. "You have me."

He moved the hand on my waist to my jaw, his thumb sweeping across my cheek. "We can be together, but we have to hide it. It has to be only in private."

"Okay."

He glanced down to my lips. "And I can't wait until the next time I can do that."

The mere idea of there being another time he'd kiss me with that kind of intensity heated my cheeks.

Reid sat back in his seat, started the engine, and gave me his flirty half smile I'd grown to adore. "Let's go."

I flipped down the visor and peeked in the mirror. Some tendrils of hair were wavy, some straight, and all of it completely out of control. My hair might as well be Captain Davey Jones's tentacles from the *Pirates of the Caribbean* movies.

With the next blink, I Pushed and a hair band appeared in my palm. I no longer felt sick each time I Pushed or Retracted reality.

Inspecting my hair, I Pushed my hair straight then pulled it into a ponytail. Every Push or Retraction came with a price. Each Oculi had a bank of energy that was limited and every manipulation of reality was an energy withdrawal. When the bank was empty, it was empty. Oculi were encouraged to not waste Pushes and Retractions on little things we could do ourselves.

I, on the other hand, was the daughter of the two scientists who'd taken the amplifying serum. My energy bank, like my older brother's, seemed to work a little differently than other new Anomalies. I seemed to have endless energy. In fact, I had to use my energy, release some by Pushing and Retracting, just to take the edge off. My energy had grown in the last three days even, almost radiating off me at times. I'd only had these abilities for a couple of weeks and I was growing more powerful each day.

"Is what I'm wearing okay?" I asked, checking out my retro Princess Leia tee and holey jeans.

"Yeah. You look…" He glanced at me as he drove and a mischievous grin slid across his lips.

"What?" My nerves were shot and we weren't even to the Hub yet.

He shook his head, smiling to himself. "You're fine."

"Okay. I guess I'll trust you on that." Even though everyone at the Hub would know who I was, I wanted to make a good impression. Everyone in the Hub would have varying expectations of me, since I was the daughter of one of the founding families of the Resistance. Plus, my older brother had an Oculi degradation in the Hub, a rare consequence of observing reality into existence. Our observations traveled through the optic nerve to our brain. Sometimes our observations could randomly fry our nerves, which could lead to degradation of the parietal lobe, cerebrum, and cortex. A possible side effect of this kind of degradation was a psychotic break.

"You can trust me." His eyes locked on mine, this time not accompanied by a smile. "With everything." He turned his attention back to the road, his profile dark against the waning sunset.

I was banking on that trust. I wouldn't be able to do anything without it. "I need to make sure I have this straight. Right now our plan is to figure out a way to expose the mole, possibly with me as the bait." I knew he didn't like that idea, so I ignored his serious side eye and continued. "This guy wants me dead, so he's almost definitely going after my family. He may also try to take the Resistance down from the inside. Aaaand, we don't know if he is working with anyone else inside the Hub, like he was with Santos."

"You got it, babe."

Anger seethed in my stomach as I watched thunderhead clouds billow from behind the mountain peaks. Energy buzzed in my fingers. This mole, this accomplice to my attempted murder, this orchestrator of the deaths of innocent people, didn't know what was coming for him.

2.

Reid

Me without Josie? Yeah, right. I'd had a thing for her since forever.

Josie had done something to me. For almost two years I'd tried to shut off my emotions, but she made me feel. She made me a better person.

I wanted to follow the rules for her own safety, but it was going to hurt us both. Hell, it'd only been since the morning that we'd broken up or whatever, and I was a freaking mess already. I'd played it cool for her, but on the ride north on my bike earlier in the day, I'd fallen apart inside. She'd chosen her family over me, and I got it. I understood. But, damn, it hurt more than I thought was possible.

When we stopped and I saw her face, I knew I couldn't do it. I couldn't be without her.

Hub rules. My rules. I was breaking them all now.

I turned off the highway onto a single-lane dirt path. Goose bumps scurried up my arms, the mountain air growing cooler by the minute. I played with the temperature control as we passed a lone sign on the driver's side. Private Property. Trespassers will be prosecuted.

Josie's head swiveled to read the sign. "Please tell me the next sign will say Xavier's School for Gifted Youngsters."

We both chuckled. I appreciated her sense of humor when things were so tense. Of course she'd reference *X-Men*.

Our bodies jostled as I navigated over bumps and holes. Colonies of newly budded aspen trees stood randomly on the rocky mountainside, like they'd gathered to greet us.

Our drive wasn't necessarily dangerous, but I did need to pay attention in case I needed to Push or Retract. This road was abandoned—or at least the Hub needed it to still appear abandoned, complete with erosion and loose boulders. Precautions were put into place, too, for the rare case in which someone chose to trespass.

Josie watched the path through the windshield of the Jeep, her head swiveling once in a while to check out a tree or something. The last rays of sunlight punched through a break in the clouds, making Josie's strawberry-blond hair seem as if it glowed, fiery and bright.

"Farther on there will be more signs on this path, as well as cameras," I said.

She turned to me in her seat, her eyes wide. I didn't

want her to panic again. That's why I thought I should bring her up to speed on Hub life. Data calmed her down. "There are also cameras inside the compound, for our security. We'll be watched or recorded everywhere. Except in our private quarters, of course."

The corners of her mouth curled up. "That's a relief."

"They'll have eyes on us once we reach the end of the road, where it looks like an old mine. Once we're inside the mine, they'll be able to hear us, too. Most likely we'll be approached by troops. They're kind of our form of security. I'll demand an emergency meeting with top officials to get them started on the search for the mole and let them know you and your family are at risk. There's only one person in the Hub I trust at this point. Cohen. I've known him since we were kids." Though, I thought I knew Santos, too.

She played with the hole in her jeans. "Cohen. Okay." Her gaze drifted back out the window. The wheels in her head were turning. When she was on the quieter side, it usually meant she was thinking.

"So," she said, watching the scenery. "Instead of assuming everyone is innocent until proven guilty, I think we need to go in thinking the opposite. We assume everyone is a mole and we cross their name off the list once we have reason to believe they're not."

I couldn't swallow. I didn't like that part of the plan, and she knew it. No reason to voice that again.

Several minutes went by and Josie still stared out the window.

"What are you thinking about?" I asked.

Her head shook. "It's silly."

With her hair pulled back, I could see the gentle curve of her neck. "I like silly stuff."

She played with her ponytail. Fidgeting. She tended to do that when she was nervous or worried. "I, uh—I wish I could talk to Hannah. Between moving so often and being homeschooled, she was my first real friend outside my brothers. And there's something special about her. Like, we're so different, but she got me, you know?"

Yeah, I knew.

Josie's gaze fell to her lap.

I pulled her hand into mine. "Hey. That's not silly. You'll see her again, okay?" She wouldn't make eye contact with me. I wasn't sure if holding her hand would help. I had to comfort her somehow, though. I squeezed her hand. "I will do everything I can to help you see her again."

Maybe Cohen could hook me up with a secure line, but I'd have to contact Hannah and divulge some info. Otherwise, she'd think something bad had happened to Josie. Another thing to think about.

Her sad eyes met my gaze and she threaded her fingers through mine. "Thank you." Her line of sight drifted back to the windshield, the pine trees growing thicker as we climbed higher. The pine scent battled the new car smell with the windows open.

My mind wandered to my own friend, Santos. Santos— one of the few people I talked to in the last year and a half, my Resistance training partner I would've died for— who'd ended up a Consortium agent.

Anger boiled in my gut. He'd tried to kill Josie for the Consortium. I'd never be able to forgive myself for not seeing who he truly was. And I wasn't sure I could trust myself, either. Self-doubt burrowed through my gut like a parasite. If I'd screwed up that badly before, how could I expect to help Josie stay safe now?

I let off the gas and steered around a hole that could've sent us flying. Accelerating again, the engine shifted as we climbed the steep grade.

I wanted to know what had driven Santos to work with the Consortium. Power or glory was all I'd come up with over the last several days. I could see why the Consortium wanted the enhancement serum—it increased all Oculi powers. It would make anyone injected with it more powerful, and it would make an Anomaly nearly invincible. The serum was dangerous. In my opinion, it was so dangerous it shouldn't have existed in the first place. If Santos failed to get the serum, he'd been instructed to take Josie back to the Consortium or kill her. But what had he been promised in return? The only thing that made sense was power, maybe a leadership role or something. No matter what his motivation was, he'd been willing to die for it.

As I braked for a turn in the primitive road, Josie braced herself against the door and shoved one of her feet against the dash. Since leaving Florida, Josie had woken at night, screaming Santos's name. She hadn't meant to kill him—it was self-defense. I hadn't made her talk about it yet, but she'd need to at some point. No one could be the same after taking someone's life. I certainly hadn't been, anyway.

Josie concentrated on the path, gripping the door

handle. One leg was bent to prop a black boot against the dash, ripped jeans exposing her knee. Her pale skin looked so soft and fragile compared to the leather and denim.

I refocused on the dry dirt road. At least it wasn't raining. Rogue boulders dotted the road to further deter possible trespassers. As we ascended, the size of the boulders increased, but then the tree coverage around us was so thick it didn't allow the twilight sky to peek through. I knew we were close. Close to home. Close to one of the only people I had left to trust. Cohen.

Cohen had been my friend since we were kids when he came to live with his uncle in the Hub after his mom passed away. Being the same age, I helped him adjust to Hub life and we became fast friends. Years later, my own mother died. Shortly after my mom passed away, I killed my friend Nick, Josie's brother. My dad was still grieving the loss of my mom. It wasn't that Dad wasn't there for me or didn't care, but he was going through his own shit. If it weren't for Coe, I wouldn't have made it through the darkest time in my life. Cohen was the one who suggested I get out of the Hub and train on the road.

Cohen was one of the only people I'd kept in contact with since being on the road. He was going to get a kick out of Josie. He knew how I felt about her from years before. He wouldn't say anything to anyone, though. We considered each other family.

And now I was basically taking a girl home to meet the fam. Not that I'd ever done that before. I'd only had a few brief relationships on the road since I'd left the Hub to train around the country. If I could even call those relationships. I mean, they were Planck girls; I had to lie about everything. But taking Josie home, someone special, where someone might try to kill her or her family? Yeah, that was a whole other level of anxiety. I probably didn't have the typical worries about taking a girl home.

The last steep ridge came into view. Accelerating against the grade, the motor revved under us.

I slowed the Jeep once we reached the DEAD END sign. From this point on we'd be continually watched. From an aerial view, the vegetation completely camouflaged the entrance in the mountainside. The overgrown trail and rusted mining equipment weren't visible from the closest road, miles away, either.

Josie's brows arched as the Jeep crawled toward the mining tunnel. The headlights illuminated multiple signs.

TRESPASSERS WILL BE PERSECUTED.

UNSAFE MINE — STAY OUT, STAY ALIVE.

DANGER.

Concrete framed the entrance, *1893* stamped at the top. Most of the other original stamped lettering had eroded away. Wide, worn boards covered the opening, in front of a wall of massive boulders.

"Let me guess," Josie said. "This is more of the illusion to keep Plancks out. But this is where we go in."

Long ago some smart-ass Oculi named ordinary humans after Max Planck, a famous Nobel Prize–winning theoretical physicist, who came up with Planck's Constant, which was used in physics equations. By definition, the constant was unchanging; it was boring.

Jumping out of the vehicle, I took two steps to a rusty

control panel. With half of the sky now dark, the bugs sang at full volume. I yanked the control box open and touched the top right screw in the back panel. A shiny metallic pad came toward me for a retina scan. I moved my head forward, and the laser passed in front of my eyeball. Two seconds later, the green light flashed. I typed in my passcode, closed the cabinet door, and climbed back into the Jeep.

Now I'd be able to Retract the wall of boulders and boards at the entrance without being escorted off the grounds by a Ranger—Resistance in disguise—who would have been "checking on the site due to recent vandalism."

I Retracted, blinked, and the entrance was clear. The boulders, the wood, gone. Easing the gas pedal down, I pulled the Jeep into the black of the tunnel.

If a Planck somehow made it into the shaft entrance, this would be as far as they would get. Hub troops would've been escorting Plancks away by now.

The front tires hit the rails of the old mining track system. I Pushed boulders back in place, blocking the entrance behind us. The rock wall in front of us slid sideways in one solid mass. "Time to get out."

I shut off the motor but kept the headlights on. Leaning forward, I saw through the windshield two red dots near the ceiling. Cameras. Josie inhaled and reached for her door handle.

"Hey."

She twisted toward me, startled and stiff.

"We'll get help finding the mole. We got this."

She faked a smile and nodded. I hadn't said it just for her.

We walked to the front of the car. It smelled like an old, dank basement. Dust and mildew. Josie stared at the rusty, cage-like elevator. A hanging light blinked on, and the wall slid closed behind us.

I motioned to Josie to follow me to the elevator. The metal door moaned as I pulled it open. A dim, fluorescent light flickered on and off inside the elevator.

Josie's head swiveled to me. "Total horror movie vibe. This is the part where I usually yell at the people not to take the elevator."

"It's safe. I promise. Security already knows we're this far because of hidden cameras and alarms."

"Okay. But if I die in this elevator, it's your fault and I'm *so* haunting you."

I smiled and urged her forward, my hand on her back. It wasn't an affectionate touch because I knew cameras were already on us, recording our every move.

I dropped my hand before it looked suspect. Josie faced me, hesitancy in her eyes. I lowered my mouth to her ear. "You are smarter and stronger than anyone in here," I whispered. "You have nothing to fear. I'm always right behind you. You are not alone. Okay?" If we weren't being watched, I would've kissed her. Not that she needed a kiss to reassure her, just because I wanted to. Maybe I needed it.

The elevator bell shrilled. She whirled forward wearing a stoic mask, but intensity burned in her eyes. Steel gears grated and the cable screeched out, echoing wails like someone screaming, warning us. We moved downward. Once we were at about twelve feet under the surface, the iron oxide–stained rock in front of us transitioned to smooth concrete. The elevator stopped when we came to the shiny metal door at the Hub level.

The door slid into the wall and the elevator door groaned open, creating a definite line between the dimly lit elevator and the dark hallway. With every breath of the cool, damp air in the mine shaft, fear stung my lungs—fear for Josie's life.

Josie took one step out of the elevator, into the darkness, her hands balling and flexing at her sides. Her one step cracked through the fear that had controlled me the last thirty seconds. I would give whatever it took to keep her alive and safe.

3.

A blank concrete wall greeted us. Reid stepped into the empty, tomb-like hall past me and I followed. Surprisingly, it didn't smell like a basement; the light lemon scent reminded me of a clean kitchen.

Goose bumps skittered down my arms, but I wasn't sure if it was from being in a place Indiana Jones would explore, or the cool air.

On my right side was a dead end, so the only way to go was to the left, where a dim light beckoned.

Two dark figures rounded the corner in front of the light, casting long shadows. By the shape of their bodies, one was male and the other female. My feet stopped without permission.

Reid paused. "They're Hub troopers. Stay next to me."

What he didn't say was that one of them could be the

mole. *Stay next to me* was his subtle reminder.

I didn't care if they were freaking Big Bird and the Cookie Monster. It was dark and I didn't know them, therefore I didn't trust them. I reached for his hand, but stopped myself before our skin touched. Not showing my affection wasn't going to be easy, and I wasn't even what I'd consider a "touchy" person. I'd become used to his closeness, though, showing we were a united front.

Reid's hands hung loose at his sides and his stance was wide. He was ready for anything.

"Reid Wentworth," one of the troopers barked, flashing a light in Reid's face. He didn't flinch away, though, only squinted. Good sign. If the light had been a weapon, Reid would've kicked their asses. And I would've, too.

Reid held up a hand to the uniformed dude and glanced over his shoulder to me. "They're confirming who we are. This is protocol." He knew how my mind worked. Information always helped me cope.

Reid turned back to the troopers. "This is Josie Harper, daughter of the Harper family, Resistance founders. We have an E3. An emergency meeting needs to be called immediately."

"Please follow us to the holding rooms," the female trooper said.

Reid nodded to me and we fell in behind the troopers, our steps echoing through the tunnel. "This is policy," he said over his shoulder. "We'll go into a room for a brief search, making sure you're cleared for entrance into the Hub." His head swiveled forward. "Can one of your troopers please radio in the E3 to the Eye in the Sky? Now?"

"I will once we get you to your rooms," the male trooper said.

Rooms. Plural. Separate rooms. Meaning alone.

Come into this dark dungeon where we'll separate you from your eye candy and examine you. Yeah, like that didn't sound like a horror flick.

Reid stopped and I stumbled into his back.

"Hold up." Reid's voice reverberated through the hallway. "No. Josie will not be left alone. I will accompany her, and you will communicate an E3."

The trooper squared his shoulders, the dim light behind him. "Mr. Wentworth, that is not protocol. I don't have the authority to override that—"

Reid raised his chin, stepping closer to the trooper. "I. Do. Make the call and take us to the same holding room."

Neither trooper moved.

"Now." Reid's voice gained strength, the pitch low and smooth.

Reid approached the troopers, but they turned and quickly marched ahead to keep the lead. The man pulled a phone out of his pocket then held the door open as we tailed the woman into a square concrete room with flickering fluorescent lighting. I could finally see our greeters better. They wore matching blue button-down shirts and blue cargo pants, along with a firearm on their belts. The young woman's black hair was pulled back in a tight bun.

Each wall of the small room housed a metal door. The door behind us banged shut, making me jump. The guy trooper moved to the door on the left wall, and the girl moved to one on the right.

She tipped her head to the other trooper. "He'll call in the E3. This way, Mr. Wentworth and Ms. Harper." The girl, maybe a few years older than myself, opened the door, waiting for us to enter. Anxiety danced under my skin.

Reid watched my face. "Stay behind me." I was on his heels. A red light caught my attention, and a tiny camera in the corner of the room followed my movements.

I stepped through the threshold onto white tile, and noticed two other doors on two of the four white walls. A white table and two clear chairs sat in the middle of the room. Sterile like Magneto's prison cell.

"Your exam will start in a moment." The girl's voice had as much warmth as the room.

She disappeared through one of the other doors and returned immediately, pushing a cart. Empty vials, syringes, cotton, and alcohol wipes filled a plastic organizer. "I need to get a small blood sample."

"I know a blood draw and health exam are policy for new Oculi coming to the Hub." Reid approached the cart. "But this can't be done right now." He paused, pivoting to look at one of the cameras perched in the corner of the room. "Do the body search and get us to that meeting."

Body search?

The door to the unknown room swung open and I jolted. A middle-aged man in a white coat moseyed to the cart. Script letters embroidered the left side of the coat: Doc.

"Mr. Wentworth," he said with a grin, pulling on latex gloves. His salt-and-pepper hair swept over his forehead.

"Good to see you, Reid." The medical trooper stood behind him, hands behind her back.

The corners of Reid's mouth curled slightly, his stance still as rigid as when we stepped out of the elevator. "Doc."

The physician stopped a couple of feet in front of me. "I'm the lead doctor here in the Hub. Everyone just calls me Doc. We need blood." He glanced to Reid. "Sorry. We have to know if she or you are carrying anything contagious. You know this is always done." Turning back to me, he gave me a sympathetic smile. "This is a small community. A major sickness could have a devastating effect on us. We're also going to do a body search for anything harmful. Reid, you can wait on the other side of that door."

I twisted to Reid, my heart suddenly in my throat.

"No can do, Doc." Reid didn't move. "Josie's in danger, which is why I called the E3. I'm not leaving her."

"He stays." It came out loud and shaky.

The doctor shrugged.

A buzz sounded from the corner and a curtain dropped from the ceiling. "Please remove all clothing, besides your underwear, and put the gown on with the opening facing the back."

I looked to Reid. I didn't want to leave him, even for a minute while behind that curtain. Instead of using it, I simultaneously Retracted my clothes and Pushed a hospital robe on my body.

Doc let out a long sigh. "That's one way to do it." The trooper handed him the wand and he slowly maneuvered it around my head, close to my skin. When he pulled my hands away from my body to examine the rest of me, I peeked to Reid. He focused on the doctor but his gaze flickered to me. As soon as our eyes met, he looked back to the doctor and shifted his stance. His hand swept across his jaw, as he tried to avoid looking at my body. If I wasn't mistaken, Reid was slightly uncomfortable.

Doc stood. "Done. You may get dressed, then I'll draw some blood."

I Pushed my clothes on and Retracted the gown. Moving the cart to my side, the doctor let Reid examine the needle and equipment he was using, pulled a stool out from the bottom of the car, gestured for me to sit, then he took three vials of blood. It was like any other time I'd had a blood draw. But it wasn't, really. A killer, or at least an accomplice, was in here with me. They could have access to my blood, to my personal records. Tingles up the back of my neck made me shiver.

Reid examined another set of fresh equipment which would be used on him. He sat on the stool, and Doc tied the rubber band around his bicep then inserted the needle. Three vials of blood like mine.

When it was over, Doc smiled. "Reid, you'll be asked a few questions momentarily. Welcome, Josie. If you need anything, please know you can come to me." The doctor was warm and gentle, in complete contrast to the rest of this place. Doc and the trooper left the room and a different woman marched in, her shoes clicking on the tile.

The woman stepped to one side of the table. "Mr. Wentworth. Nice to have you back in the Hub. I'm from the Council's office. I'm sure you are aware that you have disobeyed orders in the field and now back on Hub grounds."

"I've done so with good reason." Reid walked to the table, positioning himself directly across from whoever this official was. "This is Josie Harper, daughter of Meg Harper, one of the founding families of the Resistance. There is a mole in the Hub that worked as an accomplice to my former partner, Santos. That mole helped Santos try to kill Josie. The mole wants her dead."

The blond woman held her palm up. "This will have to be written in your file, going on your permanent record."

"Miss, if you'd—"

"Leadership may decide consequences are in order." She talked over him and the muscle in Reid's jaw flexed.

Wait. Consequences for Reid? I don't think so.

"Fine!" He threw a hand up. "I don't care if I face repercussions. The entire Hub is at stake." He swung his hand toward me. "Josie is in danger. The *daughter of a founder* is in danger. Possibly the most powerful Oculi in history is in danger."

The official tipped her head to one side, and her finger rapped on the back of the chair.

"We don't know what the mole wants with her. If they'd prefer her dead or if they'd take out the entire Hub to kidnap her. But I don't think that's something we need to chance, do you?" Reid stared directly at the camera in the corner. "The spy who informed and instructed Santos is here," he yelled. "Inside the Hub."

Reid had already been warned about consequences and he was yelling—on my behalf. I didn't want him to suffer because of me, but at the same time, a profound gratitude warmed my insides.

The lady pressed an ear piece I hadn't noticed before. She was being prompted by the people behind the camera, most likely the Council. She glanced to the camera and gave one nod.

She began to leave, pausing in the doorway. "Mr. Wentworth, someone needs to speak to you before the meeting."

Reid stepped away from the table, to me. Who would want to talk to him before an emergency meeting? An uneasiness caterpillared up my neck.

I needed to say something, but all I wanted to do was hug him. "Thank you for trying to protect me. I don't want you to get in trouble becau—"

The door swung open, the latch echoing through the room.

Reid's father stood tall in the threshold.

I couldn't manage a complete thought. My mind was confused by what I saw.

I peered to Reid, his face pale and eyes wide.

Reid's look of confusion and surprise jump-started my brain again. This person could be trying to shock us and throw us off. He could pull a gun.

It was suddenly hot in the room and Reid was too far away from me. A couple of steps was too far if this person tried to hurt Reid. I tried to swallow and forced my heavy feet toward Reid. Reid's father would be the perfect disguise for the mole, getting him special clearance and a way to get close to me.

4.

Reid

I couldn't make my body move. I was a statue of myself, unmoving and full of cracks. If someone had shoved me to the floor, I probably would've broken.

Dad's eyes wandered over me. "Cal," he said. The word came out loud and strong, the way I'd always remembered him. He glanced to Josie. "Josie, you've grown up."

I'd thought he was dead. Everyone had thought he was dead.

How did I know if it was really him? This person could be the mole. What a perfect way to get close.

After my mom died, I became suspicious of, well, everyone. And after everything else that had gone down since that day, my paranoia had only grown. Throw in a mole who wanted Josie dead now, and I couldn't take any chances.

He'd just called me Cal, my name until a couple of years ago.

The Consortium had killed my mom about a year before I'd had to kill my best friend, Nick. After I was urged to change my appearance for safety reasons, my new partner, Santos, and I became field trainers, Resistance Oculi who trained new Oculi around the country. The day after I left the Hub on my first mission, my dad went missing. He was never confirmed dead, but if an Oculi was missing for over a year, most assumed death. And the Consortium had already killed my mother—everyone assumed he went down the same way. Dad only knew me as Reid for a short time before he disappeared. But if this man was the mole, well, my new name could be something he didn't know.

"Reid. It's Reid now." My voice was small, like I was ten years old again.

My dad was a talented Oculi who'd helped form the Resistance, and I never thought I'd measure up to the amazing person he was. To many, he was a leader. To me, he was a legend. Tough as nails but a heart of gold. Gentle strength.

He shook his head. "Yes, Reid. I, uh—well."

"I need to know it's really you."

My demand didn't seem to surprise him as he nodded. "Your mom and I took you to Winter Park one weekend when you were four to teach you how to ride a bike. We wanted you to have that experience like every other kid."

He could have heard that from someone.

His brows arched as he placed his hands on his hips.

"Your mom used to get frustrated when we were late to dinner because we were playing basketball in one of the training rooms." He grinned, one side of his mouth pulling up higher than the other.

I loved shooting hoops with Dad. I smiled.

He stepped toward me. "Your mom's favorite flowers were gardenias, and you placed one in her hands the day of her funeral."

This hurt to hear but relief swelled in my chest, because it was true. No one knew that detail about Mom's funeral apart from him and me. This was my dad. He was alive.

He shrugged and approached me with open arms. It wasn't until his hands landed on my back, giving me a couple of hard pats, that I woke up.

I hugged him back, squeezing him to make sure I wasn't hallucinating. "Dad?" I croaked. We'd shared so many joys and sorrows as a family, and he was here, he was real. This was the person who would back me, no questions asked, despite my flaws. My sinuses burned as I fought off tears.

"Missed you, son." His voice cracked slightly on the last word.

My mouth stretched into a grin.

Letting go of me, he motioned for me to follow with a proud smile. He looked the same as he did a couple of years ago, besides a little more silver painting his temples. Tall, dark hair, broad shoulders.

I glanced to Josie. She fidgeted, weaving her fingers through each other, raking her fingertips over the palm of the opposite hand. She was nervous, thinking.

Turning back to Dad, I couldn't contain my question any longer. "Where have you been?"

"I went undercover. To keep everyone safe, mostly you, I couldn't let you know my whereabouts."

He'd willingly left without warning. My chest stung when I sucked in air, the truth that he *left me* pricking holes in my lungs.

"I'm sorry. I didn't want to hurt you." His words rasped out, just above a whisper.

How was I supposed to respond to his apology? Focusing on his eyes, I nodded.

His hand went to his left ear as if he were itching, and I wouldn't have thought anything different, until his thumb and index finger lingered on his earlobe and pinched. He wasn't making calls for a baseball game. My dad had created a few visual codes for our family when I was little. An index finger salute meant *something wasn't right*. This hand gesture was used between my parents, me, and my closest friend in the Hub, Cohen. There were a couple of other hand signals that were only for my parents and me. Brushing a shoulder meant *run*. Luckily we hadn't had to use that signal as often as the others. Pinching an earlobe meant *talk in private*.

It really wasn't a surprise that he'd want more privacy to talk about this. We were father and son and I needed more explanation than what he was giving. But for now, Josie and I had an ally, and that was big. Counting Cohen, we now had four of us.

I wiped under my right eye with my forefinger, indicating to my dad that I saw his sign. The gesture to the eye wasn't always needed or used, but in this instance, I needed him to know that I'd caught his secret message. Out of the corner of my eye, I could see Josie staring at me. She had no idea we were throwing signals. Or maybe she did. She was a smart one.

Clearing my throat, I said, "I know you didn't want to hurt me." We were both acutely aware that every word and action was being recorded by the camera in the corner. It was second nature to alter conversations, saying just enough, in the Hub. One con to living in a secret society stuffed inside a mountain.

He raised his right hand to scratch the left side of his chest, over his heart. It was the code for *trust me*.

Got it, dad. I nonchalantly rubbed my hand over my brow. Again, the eye to let him know I saw his sign. My muscles relaxed more with my next breath.

"Let's talk on our way to the Council meeting." He held the door behind him open, letting Josie pass through the threshold. He patted her on the arm. He'd known her since she was a baby, but they hadn't seen each other since her brother's funeral two years ago. He saluted me with his index finger as I stepped past him through the doorway.

Yep, I agreed. Something wasn't right. I returned the secret salute, anxious to get out of the heavily monitored room.

"Dad, have you been brought up to speed on what's been going on, what happened with the Harpers in Florida?"

Dad stopped and clamped his hand on my shoulder. "I got in a couple of days ago and was briefed on what happened. You trained her in record time to ensure the enhancement serum Meg Harper worked on would be delivered to Vice President Brown. Santos ended up being a double agent, working for the Consortium, and attempted to steal the serum and kill Josie."

He looked past me to Josie. "Sounds like you did a great job, Josie. Your mom should be here soon."

All of Josie's exposed skin, her face and neck, flushed as she shifted her weight to the opposite leg and crossed her arms. "What? She's not here yet?" Her voice was high and strained. "She was supposed to be here by now. Harrison, where is my family? Have you talked to her?" Through her stance, voice, and now the distraught eyes, her anxiety was almost tangible.

Dad moved to the side of the hall. "Not yet." He turned to face both of us. "I called her in because we need another Founder here. The Davises disappeared."

My stomach sank. The Davises were the closest thing I had to grandparents. They helped form the Resistance and lived in the Hub most of the time. They were good people, Oculi with empty energy banks who took care of others. "Disappeared?"

He leaned toward Josie and me. "The day before I returned, they vanished. No trace."

Josie's hand swept up to cover her mouth. "Eli." I barely made out the quiet muffle behind her hand.

Dad leaned an inch closer. "We don't know if they were taken, killed, or what. But with Stella disappearing, Nick dying, and now the Davises missing, and—" He paused, his Adam's apple bobbing in his throat. "And you after your mom. Well, we need to solidify more than ever. That's why I thought it would be best to get the Founders and their families together."

"Stella is missing?" A crease formed between Josie's eyebrows. Stella had visited Josie's family growing up just as I had. When they were younger, they were friends.

I nodded. "Right after Nick died." My guts twisted. I hated saying those words, reminding her, once again, that I killed her brother, my best friend, because he was dangerous. "Dee was devastated. All the Founding families have now been hurt in some capacity."

Dad started walking again. "Meg was the one who told me about a mole in the Hub."

Josie nodded and Dad turned to lead us to the garage.

The hall to the garage was more like a mining tunnel with rough rock walls. Our footfalls echoed in unison on the concrete floor.

We rounded the corner into the expansive open area that held our vehicles and larger equipment. The fleet of black vehicles made three lines behind the Eye in the Sky, our large control tower that overlooked the area. The garage was home to Hub security, which included military and defense equipment and transportation.

Dad walked between Josie and me as we crossed the garage floor to the opposite side. Keeping his sights forward, he cleared his throat. "We'll talk soon," he whispered. "There is more going on than you could possibly imagine. Unfortunately, you and Josie are now a part of it."

Not wanting to show an outward reaction, since anyone

could be watching us, I said, "Got it." Anger simmered deep inside me. Josie didn't deserve to be dragged into the middle of this ridiculous world.

A uniformed trooper I didn't recognize approached us, looking at Dad. "Sir. Max directed me to contact you but you weren't answering your phone. Is there a bomb threat or found weapons included in this E3?"

"No. But we still need all Council and Founder members in the meeting. Double-check to make sure all are present."

The trooper nodded, then led us to the Council's hallway.

I focused on the door ahead that would guide us to the Council's row of offices and meeting rooms. The door the trooper had just run through.

Josie glanced to me, concern dancing in her eyes.

"You'll need to do another retina scan. No biggy." I guided Josie to the scanner on the wall next to a large metal door. "Place your forehead on the rest. Wait for the blinking green light." She stepped to my side in silence. I used the retina scan and Dad followed.

Someone tapped my shoulder from behind. Dee, a dark-blond-haired middle-aged woman. She stood with her arms open and a big smile that made the corners of her eyes wrinkle.

Dee was a founder of the Resistance, and I'd known her for as long as I could remember. She was like an aunt to me, and her daughter, the one who disappeared after Nick's funeral, was like a cousin.

With no words, I leaned down to embrace her. Dee

finally pulled away, releasing me from her death-grip hug, and she paused to study my face. "Look how tall you are now."

I couldn't help but smile. "No offense, but I've been taller than you for years, Dee." She laughed. I had to give my condolences but didn't want to say the wrong thing. "I'm sorry Stella hasn't been found yet."

She pursed her lips together as her head shook quickly. "Thank you."

Dee stepped to the eye scanner, and I held the door open as Dad, Dee, and Josie filed through.

Dee spun around. "Josie?"

A bashful smile slid onto Josie's face.

"I hardly recognized you! Nice to see you, my dear." She patted Josie's shoulder then continued down the hall, leading the way.

Decorative lights every six feet illuminated the hallway and the floor was some kind of polished stone. It smelled different in this wing. Cleaning supplies covered by a sweet-scented air freshener.

Instead of turning into the usual meeting room, where I'd been many times, Dee led us to the end of the hall where two troopers stood guard with rifles in their hands. Josie tightened her ponytail and rubbed her palms on her jeans.

Dad slowed and glanced over his shoulder to Josie and me. "Extra security in a nonstandard room due to this meeting being classified as E3."

We marched into a large room where a couple of handfuls of people waited. Dad and Dee crossed the room to the Council members, who stood near a long table.

Shoving my hands into my pockets, I pivoted to Josie. Her arms crossed in front of her chest and her long legs stood wide. She was on the defense; ready for anything. Smart. Her lips parted while her eyes roamed around the room. She was nervous, scared. Hell, so was I. She was such a strong person, yet in this fleeting moment her vulnerability was almost tangible. I wanted to pull her against me, to comfort her, to help her feel safe. Instead, I simply asked, "Are you okay?"

Josie nodded. "Are you?"

"I'm fine."

A bell rang, cuing the start of the meeting. I guided Josie to the handful of empty chairs facing the Council. The Council members, five total, took their seats at the front of the room, behind a long metal table. Max, Nico, Ming, Shreeya, Jared.

The Council represented the people of the Resistance across The United States. If the Founders of the Resistance were at the Hub, they could also sit with the Council, adding their perspectives and knowledge. The Founders introduced the democratic system specifically so they wouldn't make decisions for all Resistance members.

My father and Dee sat to the side of the Council. Next to them, empty seats where the absent Founders should have been sitting. My stomach dipped. My mom, Josie's parents, the Davises.

Max, the Speaker of the Council, stood. Everything about him was long and angular. "Thank you all for coming to this emergency meeting." Only three other people sat in the "audience" along with me and Josie. They had to hold some importance if they were allowed to sit in on an Emergency 3, a meeting held in a different location than public meetings and including only the highest authorities in the Hub. Thankfully we'd never experienced an Emergency 1, an evacuation, or an Emergency 2, attack from outside forces. Wish I could've said the same about E3's.

"This meeting was called by Reid Wentworth, formerly known as Callum Ross, son of Founders Harrison and Mary Ross. We have several pieces of important news to share, since we have so many of you together in one place, but we'll allow Reid to have the floor first."

I stood and pulled my shoulders back. "Thank you, Max, Council, and Founders. I called for an E3 meeting because we believe a mole resides in the Hub, the same Consortium mole that worked with my partner, Santos, in trying to kill Josie." I hated saying those words. "Santos and the mole also tried to intercept the enhancement serum Josie delivered to Vice President Brown. This mole is a threat to Josie, to her family, who is on their way here now, and to the Resistance as a whole. Josie's family being here, given the attack and her being an Anomaly with exceptional skills, will likely push the traitor to a second, even more desperate attack." In my peripheral vision, I could see Josie watching me, and I hoped I'd spoken well enough. She would've conveyed the urgency of the problem better, probably using bigger words than I did.

Max held up his palm. "One moment." The council members leaned toward Max as they whispered. "We have debriefing questions, Mr. Wentworth."

After ten minutes of questions pertaining to dates, times, places, and such, the Council finally got to the questions they really wanted answered. "You were supposed to make contact with the Hub after you encountered a Consortium agent the night you met Miss Harper, and again when you and your partner ran into another agent. Why did you not follow protocol?" Jared, the Council member with a ponytail, asked.

I shoved my hands in my pockets to keep from crossing my arms and appearing overly defensive. "I made a judgment call. I've always made decisions based on what is in the best interest of the Hub or the Oculi in training. The Consortium goon could have only known where we were if they had inside information from the Hub. The Hub was—and still is—compromised."

"You had no reason at that time to suspect Santos of being a mole?" Ming, another Council member I didn't know well, raised her chin.

The muscles in my upper body stiffened. "No. He gave me no reason to question his actions. We'd worked together as a training team for a year and a half."

A dull burn spread through my chest. I wouldn't mention how he was my confidant—how he was one of the few who really knew the hurt I felt about killing my friend. I couldn't tell the Council he was one of two people in the world who had known of my feelings for Josie.

Josie sat tight-lipped during the briefing, her gaze traveling between me and the Council members.

"When did you realize Santos was actually working for

the Consortium?" Max asked.

"Not until I saw him try to *kill* Josie. After the fact, I learned he was after the vial Josie handed off to the Vice President, a request made by her mother. You know her mother? One of the founders of the Resistance, who should be on the premises by now."

I shifted to my other leg and peered down at Josie, who was laser focused on the five Council members in front of us. Her bottom jaw jutted forward slightly, her eyes narrowed, and she leaned forward onto her forearms like she was ready to pounce. If looks could kill, the entire Council would be dead.

Ming wrote something in the file in front of her. Without making eye contact, she continued questioning me. "Yes, Dr. Meg Harper. Did Dr. Harper give you any other orders?"

"No."

"Do you know why Santos wanted the vial of enhancing serum? Was it for personal power? Did he indicate that he was working alone, or did he mention Schrodinger's Consortium?"

I threw my hands up, then let my palms fall to the table with a bang. "How the hell am I supposed to know why he wanted the serum?" This had been distracting me for days. "It could've been for personal power, but since he did mention the Consortium, and even asked Josie to join them, I'm guessing not. Maybe he'd get more power from the Consortium, or recognition, or glory for hauling in the incomparable Josie Harper." Josie snorted next to me. "All I know for sure is that he fooled me, and he had to have a source inside the Hub."

"Did you, in fact, train Josie Harper?"

"To the best of my ability, I did."

"Did you reveal your true identity to Josie?"

Okay. I was over this. We needed to finish this up before I got really pissed.

"Did I tell her that I had to alter my appearance to keep hidden from the Consortium? Yes. Did I let her know I was really her brother's friend? That she had known me almost her entire life? Yeah, I did. Was it awkward? Yeah, just a little bit. Does she trust me now, though? Yes. Okay, are we done? Josie is in danger. We're all in danger."

I stared directly at Max. "The spy who informed and instructed Santos is here." My voice echoed off the high ceilings.

Clasping his hands in front of him on the table, Max closed his eyes for a moment. "I understand your anxiety. I assure you, we do not have a mole inside these walls. We've vetted everyone here. We've also ordered data analysis for all correspondence with both you and Santos. The odds are that Santos had an informant outside the Hub."

Turning his attention to Josie, Max smiled. "Josie, did Santos say anything to you that would give you any indication as to what his motives were with the serum? Or even in killing you?"

She adjusted her posture to sit taller. Shreeya and Nico, the other two Council members, whispered to each other, covering their mouths with their hands. Rude. Way to make Josie feel welcomed.

Josie hadn't talked at length about that night a week

ago when she'd killed Santos. "Yeah." The word came out strangled. She coughed into her hand and stood. "Yes. He said a couple of things. He needed to stop the hand off of the serum because things weren't what they'd seemed. The VP couldn't get the enhancing serum. He said if I came without force the Consortium wouldn't hurt me, but if I didn't come with him, the Schrodinger's Consortium would consider me a threat. That's all I can remember." A crease had formed between her brows.

"Thank you, Josie. We'll be speaking with your mother when she arrives, as well."

"They should be here already."

"Yes, we'll look into that. You may sit."

Josie sat, crossing her legs and arms. Her fingers played with her jacket. She wasn't happy about Max's quick dismissal of her family.

"Now, moving on to another important issue," Max announced loudly. "As of this morning, the Vice President's whereabouts are unknown. The media is reporting that he's gone on a private vacation, which is not uncommon for a person in his position to do. We hope to get a confirmation on his whereabouts soon. At this time, we will not panic."

I peeked to Dad and met his stare. A private conversation needed to happen soon. What had he done all this time, where had he gone? And what did he know now? Looking at him was surreal. For almost two years, I'd thought he was dead. Losing him had nearly undone me while I was on the road.

"We'll be reviewing the transcript and recording from

Reid's debriefing on this mission to train Josie Harper and deliver the serum," Max continued. "We will also investigate the events that led to the death of Santos, but right now we don't see adequate evidence for extreme action."

We *will*, meaning they weren't doing it before? A mix of anger and disbelief simmered in my gut. "This investigation needs to happen now. It should have already started."

Max held his hand up, as if to calm me. "Please, Mr. Went—"

"No." The snarl in my voice gained the Council's attention. "Everyone in here needs to understand that I was closer to Santos than anyone. And he was working for the Consortium. He couldn't have worked inside the Hub—our home, the Resistance base—unless he had help. That person is still here and wants Josie dead. They are also still working for the Consortium, the very organization that wants to eliminate most of us in the Hub."

Max raised his chin, looking down his long, slim nose at me. "I assure you, and everyone else"—he scanned the crowded room—"there is no way a traitor is among us. Our security would not allow one inside the Hub to go undetected." His head panned back to me. "Josie, and all other Anomalies, are safe in the Hub."

Rage crawled up my throat and burned my face. I cleared my throat, aware that my words couldn't come out harshly. "We have reason to believe the person who helped Santos is still here. They may be relatively new to the Hub, they may travel more frequently, they may have more correspondence outside the Hub, they—"

"Our arrivals and departures for the Hub are public record. We already periodically review the documents for security, but you can check them yourself. We are quite certain Santos experienced the same psychotic break that happened to Nick Harper."

So we were on our own. We didn't have the Council behind us. It was up to Josie, Dad, and me. And Cohen, once I found him. Only four of us in the entire Hub. As disappointment took over my brain, panic slinked up my spine. We needed more help. We needed to find a way to eliminate more suspects. At this point, it was just as Josie had suggested—everyone was a suspect until proven otherwise.

Max glanced to Dad. "Also, fellow Council members, this is a good opportunity to mention that Harrison's contact, our operative inside the Consortium, sent intel."

Dad had a contact inside the Consortium?

Josie tapped my arm. Her mouth was open as if to speak, but instead she shrugged.

I leaned toward her ear. "I think we have to take matters into our own hands."

She let her head hang and nibbled her bottom lip.

Max was still talking. "The Consortium labs are working on a way to detect Anomalies."

I nearly choked. One of the Council members, Shreeya, gasped.

Nico, a well-respected Council member about ten years older than me, leaned forward. "Meaning?"

Max glanced to my dad. "We're still working on

figuring out how it works and how, if at all, it could be combated. We have very few details right now."

Hushed murmurs bounced off the walls. Josie's head shook slightly as if she was objecting to the news.

I couldn't even fathom the idea. If we were born as an Oculi, how did the Consortium have the right to take our abilities away, to change us, to kill us? I opened my mouth to express my disgust and disbelief, but nothing happened. No words came out because I couldn't even form a coherent thought.

Max raised his hands again. "Please. This knowledge is confidential and will not yet be shared with the greater Resistance population. The intel is not definite."

My dad crossed his arms on the table and his brows pinched. I knew that look. He was thinking. His eyes drew up from the table to meet mine, and his hand went to his temple. Then he saluted me with the index finger slow and discrete.

Okay, so besides the mole, we probably needed to talk about the new danger from the Consortium. I had a feeling that was the reason my dad was back in the Hub. If he'd been so committed to going undercover for a mission that he let his only living family member think he was dead, only something extreme, something like this, could've brought him out of hiding. That meant this was a bigger deal than Max was letting on.

Ming leaned forward. "Max, Josie's skills development."

"Yes, thanks, Ming. Josie, we are aware that your Oculi abilities are quite advanced. With the threat from the Consortium being real and growing more dangerous daily, you need to be tested. You have the potential to be a considerable asset, and with this new threat from the Consortium, we need you reliable and useful as soon as possible."

Ming smiled at us. "Josie, if you are half as good as they say this soon after your seventeenth birthday, you are valuable. You are a remarkable weapon. We need you."

My lungs shut down for a few seconds. Weapon? A weapon was a tool, not a person. Weapons were often targeted. Making Josie a weapon would put her further at risk. Everything about this label and idea felt wrong. I opened my mouth to protest, but I also knew it wouldn't help right now.

Josie's forehead scrunched as she nodded to Ming. "Okay. I'll do anything I can."

"We'll plan on assessing you tomorrow morning." Max stood, and everyone else at the long table followed his lead. "Public records are open to you, Reid and Josie. We won't prevent you from taking independent precautions and looking at the records yourself, but we just can't allocate the resources to it. We'll alert everyone if and when we have more information about the Consortium chemical weapons. We'll all meet tomorrow morning. Dismissed."

The Council members, my dad, and Dee all moved out from behind the long table and down from the platform to the door.

That was it. We were done.

We hadn't resolved anything. We needed a team to investigate the traitor. We needed protection for Josie. Frustration itched the surface of my skin, covering my whole body, but there was no scratching it away, no immediate relief. There wasn't an easy way to solve problems when our leaders abandoned us.

Everyone passed by me and Josie without a second glance. We were being disregarded. I had been treated with more esteem when I was seventeen than I had in the last couple of hours. I didn't know some of the Council members, sure, but this was something bigger.

There had definitely been a shift since I'd left the Hub.

Dad walked alongside Max out the door.

Josie stuffed her hands in her pockets and let out a huff, plainly distressed and confused. Hell, I was, too. I watched Jared, Ming, and Shreeya leave the room, one after the other. All new members to the Council since I'd left. Any of them could be the mole, or all three of them could be.

An armed trooper stood behind us, waiting for our departure so he could lock the room. I swept my hand toward the door, prompting Josie to go before me. "Let's go find your room and come up with a new plan." Once in the hallway, away from the trooper, I lowered my head to whisper within her earshot. "This isn't the same Hub I left. Something's off."

5.

JOSIE

We hustled out to the garage from the council room, where the vague smell of gasoline and oil lingered. Fewer people were around than on our way to the meeting. Reid pointed to the largest opening in the garage. "There."

Our feet moved in unison, the sound of our steps reverberating off the rock walls around us as we entered the hall. Maybe "tunnel" was a more appropriate term since the circumference was large enough to fit SUVs on a two-lane highway. Two random troopers walked past us from the opposite direction.

Once they were past us, without looking at me, Reid gave my back a gentle slap. "You okay?"

I mumbled, "Yeah." I wasn't okay, though. The Hub, the new info, the shutdown from the Council, it was all too much, too soon.

"Cohen texted me your room number." Reid glanced at me. "Let's go let you chill for a few minutes. Regroup."

I let my fingers skim the rough surface of the rock wall. "Sounds good." The varied colors of earth were fascinating, and the random iron oxide stains were strangely warm and welcoming. We walked in silence down the long hallway, but my mind was utter chaos.

Reid's dad, Harrison, was back from the dead. I couldn't imagine how Reid was dealing with that life-changing revelation. It did reignite my hope that my own dad could still be alive somewhere. Was it logical at this point to think he was alive? No. But in the last couple of weeks, I learned the world didn't always work logically. The changes in my relationship with Mom were proof.

The hallway widened into a long, cavernous room. Each side had two floors of doors that opened to the middle of the room, a walkway and railing surrounding the rooms a level up. It resembled an old motel, only dug into rock.

Aware of the cameras everywhere, Reid led me up the stairs to the second floor without touching me. All I'd wanted a couple of weeks ago was to be eighteen, to have freedom and choices. Now I was getting my own place and I no longer wore my mother's tight leash, just like I'd wanted. But this independence made me feel kind of empty.

Pausing in front of my door, he held the key out to me. "Obviously you can lock and unlock the door without the key, but we encourage Oculi to conserve energy where they can."

I pulled the gold key out of his hand, making sure not to make skin contact. I unlocked the door, let it swing open, and reached around the corner to flip on a light.

Before I found the switch, Reid caught my arm. "Can I help you sweep your room? Better safe than sorry."

I stepped to the side. "Safety first." That's what I needed to say for the cameras since maybe he shouldn't be hanging with me in my private quarters. I needed a reason for him to be in my room. When really I just wanted all this to be over, to treat Reid like my boyfriend, to say *someone wants to kill me, of course you're coming in my room.*

Reid flipped on a row of lights just inside the door. I closed the door and followed close behind him. An electronic device appeared in his hand. "What is that?"

"It detects bugs and cameras. They have them in the garage, but I forgot to grab one." The small machine helped calm my anxiety a notch.

My *room* was more like a tiny apartment. The carpeted living room area had enough room for the beige sofa and coffee table. Reid moved to the kitchenette that held a small table, checking the cupboards and appliances. I followed Reid into the bathroom, then into the small bedroom furnished with a twin bed, bedside table, and a dresser. The only closet held empty hangers and a couple of towels. The smooth, painted walls were the most impressive feature of the place. From inside the miniature apartment, I would've never guessed we were underground, besides the lack of windows.

I sat on the bed, letting myself sink into the mattress and allowing my shoulders to slump. The softness of the brown comforter surprised me, but I kind of longed for the ugly paisley bedspread hidden away in New Mexico. "Reid."

He sat next to me and pulled my hand into his, callused and warm. "I know." His brows furrowed. "We're back to the drawing board with no plan."

Weapon. The words Ming had said pinballed inside my head. She was right. I'd killed someone only days before and I hadn't laid a hand on him. I was a weapon. I didn't want to be a murderer, but I could be a protector. "They called me a weapon."

"Josie—"

"It's okay. If I'm a weapon, I'm going to learn how to use myself, so I can protect my family. Without knowing my limits and without experience, I'm unreliable in a fight, and I can't be unreliable with this traitor around. Every day counts, every minute. Especially once Mom and Eli get here. I have to be able to protect them." Desperation had leaked into my voice despite my efforts to hold my fear in check. My throat ached.

I pulled my hand free from Reid, and sprang from the bed. Pacing to the other side of the small room, I opened the drawers of the dresser just for something to do. I didn't want him to see me struggling.

Reid's hands clamped onto my shoulders, giving a light squeeze. The warmth of his palms seeped through my shirt, helping relax my muscles. I shrugged and stretched my neck as he massaged my shoulders, kneading my back with his thumbs.

"Everyone is a suspect besides you, me, and dad. I think

Cohen is clear, too. Cohen and I can help you practice and can help keep you safe." His hands paused. I didn't realize how much I enjoyed his little massage until he stopped doing it. "My dad doesn't do much Pushing and Retracting anymore, since he reserves what's left of his energy supply for emergencies. But he'll look out for you. You have to be with one of us at all times. Always. Remember? Strength in numbers." His hands slid from my shoulders to my upper arms. "As long as the traitor hasn't recruited help, two of us would most likely take him down."

I turned slowly and he removed his hands from my arms to interlace his fingers in mine. "I'll convince my dad to pressure the Council on an investigation. We can't give up on the leadership after only one try." His light blue eyes were big and inviting. Patient.

I was beyond grateful to have Reid watching out for me and rallying others to do the same, but I didn't know Cohen and hadn't seen Harrison for years. I'd accept their extra eyes, but I would still watch my back. I'd learned my lesson from Santos. I didn't want to make Reid feel any worse, so I'd just stay quiet on the topic. Reid was right, though—the more people we had working against the mole, the better our odds at finding them. And beating them if it came to it. "I agree. We need backup. We have to have some kind of support doing this. I mean, dear Loki, we're trapped in a freaking mountain with a person who has aided an attempted murder. And where in the hell is my family? Why isn't the Council concerned about this? My mom and Eli could be stranded. Or what if there was an accident? Oh." My heart missed a beat. "Reid, what if they were kidnapped. Or—" The pitch of my voice had climbed. "What if they were killed? How would we know? How long are they going to wait to do something about my family not being here yet?"

Reid gathered both of my hands between his and pulled them up between our chests. "Hey, hey, hey. It's okay. I know, I know."

I swallowed and exhaled slowly. *Turn the worry and fear into action, J.* "I don't like this. We need to find them." I loosened my hands from his, sweeping loose strands of hair out of my face.

"I don't, either. I'll have my dad find them. Okay?"

Could we trust Harrison that much? I wasn't sure, but he was probably my only way of getting help in finding my family. "Yeah."

"We'll grab something to eat, I'll talk to Dad, then we'll call it a night. When we wake up, we'll get started on developing your skills with Cohen right away. Then we'll look through the public records."

If my family wasn't in the Hub by the next afternoon, I'd go look for them myself. Then I'd be all kinds of ticked. Reid would probably object to that idea, so I wouldn't say anything unless I had to. "Sounds good."

"But first, let's figure out what skills you need to master. Wanna get a glass of water from the kitchen, and I'll work that knot out of your left shoulder while we brainstorm?"

I thrust my hand toward Reid. He tugged me behind him toward the kitchen. Figure out what skills I need to defend us from the Consortium and beat this traitor's ass? Yes, please. This traitor messed with the wrong girl.

Reid

A knock on the door made Josie jump. I glanced at my phone. It was already seven. We'd been in her room for two hours. Crap. This would look bad, my being in her room this long. I didn't need the Council breathing down my neck about my relationship with Josie. We could be kicked out of the Hub and I could be stripped of my trainer privileges, which was the opposite of what we wanted. Right now, we needed to be in the Hub where we had access to data and people, specifically, the mole.

And we still hadn't eaten anything, which would mean more time we were together. "I got it." I cracked the door and peeked into the hallway.

Cohen, my childhood friend, stared back at me, grinning. "Hey, man."

I swung the door open. "Coe!" I pulled him in for a hug and he slapped my back.

Stepping back, I took a look at my friend. He'd hit the weights and made some gains for sure. His T-shirt pulled tight against his dark skin. Still had that friendly face, though.

Cohen sidestepped me and directed his attention to Josie, who now stood behind me. "You must be Josie. I'm Cohen, Reid's friend and head trainer in the Hub." I was damn proud of him for making head trainer recently.

Cohen was a talented Oculi and a good guy.

Josie's lips pulled tight in an unsure smile. "Nice to meet you."

Cohen leaned toward us and pointed over his shoulder to the hallway. "Check out who joined us a couple of days ago."

A tall white kid with wavy dark hair stood behind him—Zac Brown, the Vice President's son. What the hell? He was in the media enough to be easily recognizable. He glanced our way and smiled. I followed the guy's stare to Josie. Correction; he didn't smile at *us*, he smiled at Josie. *The dude better set his sights somewhere else.*

Cohen clasped my shoulder. "I'm on VP Junior duty but thought maybe you might want to hang and give Josie the official tour." He looked over my shoulder to Josie. "You know, check out your new digs."

Cohen's easy smile dissolved when his eyes met mine again. With his opposite hand, he saluted me with two fingers. My nerves calmed momentarily. By giving me that signal, Cohen let me know that he was aware that something was off.

Josie stepped through the doorway between the two of us. "Yeah, a tour would be good. I'd like to get comfortable with the layout."

Cohen waited for Josie to descend a couple steps then turned back to me. "We need to talk."

"Dude. Yeah."

Cohen sauntered down the stairs behind Josie to Zac, who waited with his hands stuffed in the pockets of his pants. Zac watched Josie, his eyes examining her lower body. *Nope. Nope. Nope.* I was going to have to nip that in the bud.

I leaned down to Josie's ear. "You can trust Cohen, but besides my dad, he's the only one." I inhaled the scent of her perfume I'd come to love. Gardenia.

Her slightly parted lips pressed into a line, then she nodded. "Got it." She followed Cohen. Her courage gave my own a boost.

We started down the long hallway to the garage. "So," Cohen said, twisting back to us. "Zac, this is Josie Harper and Reid Wentworth. You've heard who they are the last couple of days. This is Zac, Vice President Brown's son."

Yeah, Zac, captain of all douchebags. He talked a good game in the media as the VP's son, but I wasn't falling for his politician act. Besides, his dad had just disappeared on some mysterious vacation and then he showed up here? Weird coincidence. "What's he doing here?"

"This is the safest place for Zac to train."

"Yeah, putting everyone else here at a higher risk *because* he's here."

The upper-crust politician white boy paused and faced me. "My dad just wants me to receive proper training. I want to be treated like any other trainee while I'm here. We're on the same side, you and me."

Aware that Cohen, Josie, and the cameras were watching us, I decided to keep any insults quiet. "If you say so."

Cohen and I tag-teamed giving info about the Hub to Josie and Zac, the newbies, as we trekked down the long hallway. The Hub used to be a military base, and I could see Josie making mental notes of where we were and what turns we made. It was a good idea for her to have a mental picture the place.

"The entire compound is shaped roughly like an upside-down letter T." Cohen made the time-out sign with his hands. "The garage is on one end along with the Council corridor. At the opposite end, we have the living quarters, the Caf, and the Open, which is literally an open area inside the mountain. I guess you could say it's kind of like our version of main street in a village—a gathering area, shops, stuff like that. Along the way, from one end to the other, there are the training rooms and the infirmary."

Cohen led us up the stairs of the lookout tower in the garage. We stepped into a room full of screens, computers, buttons, and at least a dozen people. "Welcome to the Eye in the Sky—the control tower," Cohen said. "This is where security is headquartered. The entrances are monitored from here, and this is where much of the communication is located."

Screens covered an entire wall, all showing different pictures. Of the Hub. The secret "mine" entrance Josie and I had used. The door to the Council corridor. Doors I didn't recognize.

"Why is there a camera aimed at the wall of the garage?" Josie asked.

Cohen pointed out the window to the wall Josie was talking about. "That's the hangar. From the outside of the mountain no one can tell there is a door there. It will accommodate a chopper, a small airplane, that sort of thing. Reid's dad personally owns the land on the other side of the mountain with a private, registered landing strip. It's really just for show—that way no one suspects occasional flights around the area."

Josie nodded. "Smart."

Zac stepped closer to the wall of screens. "Are there cameras in the living quarters?"

"There aren't cameras in personal spaces, public restrooms, or locker areas." Cohen left the screens and crossed the room to the stairs. "The cameras can get old when you want to have a private talk or whatever, but they're there for our security. You know, those who come and go, possible intruders, odd behavior, or if someone goes rogue."

He was talking about what happened with Josie's brother, who'd had an Oculi degradation. I looked to Josie as we descended the stairs to the main floor. She didn't outwardly give a reaction to the mention of what happened with Nick, but I knew it didn't go over her head.

We followed Cohen, but Josie's eyes were everywhere but forward. She stared at the walls that sloped up to the top of the mountain. Her gaze flitted from the rows of vehicles to the locked weapons cage, back up to the Eye in the Sky above us.

"What do you think?"

Josie whirled around. "Heh. I don't know. I kind of feel like I'm in a Marvel movie."

"You mean, like this could be Batman's second home?"

Josie laughed. "Batman is DC, not Marvel."

"Whatever."

"No. Not whatever."

"You're such a nerd."

"Yes, I am. Thank you." Her face broke into a giant grin.

"Hey." I stepped closer. "Notice the exits in here. Lots of places to hide for the mole, but also for us, for you, if something goes south."

Her green eyes grew darker by a shade. "Yeah. I've been taking mental notes. Also, where are Mom and Eli? I'm getting nervous. They're not here, and still no word from anyone."

I bumped my shoulder to hers and motioned with my head to follow the others. "I know. I'll check on it."

We backtracked down the longest and widest hall with rough, rocky walls. Some halls showed exposed rock, reminding us that we were indeed inside a mountain, while some were more industrial, with cement walls and iron thresholds.

We made our way to an area where enormous, numbered doors lined both sides of the hallway.

Cohen held door number five open for us, and we walked into a temperate forest. The floor was littered with dirt, grass, leaves, and small undergrowth. Josie ran her hand over the rough bark of an enormous walnut tree.

The forest reminded me of the first trees Josie Pushed in the warehouse back in Florida. The bright memory faded to gray as I recalled Santos living in the warehouse with me, helping me train Josie.

"Rooms one through five are special," Cohen said, sticking close to the door.

Zac leaned against the tree. "You mean these are the rooms Oculi in the Hub go all *Fight Club* in?"

Cohen's lips turned upward and he stifled a chuckle. "Naw, man. Check it out." Cohen opened a box on the wall, revealing a digital touch screen. He tapped on the surface and everything around us was replaced with a busy city street and buildings. I watched Josie's gaze follow the buildings up toward clouds moving across a blue sky. They were skyscrapers.

One corner of Josie's mouth curled up slightly, her eyes wide in amazement. Ten bucks said she was trying to figure out how the room worked. Zac's mouth fell open in disbelief.

"What. The. Hell," Zac said, his head whipping around.

"It's basically a hologram for training purposes," Cohen said behind us. He was head trainer, so this was his job. I'd let him take the lead in here. "Obviously, the top of the buildings don't really go through the ceiling. It's all a picture, more or less."

Our surroundings changed again. We were on top of a building, and rooftops spread out before us. We had a great view of a city.

Josie glanced to me. "So, it's like the holodeck from *Star Trek*?"

"What?" I had no idea what she was talking about. I'd brushed up on *Star Wars* before training her, but knew nothing about *Star Trek*.

She turned to Cohen. "Or it's like the *X-Men* Danger Room?" Excitement laced her voice.

Cohen stepped away from the wall, in between Zac and Josie, toward the edge of the building. "Yeah," he chuckled. "Guess I hadn't thought about it that way. But that's exactly what it is. Holograms projected on real surfaces. This isn't a real building under our feet. This is just an elevated, hollow concrete platform, that way it can feel and react like a real surface. We call it VR, or virtual reality training. Anyway, it's about a seven-foot gap between this rooftop and the next. When we look over the edge of the building, it looks as if we'd fall to our death, ten to twenty floors to the street below, but really, it's only about a three-foot drop. The hologram and your brain fill in the rest of the illusion. As a trainer, though, I can Push and Retract real obstacles to enhance the training session."

The carefreeness left Cohen's face and he turned to Zac. "If a Consortium agent was running after me, what would I need to do?"

"Jump," Zac replied with not a second of hesitation. He stepped backward as far as he could until his back hit the wall. With one foot on the wall, he shoved off and sprinted. Jumping at the last second, he landed on the virtual rooftop of the next building. Turning to face Cohen and me, he said, "Like that?"

"That's one way," Cohen said.

Josie cleared her throat and grabbed our attention. She ran and Pushed a small bike-path bridge the moment her foot left the pretend building. I Retracted it and she Pushed it again. She needed practice with the unpredictable, so I Pushed a cinderblock wall just inside the edge of the other building. I could Retract it if she didn't.

But as she sprinted to the other building, the cinder-blocks didn't disappear. They weren't Retracted. They were blown backward, leaving broken pieces all over the ground. Like Josie had emitted an invisible blast of some kind.

Shock locked my legs, but intrigue and panic made my head spin.

She landed on her feet, but fell forward onto her hands, blocks scattered around her. Oculi didn't do that. We Pushed, Retracted, or both. That seemed different somehow. Which meant Josie was different somehow.

This was potentially something big. I nonchalantly wiped my sweaty hands on my jeans and inhaled to slow my racing thoughts. If Josie was different than other Anomalies, that would make her even more desirable to the Consortium, and possibly as a weapon to the Council. The fear I had for Josie just multiplied two-fold.

JOSIE

I paused, crouched on all fours for a moment while I let the last few seconds sink in. I hadn't Retracted the cinderblock wall. I'd used my personal shield. Well, in a way.

I was still getting used to the shield thing where I Pushed energy outside myself, creating an invisible field of protection. This was different than a shield, though. It reminded me of my confrontation with Santos and how I'd somehow made him fly backward. I thought I'd done the same thing again with the wall. This was more like a burst of energy from me to the point of my concentration. Electricity had pulsed through me in a way that left me feeling a bit woozy.

I stood, my legs wobbly, and examined the fallen wall, my hands on my hips. Zac stared at the shattered blocks.

Reid was suddenly at my side. "Josie?" He looked about as good as I felt.

Cohen made a beeline for me, not minding the so-called "space" between the pretend buildings where he'd fall to his death if they'd been real. "What was that?" His glance oscillated between me and the scattered cinderblocks.

Reid moved directly in front of me. "Josie. How did you do that?"

"I don't know, really. I had a fleeting thought about it moving out of my way. That's all."

Cohen ran a hand over his buzzed black hair and down his neck. "Huh." The black guy was the same height as Reid and super built. Like, Reid was muscular, but if they were in a video game, Cohen looked like he'd leveled up. He definitely made me feel safe, but more importantly, he made me feel welcomed. Some people just had a knack for that. "Okay. Well," he said. He and Reid exchanged confused looks and shrugs.

Reid crossed his arms. "That's, uh, never been done before, to my knowledge. Always an overachiever, Josie." He wasn't smiling or joking, though. In fact, I watched the muscle in his jaw twitch, something he did when he was nervous or thinking.

I got it. This wasn't necessarily a good progression. It could attract attention I didn't want.

Cohen shook his head, his eyes wide as he kept checking out the collapsed wall.

The door to the training room banged open and a tall white guy about my age bounded through the threshold, a Korean girl following behind him. As soon as he saw us, the guy halted abruptly and held his hand up to the girl. "Sorry if we're interrupting, man. Didn't know you'd already be in here."

Cohen checked his watch. "You're good. We're a little ahead of schedule."

The guy, sporting a *Super Mario Bros* T-shirt, moseyed over to the three of us, his long limbs loose and relaxed. The dark-haired girl watched me with apprehension as they approached.

The dude fist-bumped Cohen then lifted his chin to Zac and me. "Hey, I'm Chase. When not playing with reality, I game. The honeys love it."

Cohen barked a laugh and Reid made a *psh* sound.

Chase reached his fist out to Reid. "Been a while, man."

"Hey," Reid said, as he bumped his knuckles to Chase's.

It was kind of jarring to see people about my age in the Hub. I kept reminding myself that people of all ages, and even families, lived here. I forced a smile. "I'm Josie."

The girl, who could've easily passed for a stunning Hollywood actress, bounced toward me with an extended hand. "I'm Kat Shin." She shook my hand with a firm grip, exposing a toothpaste-commercial smile. "It's so nice to meet you, Josie." She seemed to glow from within, with flawless skin and her black hair in a trendy pixie cut that I could never pull off.

"You, too."

Zac greeted Chase with a handshake. His stare lingered on Kat's face a bit longer before he finally said, "Kat. It's a pleasure."

"Likewise," Kat said through a smile, her cheeks rosy. She tucked a chunk of hair behind her ear.

I dropped my gaze to the floor, averting my eyes from the obvious instant connection between two people. It didn't necessarily make me uncomfortable or embarrassed. It was more like I wanted it. I wanted that look they exchanged. I had that with Reid and I couldn't wait to stop hiding it. I couldn't wait until we left the Hub or the Council somehow deemed me no longer a trainee. I didn't even know what I had to do in order for the Council to make that decision.

We stood in a circle, in the middle of the practice room, on top of pretend skyscrapers. Cohen cleared his throat, breaking the staring fest between Zac and Kat. "Zac and Josie, these two will be helping you acclimate to your new home. They're close to where you are, Zac, with their abilities. They're still training and honing, but know the ins and outs of the Hub."

They all seemed nice and welcoming, but they were all here, in the Hub, which meant any one of them could've been the mole. And this room was not only a great place to hide if in trouble, but it could also harbor the mole, especially if training was taking place. Simultaneously a safe haven and potential deathtrap.

Cohen hit a few buttons on the control panel, making the holograms vanish and the props disappear into the floor, walls, and ceiling. The room was a blank slate again, white and empty.

Cohen headed toward the door. "Let's chow."

The Chase guy whooped and ran out the door, and we followed. I wasn't in any kind of mood to socialize, let alone pretend like I was excited about eating with a bunch of people I didn't know. And I just performed a trick of some kind, probably a not-good one, and had no idea how I'd done it.

This unique ability was just added to my list of things to worry about. This was enough to move my freak-out meter from "I have a bad feeling about this" to "so overwhelmed I can't even."

That's all I'd had for two weeks. Life-altering change after life-altering change. My life was standing on a sand dune; one move and everything shifted under my feet. I'd adapted and readapted and I wasn't sure I could do it much longer. When was this going to end, or at least slow down?

My lungs squeezed. I inhaled deep and exhaled slowly. *It's okay to feel this way. You will get through this. Everything will stabilize eventually.*

As soon as we were in the hallway, Reid grabbed my arm. "Hey. My dad." He pointed down the hallway to where his dad and Max stood talking. "Cohen, can you stay with Josie? Like, don't let her leave your sight. I need to get Dad to convince the Council to launch a real investigation for the mole and I need to check the status of your family. They have to be close."

"You got it, bud. Josie, let me introduce you to *the* hot spot in the Hub."

"'Kay." This was the first time I'd not been with Reid since I killed Santos, and I wasn't ready for it. My lungs squeezed again as I watched Reid turn to catch up with Max and his dad.

"Reid." My voice stretched his name.

He swung back to me, his face only inches from mine. "I know. You can do this, though." He knew I was hesitant without me saying anything but his name. "It's also making a statement to the mole—that you are more powerful than them because you aren't letting fear control you. Remember that, Josie."

I nodded, he pivoted, and I turned to follow Cohen, who was patiently waiting about five feet behind me.

Reid was right. Even if this was all destabilizing, I wouldn't give the mole the satisfaction of seeing fear affect me.

6.

Reid

My footfalls echoed in the hallway, alerting Max and my dad to my approach. They paused their slow walk toward the garage, and dad waved me to them. Max clasped his hands behind his back, his eyes on me as I matched their stride. His position as Speaker of the Council seemed to have elevated to something of more responsibility since I'd last lived in the Hub. It had to be because of the increased threats by the Consortium in the last couple of years.

"Reid." Max drew out my name. "We need to know if Josie is stable. We need to make sure there are no more 'accidental'"—he gestured air quotation marks—"victims. After the news we received of the Consortium's advances, we can't afford to have another Nick on our hands."

I knew exactly what the Council would want to do if I said no. They'd eliminate her. The very thought made my stomach turn and my pulse skyrocket.

"No need to worry." My words were sure and voice confident. "She is mentally and physically stable. She's grown exponentially in less than two weeks. Josie's Pushing and Retracting are already superior to Nick's, which means they are superior to almost everyone else's here."

Max tilted his head, as if processing these facts, or maybe he was trying to read between the facts. I continued to explain, not wanting Max to get the wrong idea about Josie. "At the same time, Josie knows and obeys the rules. She's not a risk."

"Okay," Max said, glancing to Dad, "then we will need her to develop and master her Pushing and Retracting skills, including the use of her shield."

Max turned right toward the Council rooms as we entered the garage. "In addition, you'll need to ready her close contact and combat skills. We need to make sure she can handle being provoked, especially after what happened a few days ago."

We stopped outside the door leading to the Council rooms. Dad gripped my shoulder for a second. "We need our strongest and most talented Oculi ready, should the Consortium make a move. They're gearing up for something, I'm positive. Cohen is powerful, but we need as much help with training as possible. We need someone to take Santos's place."

The Consortium's new ability to detect Anomalies and a chemical weapon to disarm them was a serious threat if the Council was asking this of Josie already.

I nodded. "She surpasses Santos's skills in every way. Once she practices more, she'll surpass mine. We'll start right away to make sure she's ready to take on the Consortium, or the mole. She needs to be able to protect herself against this traitor ASAP." Plus, to get rid of the traitor, she needed to be consistent and confident in her skills—which she wasn't yet. She was getting there, but small mistakes could mean she'd lose her family. I wasn't going to let that happen.

Max glanced to my father.

"Agreed," Dad said. "If she's this good already, she'll be a valuable asset."

Facing both of them, I held my hands in front of me. "In the meantime, Josie is concerned that her mother and brother haven't arrived yet. Do you—"

Dad was already nodding before I could even get my question out. "I wondered the same thing and sent out a couple of troopers this afternoon to meet Meg and Eli. I'll let you know when she gets in or if I hear something."

"I'm sorry, if you'll excuse me." Max slowly backed away and turned to scan his retina for entrance to the Council corridor.

"Thanks. What about the mole?"

"Son, I'm on it." Dad started across the garage, which was definitely quieter in the evening than it was during the day. I watched him for a second, my mind still trying to wrap around the idea that he was alive and right here in front of me, before I caught up to him. He glanced over his shoulder to me. "I already talked to Nico and Shreeya and convinced them the possibility of a mole was worth at least looking into, especially now with the news about the Consortium."

"Really?" I blew out a long exhale.

Dad turned and leaned his elbow on one of the shiny, black Escalades in the garage. A vehicle somewhere behind Dad rumbled to life.

"Thanks, Dad. Can you help us guard Josie? If they aren't assigning anyone, it's up to me and Cohen."

A ghost of a smile played on his lips. "Of course I will."

"Talk later or tomorrow about where you've been? And why you're back?" I still didn't have details, but he showed up just as the Consortium tried to recruit then kill Josie and we learned they have a weapon to identify Anomalies? That wasn't coincidence. I trusted my father, but I knew there was something more behind his disappearance. And reappearance.

"Yeah." He hit my upper arm. "Now go eat. You look like you're going to fall over."

"'Kay."

I jogged across the garage and down the hallway, passing the training rooms onto the Open. A small patch of grass anchored the center of the large open area, along with a couple of benches, flowers, and a small decorative pond. It was our version of Central Park, just inside a mountain. Various businesses and rooms bordered the Open. The Hub Pub, our local bar and grill; the Caf, short for cafeteria; and a coffee shop with pastries were our eating choices. When I was a kid, I thought a coffee shop inside the Hub was odd, but then I started drinking coffee and understood. The Open was also home to our tiny library, a mail room, a small grocery store, one large banquet room, and several smaller meeting rooms which were used as a school for the few Hub kids.

The thing I liked the most about the Open was the natural sunlight. With the use of small reinforced holes in the mountain surface and carefully placed mirrors, we got to enjoy daylight inside the Hub. Sunlight could be found in other parts of the Hub, but the Open, including the shops surrounding it and the Caf, had the highest quantity, helping give the feel of day.

My phone beeped in my back pocket.

Cohen: *Eating @ PH.*

Of course he'd take them to the Pub Hub. The Hub was where people went when they wanted to be social. It was our version of the corner bar, chain restaurant, and local hang-out rolled into one.

Through the Pub Hub window, Josie waved to me. The person in front of her turned around. Zac. He graced me with his slimy politician smile.

I was liking this jackball less and less by the minute.

I greeted the server at the entrance and found Josie's table. They sat across from each other, talking and smiling like they were at freaking Chili's on a date before a movie. I wasn't really worried, though. I knew how she felt about me, about us. Besides, Cohen sat next to Zac. And I definitely couldn't let my twinge of jealousy show. It looked like Chase had found some friends to join, and Kat sat at a table with her mom.

Josie caught me staring at her and watched me until I sat on a stool next to her. She pointed at the plate sitting at an open seat next to her. She'd ordered a club sandwich and fries for both of us, one half of her sandwich already gone. "Thanks for ordering me food," I said.

A corner of her mouth pulled upward, and that was enough to calm my nerves a little. She peeked over her shoulder at someone behind us, then leaned into me. "Everything okay?" she asked in a hushed voice.

"Yep. Fine." I shoved a fry in my mouth. "So, why are you here, Zac?" Like Josie said outside the mine, everyone was a suspect unless proven otherwise. He did just arrive, but the timing of his arrival was what worried me. Why now?

Josie bumped my leg with her knee. "What?" I asked around a bite of sandwich. I was so hungry I didn't even taste it.

Zac's plate was empty. He wiped his mouth. "It's okay. He has the right to ask. I'm probably a threat to his self-esteem."

Laughter erupted from me. "You don't threaten me." Josie let her face bow toward the table, clearly uncomfortable. "I want to know if you being here will threaten anyone else." Innocent people lived in the Hub, which now included Josie. It couldn't have been a coincidence that he showed up about the same we did and his dad had gone AWOL.

For the first time since I sat, he made eye contact with me with a sober face. "I really hope it doesn't. We're fighting for the same cause. Go easy, tiger." He stood, focusing on Josie. "It was nice to meet you."

Josie lifted her head. "You, too."

Zac slowly made his way toward the entrance, stopping at tables and shaking hands along the way. If there were babies here, he probably would've kissed them.

When Zac approached the doorway to the Open, Cohen turned slightly to watch Zac. To know there was at least one person in the Hub who had our back let my heartrate come down another notch. Cohen gestured to Josie, who was trying to get a better look at a little blond-haired kid. I nodded, conveying my thanks with a smile. He shoved his last french fry in his mouth and stood. "See ya later." With a wave, he was gone. It was like a hand off of some precious gem.

Josie's hair swished over her shoulder as she checked out a redheaded lady. She was looking for her family—a blond brother and redhead mother.

As soon as Cohen was out of earshot, Josie swiveled around to me on the stool, worry etched into every feature. "Can we talk?"

"Yeah." I threw money down on the table, and Josie's gaze ping-ponged between the cash and me. She'd probably assumed we didn't use money in the Hub. People visiting for the first time often thought that.

"The Hub runs just like a town," I explained. "We can't Push everything we need, use, or eat, or we'd use up our energy stores."

"But Zac walked away. I don't think he kn—"

"I got it, come on." Grabbing her wrist lightly, I tugged her behind me toward the back of the room. The place was an ordinary bar and grill, so it was as noisy as any other restaurant in the Planck world.

I stopped and pulled her beside me, letting her hand fall.

Her mouth fell open. "It's the billiards room you Pushed in the warehouse last week." She examined the pool table where we kissed with flushed cheeks.

I nudged her shoulder with mine. "Hey. I didn't show you to embarrass you. I wanted you to know I wasn't making it up. It's a real place and wasn't some ploy to get you to kiss me." I also wanted to remind her that the kiss happened. It was real.

A slow smile parted her lips. "I believed you, but thanks for showing me."

Jerking my head, I signaled for her to follow me. Once outside the Pub, we high-tailed it down the hall to the living quarters.

I swept her place, even having done it less than two hours before. We ended in her bedroom. "It's clear."

My phone vibrated with a text from Dad.

Me & Cohen switching off to guard J's room tonight. Get a good night's sleep. A guard will also be on duty at the hallway intersection.

That was a load off my mind. My muscles immediately relaxed and I gave in to the tiredness.

Josie leaned against the doorjamb. "Thank you." She blinked slowly. "For everything."

"You don't have to thank me."

"Yeah," she huffed, "because you're Mr. Bigshot Trainer. That's just part of the job, ma'am." She said the last part in a deep, southern twang, as if she were an Old West sheriff. Her light laugh filled the space between us.

Seeing her laugh lifted my mood. "No." I smiled. "Everything I've done for you in the last week is because I care about you."

The slight smile that lived on her lips faded. "I know you can't—uh, I know we can't have the same sleeping arrangements as we have had, due to the whole no trainer-trainee relationship rule here." She ran her fingers through her ponytail and shuffled her feet. "But can you stay long enough for me to fall asleep?"

Her expressing that she wanted me, even if it was to help her fall asleep, made me happy in a way I'd never felt before. A warm sensation filled my chest and crept up to my face. I couldn't have hidden the huge-ass grin on my face if I'd wanted to. "I didn't even think that was up for debate."

Her smile reached her eyes. She spun to the bathroom to get ready for bed and came out a few minutes later dressed in R2D2 pajama pants with her hair down. She plugged her phone into the outlet by the bed and set it on the nightstand, then climbed under the covers. Scooting against the wall, she left the comforter flipped back then gazed up at me.

I laid down next to her, pulling the covers over us. "What did your dad say?"

"He talked to Nico and Shreeya on the Council. They at least seem a little more concerned than the rest of the Council. That's a start. Dad and Cohen will be helping me guard you. One of us will be with you at all times." My hand found her waist. "Tonight, they'll take turns at your hallway door so I can get a full night of sleep. I still haven't had a chance to talk to him about where he's been doing undercover work."

She rubbed my arm. "Thank you. To all three of you."

We watched each other in silence. The soft light from the lamp illuminated her makeup-free face and highlighted the blond strands in her red hair.

I smoothed my hand along her jaw and kissed her softly. I pulled away to shut off the lamp so she could sleep, but she wrapped her hand around the back of my neck and pulled me to her. We kissed for several minutes, then she snuggled into my side, resting her head on my chest, just as we had done in the hotel rooms traveling from Florida. Josie was right; there was something about hiding away that was comforting. I would've given anything for us to be a normal couple, for us to be safe and falling asleep while watching one of the movies she could quote from memory. There was something intimate about lying next to the person I cared about most as I fell asleep. Maybe one day I could have that kind of normalcy with her.

Josie fell asleep quickly, and I snuck out without her noticing. Cohen gave me a fist bump when I left Josie's room. "Go catch some winks, man. We'll talk in the morning."

I fell into bed and the next thing I knew, my phone buzzed loud enough to wake the dead with a text from Dad.

Josie's family has arrived. They will be in one of the training rooms with me. Cohen is back at Josie's room until you get to her.

It took me a matter of minutes to get to Josie's door.

"Thanks a lot, Coe."

Cohen slapped my back as I knocked. "No prob. See you in a few."

I cracked the door. "Josie!" There was no sign of her. I slipped into her place, closed the door behind me, flipped on a light switch, and took a step out of the entryway into the tiny living room.

"Stop." Josie pointed a Glock at me from the end of the short hallway.

I jumped, along with my heartrate, and pulled my palms up. "It's me! Your mom and Eli are here."

She lifted her forefinger toward me. "Wait. I need to know you're Reid before I go anywhere with you."

She was right to question me. But how could I prove I was me? I chuckled. "Well, I'm pretty sure no one else knows that I was in here, holding you so you could sleep."

She nodded. "Yeah, but that's not good enough. Someone could've seen you leave my room."

"You liked that motel room in New Mexico that was stuck in the seventies."

She shrugged.

If I went back farther in time, I could find something that was proof of something only few knew. "Nick used to call you Jojo when we were little."

Her lips parted. She took several quick steps and laid the gun on the kitchen table. "Holy shit balls! You scared the crap out of me, Reid."

"Just me. Stand down, soldier." I let my hands drop.

Her brows furrowed and she exhaled loudly. "I could've hurt you."

She was beautiful even with messy hair. "If you hurt me, does that mean you would've kissed my boo-boos?" I stepped so close our chests touched and she had to tilt her head up to see my face. "You need more proof? Before you fell asleep, we made out." My lips hovered above Josie's. "And I kissed you here." My finger smoothed over her collarbone.

The simple touch was as light as a feather, yet it cemented her in place. Tingles spread through my chest, where our bodies touched.

"Okay," she smiled. "It's you."

She let her head fall, her forehead resting against my chest. "They're here," she sighed. I could feel her warm breath through my shirt. "They're alive. Thank Thor."

I encircled my arms around her. "Let's go see your family."

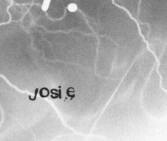

7.

JOSIE

I jogged down the long hall toward the training rooms and my mom and little brother, my heart swelling with each beat. After Reid had told me Mom and Eli were here in the Hub, I'd gotten ready in record time.

We came to the intersection of hallways and rounded the corner toward the training rooms. A short figure ran toward us. Eli smiled, his blond hair bouncing and blue eyes wide. I set my feet and bent down, preparing for his weight as he launched himself into my open arms.

Relief rushed through me, all at once like a flood. His arms wrapped around me and I squeezed. This kid and I had been through hell together—losing a sibling and watching our parents change—before the Oculi world was ever shown to us. He was one of the few people I could count on the last couple of years, and he was nine. But we shared a weird family bond, including tragedy, that made me care for him in a way that was too difficult to put into words.

He pulled away, grinning so big his chubby cheeks made his eyes squint. "Where's Mom?" I asked.

He motioned to the training rooms behind him with his thumb, down the hallway on the way to the garage where they would've arrived. Mom shouldn't have let him wander off. "Why are you out here? Does Mom know where you are?"

He nodded, making his hair bob. "I was looking for the bathroom. Can you show me where it is?"

My heart seized. Mom wasn't taking this traitor seriously, either. As soon as humanly possible, I needed to change that.

Reid pointed to the bathrooms down the hallway. "Down there, buddy."

Eli couldn't go traipsing around the Hub with a traitor on the loose. He could be taken or hurt in an instant. The very thought made my stomach turn. I wrapped my arm around my churning stomach. "Reid, can you take him to the bathroom? He shouldn't go by himself."

Reid's hand landed on my back. "Of course. You need to have a bodyguard until you're in the training room, though. Eli and I will walk you to the door, then we'll find the bathrooms."

Eli frowned. "I don't know him. Can't you go with me?"

The three of us started walking, me between my brother and Reid. I ruffled Eli's hair. "Hey. You can trust Reid, okay?"

Eli nodded. He was on the quiet side even normally, but he'd just been thrown into this world a few days ago. Poor guy. He had to be so confused.

I bumped Eli's shoulder and he bumped me back. "Where have you stayed the last couple of nights with Mom?"

He shrugged, his gaze staying on the floor. "A different state every night."

Eli shouldn't have been involved in this. Guilt nibbled on my heart. I squeezed Eli's shoulder as we approached an open training room door, where the sound of Cohen's laugh echoed into the hallway. "Stay with Reid. See you in a few minutes."

Eli glanced to me with a hesitant smile. Reid gave Eli a pat on the shoulder. "So, the Hub is pretty rad, isn't it?" They continued down the hallway toward the garage.

I turned, my heart thumping again in anticipation of seeing my mother. Stepping into the training room, I saw Cohen flash a wide grin alongside Harrison, Reid's dad. Zac and Kat stood behind Cohen. To the left, around the corner, not visible from the hallway, red hair swept into a ponytail—Mom. And Eli.

My body locked, unable to move, but my mind shifted to warp-speed.

How could this be? I was just with Eli. He was in the hallway. I touched him. I hugged him. I— No. Uh-uh.

I sank to the floor, shaking. Mom and Eli ran to me, wound their arms around me.

"Mom," Eli said next to my head. "What's wrong with J?" I looked at him, really looked at him. Worry contorted his face.

Mom didn't answer Eli, but instead struggled to sit next to me on the floor, her cane falling with a loud clang. She tightened her hold on me. "J, calm down. We need you to tell us what's wrong. J?"

Voices murmured around me between my gasps for air. Then Reid's voice resonated through the room from somewhere behind me. I could hear him running. "Eli didn't come out of the bathroom. I went in and he's gone." His voice wavered. "I need help looking for him, stat!"

Mom let go of me and shifted to see Reid. Eli stood. Everyone around us parted so Reid could see me and my family. Sucking in air through my nose, I tried to calm myself so I could talk.

Reid was already jogging toward us when I twisted to look over my shoulder. Then his eyes lifted from me to Eli. His jaw set, brows furrowed.

"Eli's been in here," Harrison said, clearly confused.

Mom leaned to my ear. "J. What's going on?"

Cohen squatted next to my mom. "Can I help you up, Dr. Harper?" Mom nodded while Eli retrieved her cane. Zac and Cohen helped my mom to a standing position.

Reid stepped closer to me and turned to his dad. "Someone just impersonated Eli."

Everyone erupted in questions. "Why would someone want to be me?" "What would someone get by impersonating a kid?" "How do you know?"

Someone fooled me with my own brother.

I'd hugged the traitor. They'd had me in their arms. Chills ran up my spine.

I watched Eli's eyes widen, gawking at everyone

talking at once. *No. He shouldn't have to be scared out of his mind right now. My family is off-limits.*

Reid offered his hand and tugged me up. His eyes darkened by a degree. "That was the traitor. I had my hand on the mole, and he got away." He said it to me, but it was loud enough for all to hear.

I pictured hugging the imposter and anger simmered in my stomach. He could have Pushed a knife and killed me right there. He could have killed Reid, too. So easily.

"Yeah, and we'll get our hands on him again." Cohen lifted his chin. "Don't you worry."

Harrison stepped to my mom. "The three of you need protection at all times. I'm ordering it myself."

An attempt to rattle me, scare me into making a mistake. To convince me to go off with him. Was that what this was?

Kat had been quiet, but she stepped to me and rubbed my arm. "Are you okay?"

"Yeah," Zac said, shoving his hands in his pockets. "What can we do to help?"

Eli threw his arms around me, his eyes watery, knocking me out of temporary shock. His bottom lip trembled. An ache grew in my throat. I moved a strand of hair out of his eyes. "You'll be okay. I promise I won't let anything happen to you. I love you, little man." He nuzzled his head against me.

Mom wrapped an arm around each of us, her eyes glimmering. My heart warred with itself. Part of me still ached from the last two years of her being so controlling, yet emotionally distant and her leaving me last week.

But she'd sent that message the night I killed Santos, explaining that she'd tried to lure the Consortium away from me and the serum drop with Vice President Brown. When I'd thought she'd deserted me, she had actually put her own life on the line. I was relieved she wasn't hurt, or worse.

Mom pulled both of us into her. She smelled like our laundry detergent, which instantly took me back to our house in southwest Florida. Eli and I had just been starting to have a normal life there.

She kissed each of us on the forehead. "I love you both. I'm sorry you're a part of this," she whispered. Her eyes shut, letting a couple tears slip. "We *need* to talk later." Her eyes opened, her vibrant green irises locked on my face, tears still pooling in the corners.

"Yeah." My voice cracked. "We do."

The Consortium had nearly destroyed her. Working for them, running from them, starting the Resistance, losing a son, my dad undercover and maybe dead. It had all been because of the organization that wanted to exterminate Anomalies.

No more.

Rage boiled in my veins as I hugged what was left of my family. I had to protect them and develop the skills to protect other Anomalies. If I was as advanced as Reid thought, I needed to master the skills to defend as many Oculi as possible and take down the Consortium. There was no waiting. The mole had already fooled me and Reid once.

I pulled away from our embrace and turned toward

everyone else in the room. "Reid and Cohen and anyone else equipped and available to help me hone my Oculi skills, teach me." Heat flashed in my face. "Mom and Eli need to stay here with me. It's the only way I know they're really safe."

If I was part of the Resistance, then I needed to start mastering the skills to take this guy down. Because this had been a threat meant to rattle me. And that meant the mole would come back.

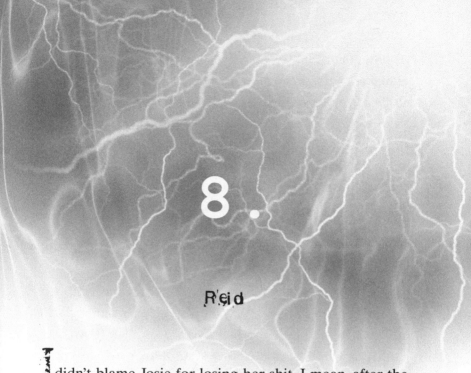

8.

Reid

I didn't blame Josie for losing her shit. I mean, after the traitor impersonated Eli, I'd wanted to throw down, too. This was a personal act on the mole's part, and that made me furious. If I got my hands on him, I'd have no mercy after he'd tried to kill Josie and then taunted her.

The door of the training room creaked open and Max walked in, the other Council members following behind him—Nico, Shreeya, Jared, and Ming.

Max stopped closest to my dad, looking at Dr. Harper. "Meg. What kept you?"

With the help of her cane, Meg approached Max. "We ran into a little trouble. Someone was following us last night. We managed to lose them in Denver, though. Max, the Hub has been compromised."

Max's head swiveled to my father. "Harrison?"

"She's correct. We have a breech in security." My dad explained what had just happened with the Eli imposter.

"Are you sure this isn't in Josie's head?" Max glanced to the other Council members.

Nico stepped closer to the rest of us. "Yes, this could certainly be the beginning symptoms of Denigration. It tends to start broad, doubting and questioning ideology. Then the Oculi tends to get fixated or obsessed about something specific."

"Unfortunately," Ming interjected, "it does run in families. It tends to be a genetic thing. And with—"

Fury flamed in my chest. "No!" Everyone whipped around to look at me. "I was there. I experienced it. I touched him." I spit the last two words. "I was *with* an imposter while the real Eli was in here with Josie and everyone else. This happened. Josie isn't showing symptoms of anything."

Ming nodded to Shreeya, who then crossed her arms. "Well, if it happened, we need to take action. We need protection for the Harper family at all times. Josie, we need you in fighting shape. A couple of our most talented Oculi should help you do this." She glanced to me and Cohen. "Let's get started."

"Agreed," said Jared.

"Yes." Max held his index finger up. "But we need to check security availability—"

Dee ran through the door, dressed like she usually was, in jeans and a hoodie. "Meg. Where's Meg?"

Max stepped away from Meg.

"Meg. Harrison texted me." Dee ran to Meg with open

arms. Both women were motionless as they embraced. They probably hadn't seen each other in person since Nick's funeral. That would've been before Stella, Dee's daughter, had gone missing. Like my dad, everyone assumed the worst. If an Oculi went missing for over a couple of weeks, the assumption was death. And now the Davises were missing, too. Oculi history had proven that it was highly likely Stella and the Davises were gone forever.

The Hub really did need Josie.

Sometimes I forgot our parents were more than the Founders; they were friends first, once all incredibly close.

Several random people entered the training room, talking loudly amongst themselves. Max turned, pointing toward the door. "This room is not for public use right now." A few others came into the room, and Max chased them all out the door.

Josie shifted at my side and sighed. "Okay, let's start."

Shreeya waved an arm. "Everyone else, please move to the side. We have work to do with Josie."

Shreeya and the rest of the Council members were anxious for Josie to practice her skills, yes, but for an entirely different reason than Josie was. They wanted to see if she'd have an Oculi degradation like Nick. And they needed her as a weapon.

I wasn't nervous, though. Josie was probably more stable than I was.

The four Council members whispered amongst themselves, and the three Founders, plus Eli, ambled to the chairs. Josie hit my forearm. "Will you sit next to Mom and Eli? You're the only one I trust. Please?" Her green eyes pleaded.

I would because I wanted to, but I also couldn't say no to her. About anything, really. "Of course. I've got it."

Zac and Kat took seats next to Eli.

Max, still standing in the middle of the large room, clapped his hands. "The Council agrees that it would be best for Josie to practice the use of her defensive shield. If the Consortium were to attack, we need to make sure she can control this skill. And if someone impersonating Eli had tried to attack her from close range, she would have needed to use it. For now, we request that no Pushing or Retracting be used." He turned to Josie. "Practice hand-to-hand combat, since it can evoke emotions, then use your shields as needed as a last resort for protection."

"Absolutely not. She has been through enough in the last couple of weeks," Meg yelled, her voice echoing through the room.

Jared stood in front of his chair, but angled himself toward Meg. "We'd like to elicit emotions through hand-to-hand combat as much as possible because that will also help you practice keeping those feelings in check. Often, heightened emotional responses can help us also identify an approaching Oculi psychological break."

As much as I didn't want to admit it, Jared was right. Meg knew it, too. We did have to make sure Josie was safe in all capacities.

Josie hitched a hand on her hip, glanced to her mom then me. Her slight agitation was apparent to me, and probably her mom, but likely not to the Council members.

Talk about sugarcoating. Jared sat and Ming immediately whispered in his ear. The dude could've just said *we need to make sure you aren't going to have a psychotic break, so we need someone to beat you up.*

Max now stood beside me. He smelled of cheap aftershave, something with a high alcohol content. "Let's see what she can do with Cohen, someone a little more experienced."

Josie stared at me then looked to Cohen. "Let's go."

Cohen was frozen in place, eyeing Max.

Max looked between the four of us. "You heard her. Cohen, don't go easy." He spun around without another word and mall-walked to an empty seat.

I glanced to Cohen, who was already watching me. We both knew he couldn't hold back too much or everyone would be able to tell. Josie was good, though; she'd studied tae kwon do since she was a kid. And she was just plain tough.

I retreated to the chairs, making Kat move over so I could sit next to Eli. Eli stared up at me, his eyes scared. I patted his back, trying to give him some kind of assurance.

Clenching my teeth, I crossed my arms and focused on Josie and Cohen, ready to Push or Retract if needed. Cohen didn't Push any safety gear on himself.

They both cautiously closed the gap between them. To my surprise, Josie threw the first punch, but it was blocked. Cohen swung his right hand, left, then gave a hard uppercut, but Josie blocked them all. Dancing in a circle, they kicked, punched, and blocked for several minutes, demonstrating their skills. Cohen kicked his leg low, but as Josie blocked it, Cohen leaned in and slammed into her. Josie lost her balance, being a third the size of her opponent, and Cohen ran toward her. Grabbing Josie's shoulders, Cohen kneed Josie in her stomach, making her double over. My stomach rolled and I leaned onto my knees.

Planting his back foot, Cohen lowered his center of gravity, spread his fingers wide over Josie's shoulders, and shoved with a deep grunt. Josie stumbled backward again, trying to find her balance, and she found it — against the wall. Not good. Bad place to be when tired.

My stomach pitched and my back muscles tensed. I knew he wouldn't hurt her besides maybe a minor injury, but it still wasn't easy watching.

Cohen was well-trained and knew he needed to take advantage of her position. He leaped and pulled his fist back to smash the right side of her face.

I'd already jumped up from my seat when a burst of energy exploded. Shoved backward by something like wind, I scrambled to find my footing, but Cohen flew through the air like he'd been power-punched in a video game. He landed at least ten feet away from Josie, on his back, not moving. My dad ran to Cohen, and I sprinted to Josie.

Josie slid down the wall to the floor like a withered plant, nothing in her left to hold her upright.

"You okay?" I tried to get a better look at her face. She pulled away.

"Perfect," Josie mumbled. She blinked fast.

"What was that? What happened?"

She pulled her head up to look at me. Fear welled in her eyes.

Oh, shit.

It was her; she did that.

"I…I didn't mean to." Her words were thin. "I'm sorry."

My heart missed a beat. If the mole was in the room with us at that moment, they just saw what she was capable of. They had a first-row seat to her strengths and weaknesses.

Squatting closer, I whispered, "Don't apologize. It's part of you. Own it. Remember? Don't show fear."

Her eyes latched onto mine like they were her lifeline. I nodded and she mirrored.

Meg knelt on Josie's opposite side. "You're okay. You're okay. You did good."

Meg wasn't a beaming parent. Her eyebrows pinched together, lines formed on her forehead. But she knew better than to voice her worries. Meg had to have known that what she witnessed would make Josie more desirable to anyone who wanted power.

I wrapped Josie's arm around my neck, and Meg tried to help with her other side, testing if Josie could stand.

Cohen sat up, rubbing his head. I hadn't realized he'd landed on a thick mat. He would have felt that landing anyway.

The Council members still graced us with their presence. A delighted grin stretched across Max's face. "This"—he waved to the middle of the training room floor—"was unprecedented. As you probably well know, Meg, nothing of this sort has been recorded in known Oculi history. We need to get these two checked out to make sure they don't have concussions. Full vitals check."

Meg nodded.

Max stepped closer and concern replaced the smile. "Josie, are you okay?"

Josie kept her gaze down, not looking at Max, but nodded.

"Good," Max said. "We'll take care of you." He looked to Meg again. "The infirmary will inform you of any findings. But one thing is for sure: she's more than an Anomaly. Josie's unique. Full of the unexpected. She's an enigma." Max quickly tipped his head to Meg, pivoted, and walked to the door.

The Council left the room, but we were all aware that the cameras were still on. Dad helped Cohen stand up. "Infirmary for Josie and Cohen."

Meg leaned into Josie. "Let me know what the infirmary says. Then find us this afternoon. Eli and I are going to clean up and nap. Someone will go with us, so don't worry."

Josie nodded in tiny, quick movements.

"Here," I said, pulling Josie's other hand up around my neck. I carefully swept her feet out and lifted her into my arms. Her head fell to my shoulder.

Meg glanced to me. "Thank you." Eli squeezed Josie's hand.

"Of course. Hey, Dad?"

He stepped behind Meg. "Don't worry. I'm taking care of these two."

Kat held the door open for us, and we started down the hall to the infirmary alongside Cohen. He seemed fine but walked slowly.

"You okay, Coe?"

He lazily glanced at me. "I'm fine, man."

"I think we need to talk about a couple of things behind closed doors." I spoke quietly and quickly.

He didn't say anything for a few seconds, glanced to me, and gave me the index finger salute. Relief washed over me. The tiny gesture let me know that we were on the same page.

"My dreams have come true," Josie said, still limp in my arms. "I have the Force. You can call me master now."

Cohen laughed and I stifled a chuckle, which reverberated in my chest. "What, now you can Force Push?" My chest ached. This was too much for one person. "Are you okay?"

"I don't know how to control this energy burst or whatever it is." Josie sighed. "And if I can't control something powerful, I'm dangerous."

Cohen shook his head and exhaled loudly.

The mole had committed an act of psychological terror by impersonating her brother. He showed that he held power over Josie—over all of us. And now Josie's new ability? She was exactly what the Council said she was: a weapon.

With the larger situation as dire as it was, the Council could get greedy. They could put her in harm's way, jumping at the chance to use her before she was ready. Trying to make her do things she didn't want to do. She took Santos's life only days ago and was haunted by it.

"We got this, Josie." I said it for her, but also for me, because at the moment, it seemed like the mole had "got this."

9.

JOSIE

After three hours of tests and observation, I was released by Doc. I physically felt fine, especially after they fed me.

I followed Doc out of the examination room. Reid was leaning against the opposite wall, a faint smile on his lips. "You okay?"

"Yeah." I really was fine, besides being scared of myself and not knowing how to control my new gift. "Where are Mom and Eli?"

Reid guided me out of the infirmary into the main hallway where voices, motors, and noises from various tools echoed from the garage.

"No worries." His voice was steady, calm. "Cohen is with them. Dad and Dee escorted them to get food to take back to their room. Once Cohen was released from the infirmary, which wasn't long, he went with them. If someone wants to speak to your mom besides the four of us, Cohen has to be *in* the room."

I blew out a breath of relief, and my lungs seemed to work easier.

I directed my attention to Reid and away from the rocks. "That Force Push thing? I used it with Santos. It was like I was Pushing my shield, and a surge radiated from the center of me. This cool sensation spread through my chest as I moved energy outside my body. It was weird, but what made it scarier was it not being intentional." I let my hand trail against the rough mountain wall. "I'm betting the mole can't do the Force Push thing, which gives me an advantage. I need to capitalize on that. I need to master it as quickly as possible."

"Hey," Reid said, dragging my attention away from the mountain wall. "I get it, and I agree that it's an advantage, but you have to be safe." He stopped in the middle of the hallway and turned to me. A couple of random people passed us in the opposite direction. "We need to practice this daily, so you can learn how to control it without getting hurt. Slow and consistent. We don't really know how it works. You getting hurt won't help anyone." There was no joking, nor teasing, just an intense stare. He was worried.

My heart lightened in my chest, making me feel dizzy for a second. "Okay." I bit my lip.

He continued walking again, and I resumed touching the wall of rock. "You seem kind of intrigued by the mountain," he said, watching me out of the corner of his eyes.

"Rocks, in mountain ranges particularly, fascinate me. It's like…" I shrugged. "Living history. Think about how old this is. It's crazy." If I was honest with myself, Reid actually fascinated me more than rocks. But they were a convenient distraction.

We rounded the corner where the people hurried through the Open, doing their own thing. "Let's check out the public records in the library to get a list of all those who have entered and exited the Hub compound, as well as outside communication. We need to check to see if anyone was here when they weren't supposed to be and activity in the Hub before Santos arrived here. I also want to check those records for last week when Santos was close to you. Then I'll get you to your family. They're safe for now, but we have work to do." The library sat across from the Caf and the Pub Hub in the Open.

Reid pulled the door open for me, and we entered one large room with rows and rows of metal shelves. No one seemed to be there, but I spotted several cameras. Reid stopped at a table in the back. "These are the computers we use to access the Hub public records."

I sat in the chair next to Reid as he logged into the system. "Here. This is the registrar for everyone who is currently in the Hub, marked with their arrival and departure dates." Reid tapped the screen. "Let's print this then do what you suggested—cross off those who aren't possible suspects. It's a start."

"Gotta start somewhere."

We printed the list and walked to the living quarters, Reid leading me to a room on the bottom level. "This is your mom and brother's room."

For some reason, I'd expected them to be in my room, even though I only had a twin bed. They weren't far from my room, though. A thirty-second walk, maybe.

I knocked and Cohen opened the door. Dee was right behind him. "Josie. I was just leaving," she whispered. She stepped around Cohen and wrapped her arms around me, giving me a quick squeeze. "How are you doing? Are you feeling okay after, well, whatever that was?" Her face twisted in concern, her dark eyes drawn in sympathy.

"I'm okay." I kept forgetting her daughter was missing.

She placed her hand over her heart. "Oh, thank God. If you need anything, I'm here."

It was kind of her to offer, but I hadn't seen her for two years or really talked to her much since I was thirteen or so. "Thanks, Dee."

She moved past me and Reid, giving him a brief smile.

Cohen waved his hand, signaling for me to enter. "I'll be outside if you need anything."

I walked through the doorway, and turned to see if Reid was following. "I'll be close. You need a few minutes alone with your mom." His eyes hung on to mine.

I knew we were both safe at the moment, but I didn't really want him to leave me yet. "Okay." It was an odd feeling, wanting to be with someone all the time.

Cohen closed the door, and Mom walked with the use of her cane to the couch, an amused look on her face.

"What's that look for?" I asked.

She sat and I followed. "Don't let the Council see how you look at each other."

Panic slammed into my chest. *Holy shit balls. Deny. Deny.* "What?" I acted like I was shocked. And I was shocked, from fear.

"You don't have to pretend with me. It's…" She smiled to herself. "Natural."

Dear Loki, please don't give me the talk, Mom.

She looked at me again. "Cal—" She shook her head. "I mean, Reid has liked you forever."

She knew Reid liked me? He's liked me forever? Was I really having this discussion with my mom? My heart raced out of control, and my mind went with it.

"Reid's mom was my friend and we talked. I knew."

She wasn't going to out us, was she? I bit my tongue, waiting for her to move to a different subject, wishing I could Retract conversations.

"It makes me feel better knowing he cares about you. Just don't let the Council figure it out. That was a Council rule implemented about ten years ago."

I nodded as if I was a bobble-head doll. My mom was okay with Reid and me being a *thing*.

And it was a Council rule, not an Oculi rule. Huh.

"But," she said. It was amazing how one word could send my vitals into a frenzy. "I did want to talk to you about our living situation while in the Hub. Do you want to remain in your own place?"

I thought she was going to say something about my and Reid's relationship, not inquire about where I stayed. I had no idea how to respond. I was so confused about wanting more independence, then getting it but not the way I wanted.

Mom watched me patiently. "It's okay if you'd like to stay in a place by yourself. You're less than a minute away, but—" She looked up toward the ceiling like she was thinking. "You could be safer here. Not that we can protect you, but there would be more people around you."

Me staying with my family could make the mole think I was scared. Or they could use my family again to get close to me. If I stayed by myself, maybe I could keep the mole from messing with Mom and Eli. Maybe he'd come for me instead. And after being overprotected for so long, I did still want a little freedom.

"I'd like to stay by myself for a little while."

Mom's gaze shifted to the floor and she nodded. "Yes. Okay." Sadness laced her quiet words. I didn't have to explain why I wanted my own place for a while; she knew.

Mom cleared her throat and twisted to the coffee table. "Here." She held a small box out to me. "Open it."

This wasn't normal. She didn't give presents.

I took the lid off and pulled the Dragon's Eye symbol out of the box. The chain uncoiled, dancing like a silver snake in the light. "Thank you."

"Do you know what it stands for?"

"Wisdom, love, and power." And coming from my mother, it was even more meaningful.

A few wrinkles gathered in the outer corners of my mother's eyes. "This doesn't make up for anything. It doesn't make up for constantly uprooting you and your brothers, for keeping this life a secret, for not being there emotionally for you and Eli the last two years."

The hurt I'd held on to for so long surfaced, scratching

at my throat, begging for me to release it. I stood up from the couch with the necklace in my hand. I needed to keep a leash on the words wanting to spout from me. "No, it—" My voice cracked. "No, it doesn't."

Her eyes watered. "I'm sorry. That doesn't make anything right, but I am sorry. You need to know that we believe in you. That your dad and I love you."

"Dad?" I squeaked. My heart slammed against my ribs.

She closed her eyes for a moment, then faced me. "Your dad is Harrison's connection inside the Consortium. I didn't find out until a couple of days ago that he altered his appearance for protection, much like what had to happen with Reid. Your dad is *our* mole. He's still alive."

I covered my mouth, trying to keep myself from crying. Tears rolled down my cheeks anyway.

"I haven't spoken with him at length. It was a two-minute conversation." Her nose suddenly became red and she sucked in a slow breath. She glanced to her lap momentarily and just like that, she swallowed her emotions and put her strong face back on.

Mom patted the couch. I sat again and she took the necklace from my hand and unclasped it. I leaned forward so she could fasten it behind my neck. Sitting upright, I stared at the shiny pendant, a gift from my parents, both of them alive. "Thanks," I croaked.

"This is just a reminder that we believe in you. We will find this traitor. And you are strong enough to help us fight the Consortium, standing up for Anomalies like you."

"But what if I'm like Nick? What if I can't handle it?"

Mom's ponytail whipped back and forth as she shook her head. "You're different than Nick, just as Eli is different than you. No two people are identical. You're smart and stubborn, but within you is a drive, a determination that will serve you well. That will serve a lot of people well. You will stick by your morals."

This was unorthodox for my mom. She was the scientist, not a pep-talker. "Is that your scientific surety? How have you come to that conclusion?"

"No science involved. It's called a gut feeling. Sometimes those are more convincing than anything logical. You use that sixth sense more than you think you do."

"What about finding the mole?" I motioned to the stack of papers on the couch next to me. "The entry and exit logs show routine behavior. I don't know where to look next."

"Make lists. Categorize people. I'm here to help; I'll see what I can find." She patted a laptop next to her on the couch. Her laptop from home.

"How are you going to use your laptop to help us identify the mole?"

"I'm one of the few who have access to the Hub database. Restricted files. Top secret files. I can see them all, but I had to be here to access a majority of them. Only Harrison knows I'm doing this. That is, Harrison and now you."

She was helping investigate the traitor the best way she could. But secretly. My pulse skipped around, happy and confused and grateful all at once.

I stood, prompting her to do the same. "I need to get this new Force Push thing down. If you need me, I'll be practicing in the training rooms. Or you can rely on Cohen, Harrison, or Reid. Otherwise, don't trust anyone."

10.

JOSIE

I opened the door after hugging Mom and wasn't expecting so many people. Reid was talking with Cohen, two troopers in tow. He turned to me.

"Dad and I talked to the Council, and they had already started the process to get a permanent guard assigned to Meg and Eli. Since Meg is a Founder, threats against her or her underage child cannot be ignored. And since Eli and Meg will occasionally need to separate for Meg's work, we have two vetted guards. But we'll still have to use Dad, Cohen, and me the most, for safety."

I couldn't hide my smile if I tried. "Thank you."

"Yes, thank you," Mom said behind me.

Reid tipped his head to Mom. "Of course. Coe, the guards want to talk to Meg and Eli about their schedules, safety protocols, and a system of signals and codes, and they'll also start installing additional security equipment in their rooms. Can you help with that so one of us knows exactly what is said, done, and planned?"

"You got it."

"Thanks, man." Reid gently wrapped his hand around my arm to move me in the right direction, and leaned toward my ear. "You and I need to go this way."

We walked away from the room down the center of the living quarters, and I could hardly contain my happiness. "You won't believe this, Reid."

"What?"

"My dad is your dad's contact inside the Consortium." I could actually feel the smile on my mouth spread. "My dad's alive," I whispered.

His smile matched mine. "That's awesome. So happy to hear that. And I have more good news. Cohen and I are now officially assigned to you as guards. The council thought nothing of it, since there had been a visible threat to Eli, and since I'm your trainer. Cohen is going to step in any time I can't."

And because of that, no one would think Reid was being overprotective for suspicious reasons. "Thank Thor."

His feet slowed and mine matched his. "That means I'll be staying in your room."

My face was suddenly on fire and my palms turned sweaty. An image of him holding me at night flashed in my mind. Then the image of him kissing me in the Jeep.

A tiny giggle escaped from me. To cover it up, I began walking fast again. I needed to change the subject. "I'm going to the practice rooms. I need to learn how to use and control that Force Push. And I want to start learning to observe without using my eyes." My biggest strength and my biggest weakness. "If I'm going to take down this mole, I have to do those things. And we've been here too long already without finding this traitor."

"Hey." Reid stopped before we reached the intersection of hallways. I turned and stopped a foot in front of him. "Okay," he said. "But the accident with the Force Push happened because you were upset. I want to make sure you're okay and not stretched too thin emotionally before you do it again."

"I— Uh, okay." I wasn't sure I understood what he was saying.

"I have a surprise for you." He pivoted and headed up the stairs behind him to my room. I followed, totally confused. Was he going to make out with me? Was that going to help me emotionally?

Well, it wouldn't hurt.

At the top of the stairs, I could see the entire living quarters area. The homes incorporated into the mountain were impressive and surreal. The overhead lights shined brighter than I'd remembered from the night before Reid lead me through the door to my room and closed it behind us. He entwined his fingers in mine and tugged me into the kitchen where a laptop sat open. "The computer?" I made sure not to sound disappointed.

His hand landed in the small of my back. "No. What's on the computer." Guiding me around to view the screen, Reid's warm hand found its way to my waist and he moved me into the chair.

I sat in the chair in front of the computer as he stood at my side and pressed keys. The screen flickered on and he squatted down next to me. "I'll be out in the hall until you're done. Keep it brief; I pulled some strings and have it untraceable for four minutes. She's already expecting this video chat so she knows you're with me. Don't tell her where you are, though." He sprung up and kissed me on the forehead, pushed a key, and darted for the door.

I had no idea what he was talking about and was utterly confused. "Who are you talking about? Reid?"

Pausing at the door, he flashed me a grin.

"Josie!" the computer yelled.

"Hannah!" I grinned, leaning as close to the computer as I could.

It had been less than a week since I'd disappeared without a good-bye, but it seemed like eons since we'd seen each other. So much changed for me in the span of a few days, yet she looked exactly the same. Lively hazel eyes, the dark hair I'd always envied, and happy.

"Where are you? Are you okay?"

"I'm perfectly fine." That was an exaggeration, but I needed her to stay calm enough to talk. "Mom and Eli are with me and we're with Reid." I squinted to make out her background. "Where are *you*?"

"I'm in my car. At school." I'd lost track of time in the real world. It was Friday; she had class. "Reid contacted me."

What could I tell her? Nothing. I wiped my sweaty palms down my thighs. I wasn't supposed to reveal anything to Plancks. But when Reid left the room, the only thing he warned me about was telling her our location.

Hannah pulled her phone closer to her face. "Josie."

She was my best friend. Sometimes, when I didn't think I knew myself, all I had to do was go to my best friend and she'd remind me of who I was. I missed that. I missed her.

"Reid told me. Well, he showed me."

My stomach dipped like I was on a rollercoaster. "What?" I whisper-yelled. He broke the biggest, most important rule. "I don't understand. *What* did he show you? When?"

"He made stuff appear. Disappear. Change." Her voice was quiet but excited. "It was so weird. I thought he was a fruit loop. Then I thought *I* was the fruit loop. He called me first thing this morning, like before the sun was up, asking for a video chat, blah, blah. The only reason I agreed was he said if I did I could talk to you." I could imagine her freaking out.

I realized what she'd said—Reid called her early this morning. He knew exactly how much this would mean to me.

Wait. Why wasn't she flipping out more now? How could she be so calm learning all this in a video chat just a few hours before? But, that was the beauty of Hannah. She was the perpetual optimist, always looking for the silver lining.

"Then," she continued with wide eyes, "Reid told me that you're, you know, like him—a reality-changer." She shrugged. "Or whatever. Why didn't you tell me?"

"Because the first the rule of Fight Club is 'You do not talk about Fight Club.' I'm not supposed to tell anyone.

Reid wasn't supposed to, either. You can't tell anyone anything. Ever. We'd get in trouble. Or, maybe, you." I pictured Santos on Hannah's doorstep. She'd already had a Consortium person at her home. "Hannah, I don't know. Just promise you won't expose Oculi. You could end up hurt. Or—"

She held a hand up. "Okay, okay. I won't. But are you okay?"

I nodded. "Yeah. But these rules—"

"Why can't you tell anyone? Why are you guys hiding from normal humans if you have these superpowers?" She twisted her mouth, her usual perplexed look. "If you're more powerful, it doesn't make sense."

"I think because Plancks, uh, regular humans, wouldn't accept us. But—" I paused, an unnerving feeling blooming in my gut. "I don't know, really."

"Who do the rules benefit? Normal humans? You? The people who made the rules?"

Good question. I'd been so stuck on learning how to Push and Retract and delivering the serum and staying alive, that there was a lot I hadn't questioned.

"I don't know. I'm out of my league. I can handle science and equations, but not the politics, the secrets. I don't know who to trust. People want to kill me and—"

"Kill you?" she screeched.

"Shhh." I held my forefinger against my lips. "Yeah, it's okay."

"No, that's not okay, Josie. In what world is that okay? We aren't in one of those Avengers movies."

"You're right, we're not. It's scarier."

Hannah's hand cupped over her mouth, her eyes bulging. I needed to stop freaking her out. *Think fast.*

"But." I held up a finger. "Reid's friend Cohen looks similar to Falcon in *Avengers.* So there's that."

Her hand dropped away from her somber face. "For cereal?"

I couldn't help but laugh. A hot dude always stopped her in her tracks. "I'm totally cereal. Oh, and you were right. I do like Reid."

She rolled her eyes. "Duh." I knew she was going to say that.

A countdown of thirty seconds started in the corner of the screen. No. I didn't want the chat to end yet. I didn't know when I'd see her again. Or *if.* An entire group of people wanted me dead, let alone someone trapped inside the mountain with me. "I have less than thirty seconds." My throat went dry. "Hannah." The word was long and raspy. "I'm scared."

"J, you were able to manipulate life way before you received superpowers. Regular people do amazing things daily." Tears puddled in her eyes. "Normal humans beat the odds, they defy reality and triumph. You have one up on us regular peeps. That means you can do, well, almost anything."

I wiped a tear from the corner of my eye before it could fall. "I'll see you soon."

She smiled through blurry eyes. "Hells yes you will," she yelled.

The screen went black. I stared at the laptop, inhaling through my nose and exhaling through my mouth, trying to calm myself, keeping a leash on the threatening tears.

My head spun. Humans couldn't know about Oculi. Who did that rule benefit? Plancks? Oculi?

That was it—the rule. Why were rules put into place? Usually to keep people safe and orderly. Or to make them do what you want them to do.

Or to help the people in power *stay* in power.

Ding, ding. *Thank you, Hannah.*

Reid

Josie and I weren't able to be alone for the rest of the day. We spent the afternoon in the training room with Cohen, Zac, and Kat. So far we'd practiced hand-to-hand combat and Josie had performed well. Her tae kwon do was still fresh. We then moved onto Pushing and Retracting, allowing us to use our defensive shields, but not Josie's new Jedi trick.

When we came back from a restroom break, Cohen had a table of equipment set out. I liked how his brain was working. The five of us stood in a loose circle, all eyes on Cohen. "We've all had combat training, but Josie and Zac haven't. With the Consortium being even closer to being able to identify and kill Anomalies, we need to know some of this info. Remember how you have to see it, know it, visualize it in order to Push it into existence?"

Josie and Zac both nodded.

"Well, take a look at the equipment on this table. Protective armor, all variations of what national militaries all over the world use."

Tables and racks of vests, undergarments, padding, guards, helmets, and ballistic shields laid before us. We spread out along the table, picking up the equipment and accessories, inspecting them.

I stepped behind Josie, getting a whiff of her perfume or whatever she used. Gardenia, my mom's favorite flower. "Just like with the weapons last week in Florida, you want to handle these pieces." My mouth was inches from her ear, giving me a great view of her neck. "Take note of how they look and feel, commit it to memory. You know, so you can Push them immediately when needed." Not only was Josie naturally intelligent, but her memory was like nothing I'd seen before.

She picked up a pair of unassuming glasses. "Ballistic protective eyewear," I said.

After examining the lightweight, souped-up sunglasses, she slipped them on. "Yeah, it's the smallest piece here but the most important."

Zac, standing a few feet down the table, turned to Josie. "Why do you say that?"

Josie turned around to Zac with the protective eyewear in place. "Without our eyes, we can't observe. The act of observation is what makes one of the two possible wave length superpositions collapse into a state. Copenhagen Interpretation, Heisenberg. So if we don't have the use of our eyes, we can't observe reality. We can't Push or Retract."

I could've heard a pin drop. Everyone stared at Josie.

Zac's mouth had dropped open.

"Whoa," Cohen chuckled. "You're right, Josie. Unless, of course, you're Reid. Then you can Push even with your vision taken away."

I tried on other protective gear, ignoring Cohen.

"Our boy here," Cohen continued, gesturing to me, "is the only one in recorded history able to do it."

"I'm going to learn to do it. I need to," Josie said.

Cohen rubbed his hands together, like he was ready to jump in. "All right. Only one way to find out. We can try—"

I stepped between Josie and Cohen. "No. I'll work with her on it in private. It's not fun." Twisting to Josie, I leaned toward her. "You don't want people watching you try the first time or two. Not pretty."

After we spent a while going through all the protective gear that could be useful if we were attacked by the Consortium, I cleared my throat. "Okay, it's time to practice Josie's power move."

Josie threw her shoulders back. "Let's do it."

Cohen moved to Josie's side. "I had a thought. I want you to be conscious of how you want to use it and the intensity, kind of like you have your own gauge. Let's keep it in the green and yellow, not venturing into that red zone. Maybe if you can categorize how you feel when you exert the energy, you can start to gauge it better. Make sense?"

Josie twirled her ponytail and nodded. "Okay. Yeah." She did that, fidgeted when she was nervous, but she put on an awesome game face.

Zac jogged out to the opposite side of the training room in his damn skinny pants. He looked like a preppy

Justin Bieber sans tats. "You can try on me first. I want to help somehow." I still wasn't fully convinced of him wanting to help as much as he wanted to maybe appeal to the girls, but whatever.

Thick pads appeared behind Zac on the wall and floor. Josie widened her stance, rolled her neck, and let her hands relax at her sides.

Nothing happened.

Kat looked to me and I shrugged. "Maybe Zac had to be closer like Coh—"

Zac flew backward. His shoulder hit the wall first, and he landed with a *thump* on the floor. He'd tucked his head into his chest, which was a smart move so as to not hit his head. A muffled groan came from Zac, face down on the mat. Cohen got him to sit up and took a look at his shoulder. "Uh, I think it's going to be sore."

Josie, now squatted at Zac's side, played with the hole in her jeans. "Ugh. I'm sorry, Zac."

He shook he head. "Psh. It'll be fine."

"My turn." Kat was at the long end of the room, blue mats already covering the walls and floors. "Now, how that felt? See if you can take it down a notch. I'm going to stand a little closer to you, though."

Josie stood and glanced to me, uncertain.

"Try to do what Kat said. What you just did to Zac would be in that red zone. See if you can bring it down to yellow at least." I walked backward toward the back wall where Kat would probably end up.

Josie lowered her chin, looking at Kat from under her brow. Kat sailed back in the air as if hurricane winds picked her off the floor. A rope appeared in Kat's hands, tethered to the ceiling. The slack in the rope caught and tugged Kat back toward Josie, essentially keeping her from slamming into the back wall.

A big fluffy, bouncy house mat manifested under Kat and she let go. Her body made the mat pucker, but she sprang back, laying unharmed on her back. Kat sat up with a smile on her face, scooted to the edge, and hopped off.

Josie's hands covered her face. I ran to her, pulling her shaking hands away. "Hey. It's okay. You did great."

We all convened in the middle of the room. "Maybe it's wishful thinking, but I could swear that was a little less harsh," I said. A light tremor shook Josie's shoulders, arms, and hands. I moved behind her. "I'm going to massage your shoulders." I announced it trying to make it seem like I was acting as her trainer, not a boyfriend getting handsy with his secret girlfriend.

Zac held an icepack on his shoulder. "I think maybe it wasn't as hard."

Cohen high-fived Kat. "Nice job, Kat. Josie, maybe it's like working out. You're going to get muscle cramps, be sore, but if it's consistently used, you'll gain more control."

Kat took a peek at Zac's shoulder. "I think they're right, Josie. I had time to think and Push my way out of your force shield, or whatever we're calling it."

Josie's shoulders shrugged under my palms, her muscles rock hard. "I don't know, guys. Right now, I feel like the Hulk. It just feels uncontrollable."

I pulled my hands off her so I could see her face. "Let's

take a break and make a list of people we know *are not* the mole."

Josie nodded and three plush purple sofas appeared behind Cohen. If anyone else wasted energy that way, I might have scolded them, but this was Josie. She still wasn't showing signs of even temporary energy depletion except after these huge blasts. She grabbed her bag and led us to the couches. I sat next to Cohen, hoping it would reinforce that Josie and I didn't have a relationship outside of Oculi stuff.

After passing out copies of the master list of Hub occupants, Josie extended her legs on the couch and made a list of everyone in the room when she reunited with Eli and her mom. Since the traitor had been impersonating Eli at that exact moment, it couldn't have been anyone she'd seen in that room.

"Meg, Eli, Josie, Harrison, Cohen, Zac, Kat," Josie announced. "Those are cleared. And Reid, who was with the Eli imposter."

Anger ignited in my gut just hearing her say those words.

"We know that everyone in that room, us plus our parents, isn't the mole. But we also have to remember that the mole could have recruited someone within the Hub to help him," she said.

Kat, sitting on the same couch as Zac, with her knees drawn up to her chest, raised her hand. "Idea. How about we divide up this master list. Like, I'll check out everyone who has regular communication outside the Hub."

I glanced to Josie, who was already eyeing me. Josie

smiled. "Great idea. What other divisions would be useful?"

"Right on." Cohen, lying way back on the couch, had Pushed a footstool under his feet. "I can check on those who hold a position of power."

Zac dropped his icepack on the floor and shifted in the couch. "I don't think I have access to much yet. I've only been here a few days."

He was right, but he could be useful in other ways. I didn't like the timing of when he showed up at the Hub, but he had been in the room with Josie at the time Eli was impersonated, meaning he wasn't the mole, so we could trust him to do something. "Would you be comfortable digging in to where your dad is, what communication he's had lately, or whatever with the people you know in his office?"

"I can do that."

"Good. I'll check on the fringe, those who may leave the Hub more often but aren't necessarily in a power position."

Josie's lips pulled upward in a slight smile. "That's a great start. Thank you, everyone. I'll keep practicing the shield Push. But not with Kat and Zac. I don't want to hurt you guys. You have to be well and ready to fight in case the Consortium attacks."

"Agreed," Cohen said, standing. "Dinner, anyone?"

Josie shoved off the soft couch. "Thanks, but I'm going to eat with my family. Reid, will you escort me?"

Zac pulled up a hand. "Later."

Kat hugged Josie. "See ya tomorrow morning?"

Josie smiled. "Yeah." Seeing her in better spirits and working on a plan to find this mole helped my own mood.

Everyone left the room and Josie and I hung back, moving slowly toward the training room door. Josie stepped beside me. "I think we're moving in the right direction. Thank you."

I pretended to tip an imaginary hat to her. "Just doin' my job, ma'am," I said with my best cowboy voice.

She giggled, and I decided it was my favorite sound in the world.

11.

JOSIE

Aknock came from the door and I nearly jumped out of my skin.

I'd been in my mini apartment for over an hour after I returned from hanging out with Mom and Eli after dinner in their room, with Harrison in their hallway on watch. Mom and I tried to have a semi-normal family dinner for Eli. Mom told Eli about Dad being alive, we talked about some of the funny stuff that had happened on our vacations, and we even played a few hands of UNO.

I fumbled to the door and squinted into the peephole. Reid. Thank Thor.

Swinging the door open, I gestured for Reid to come in. Cohen stood outside my door, laughing at him, I guessed for looking like a pack mule. He had a large duffel strapped over one shoulder, a pillow under one arm, and a sleeping bag under the other. Reid wore the same clothes he had on earlier, but his shirt was rumpled. He'd been lying down, too.

"I'm going to take off now." Cohen was already trotting down the stairs. "Later."

"Thank you, Cohen," I said. He raised a hand to acknowledge me.

Reid's gaze drifted down. "Are those floating Spock heads?"

I scanned my Vader *Who's Your Daddy?* T-shirt and *Star Trek* pajama pants. "If you're just going to make fun of me the whole time, I'd rather go lie down and fall asleep where I can dream about Captain America, thank you."

I turned away and gave the door a nudge, but Reid caught the door with one hand and my wrist with the other. He tugged me into him, his face completely sober. "You didn't let me finish. Nothing turns me on more than pointy ears on pajamas."

Heat flashed in my cheeks. Laughing, I swung my free hand and landed a soft punch on his shoulder. Solid.

He gave me a bewildered look. "What is it with you and hitting? Use your words." His lopsided grin pulled at his lips. He closed the door behind him.

Stepping into him, I said, "Wait. How do I know this is you?" I hated to have to say that, but I couldn't chance anything anymore.

One corner of his mouth curled. "You're so hot when you think logically."

I tried not to react. I kept a straight face, but this weird tingling spread through me. "That doesn't answer my question."

He crossed his arms. "Fair enough." A gleam of playfulness burned bright in his eyes as I challenged him. "You and I made out on a pool table not long ago."

Oh, for the love of Khan! Did he really just say that aloud? My face ignited and I covered my eyes.

"If you want, I can Push another pool table and we can finish where we left off." His smile made my heart falter.

Him being here was different than before. We shared a room for a few days before we were together, but then in the Jeep, he kissed me and said we'd continue whatever this was.

Reid placed his things on the floor and cocked his head. "What are you thinking?"

I leaned against the wall. "I kind of feel like the mole has interfered with so much of my life that he's even stolen our relationship. This traitor has made decisions for us. I mean, normal couples decide together that they're ready to move in with each other. You're moving in with me because I'm in danger. I just—" I glanced at my bare feet and shook my head. The awkwardness was almost tangible.

Reid's finger pulled my chin up so I'd look at him. His eyes seemed bluer than normal and happy. "I get it. This traitor doesn't get to steal everything, though. Let's take a walk." His smile made me smile.

He grabbed my hand, tugging me to the door, and I Pushed flip-flops on my feet. Being on the second floor, I had a clear view of this section of the living quarters. The lights were dimmer than during the day. "That's nice that they have different settings for the lights. The lights during the day are so bright."

Reid led the way down the stairs to the ground floor. "It's because they use blue spectrum light to simulate daylight as much as possible. The first members in the Hub experienced all sorts of sleep issues, so they introduced the special lighting and found a way to get natural light down here where possible."

"Like in the Open." I followed at his side down the hall.

"Yeah. Tiny bits of light can be exaggerated with the use of mirrors. It's also recommended to get out of the mountain every once in a while."

"Did you get out of here often?"

"Yeah, I used to hike with my dad a lot. My mom would take me into Denver to shop and go to restaurants. We traveled, took pseudo vacations, usually to other Oculi families around the country…like your family."

I loved when his family visited. "So, it's okay to walk around after quiet hours? We won't get in trouble?" I asked as the hall met the Open.

Reid paused. "No. We aren't doing anything wrong. Quiet hours are just that. We don't have to stay in our rooms, but we have to respect everyone else in the Hub. You know, especially the elders and the few families with younger kids." The last several words were barely a whisper. "Besides, we try to keep everyone healthy, which means sleeping when we should. But"—his voice lowered—"if you want to do something and don't want it viewed or questioned, you still have to mind the cameras. Like now."

I couldn't help seeking out the closest camera.

"Come on." Tipping his head, he signaled to me to follow.

He pointed to the high ceiling. "The entire Hub is lined with steel so we aren't detected. We have a closed, contained green cleaning system for the water, tapped into the natural springs under the mountain. It's not attached to a public sewer system."

The pipes were snuggled into the corners where the walls and ceiling met. Smart.

We followed the hall toward the training rooms. "We'll talk in a minute," he whispered. Clearing his throat, he continued, "The air is also on a closed purifying system. The generators are below the garage. Here."

He stopped in the middle of the hall, one of the sections that was more primitive. The walls were made of all rock. His hand wrapped around mine as he ducked under a lip in the wall of stone. "Watch your head."

Stooping under a shelf of rock, I shadowed Reid, the light from the hall illuminating the way just enough to outline the rock. Reid guided my head so I wouldn't hurt myself then moved me forward. "You can stand now."

Reid flicked on a flashlight. A narrow path lay before us, slightly uphill. Reid interlaced his fingers in mine and my stomach flipped at the simple touch.

"What are we doing?"

"We're going to a secret spot to talk." Reid's words, though quiet, echoed back to us.

The chill in the tunnel permeated my skin and sank into my veins.

Climbing a slight incline and still holding my hand, he said, "We have to figure out a way to control the energy burst thing that happened today."

"Otherwise?" Yeah, I was asking him to tell me the consequences.

"We don't want to find out."

My feet stopped working, along with my lungs. The flashlight on Reid's belt loop swung around as he turned to me, the narrow beam of light dancing on the rocky floor of the path. All I could see was the outline of his face hovering in front of my own.

"It's going to be okay. We are going to get through this."

"We." It was amazing how much comfort one word could bring. *We* were in this together. I sucked in air, breathing easier.

He pulled on my hand. "Almost there. Talk to me as we walk. Are you scared?"

"I'm petrified. Of myself." His fingers squeezed mine. "I don't know how to control what I did today. I could've really hurt Cohen. I've..." I couldn't say it aloud. But just because I hadn't said it aloud didn't mean it hadn't happened or I could magically undo it. I'd killed. Yes, I could argue it was done in self-defense, but even that didn't lessen the guilt and shame. "I've taken a life. I'm a murderer, Reid. I could have an Oculi degradation like Nick."

Using my other hand, I guided myself away from the jagged rocks. "If it gets to that, you have to promise you'll do what you're supposed—"

Reid whirled around, placing a hand on each side of my face. I could barely see him. "It's okay to be scared, but don't think for a second that what happened was your fault. Do you understand? You are a good person put into a terrible situation."

I nodded, trying not to give in to the pressure behind my eyes.

"You will not become your brother. You are not him, okay?"

He wasn't going to let me take the blame. But it wasn't that simple for me. I nodded anyway.

Reid pressed his lips to my forehead, then continued tugging me along the slightly uphill path. We followed the path over a ridge and Reid shined the flashlight ahead. A dead end. I didn't get it. Was I missing something? The next second, a massive section of the rock wall in front of us was missing, big enough for us to pass through. Obviously, the wall thing was Reid's doing.

"Watch your step," he said, focusing the light on the uneven ground.

Once we passed the wall, Reid shut the flashlight off, but a greenish-blue light glowed around the corner. Hesitating, I said, "Please tell me you didn't find the Tesseract."

"I don't even know what that means."

"The cube of unmatched power in Avengers?"

"The cube of what?"

"Never mind."

"Already did."

"Jerk."

"Am not. Would a jerk bring you to his secret childhood hiding place?"

Oh. "No. A jerk probably wouldn't do that." I bit my bottom lip, attempting to keep the grin off my face.

His fingers unlocked from mine, leaving my hand feeling unexpectedly cold and empty, and migrated to the small of my back. Goose bumps covered my arms, and, almost like he could read my mind, a hoodie appeared on me.

We turned the corner and I was speechless.

A single moonbeam radiated down from above, splitting the darkness like a bolt of lightning in the night sky. The ray of light showcased a ledge of blinding sparkles, like a spotlight. Breathtaking.

"I thought you might appreciate the quartz formations." His words whispered against my neck like a feather. I stared, slack-jawed, admiring the ledge of quartz.

Tiny green plants sprouted around the bed of quartz, casting a green-blue hue onto the pale cave walls.

"It's…" I couldn't find the words. It was beautiful, but it was even more special because it was *his* place.

Urging me forward, he said, "Over there."

A blanket lay on the ground, the moonlight streaking the air overhead. My heart shifted into warp speed.

"Have you brought anyone else here before?" I didn't mean to say it. That was supposed be a thought in my head, not said aloud.

He chuckled as he ushered me toward the blanket. "Never. And I swear my intentions are pure."

I side eyed him.

"Okay, so my thoughts may not be pure, but my intentions are. Otherwise, I would be trying to take your clothes off." He yanked on my hoodie. "Not putting more on you." And just like that, my face was on fire.

He pointed away from the glittery ledge. "Lie down on your back, your head at that end."

I didn't question him, mostly because I didn't know what to say. No one had ever flirted with me the way he did. Definitely no one other than him had done anything vaguely romantic for me before. I also wanted to shove all the scary stuff away, my weird ability and a mole in the midst, even if only for a few minutes. I positioned myself on the blanket like he instructed, then watched as he lay next to me, his shoulder touching mine.

Reid turned his head to me, our noses almost touching. "Look up."

Rolling my head, I gazed to the ceiling, only it wasn't exactly a ceiling. A small hole in the cave opened to the sky, giving us a sneak peek of the moon and stars. It was as brilliant as the shelf of glowing quartz. But what mesmerized me most about this little adventure was this side of Reid I didn't anticipate. This part of Reid dazzled me more than shiny stones or a breathtaking view.

"Josie?" His index finger hooked mine.

"Yeah?"

"I—" His voice scratched. "I apologize for what happened with Nick."

My eyes closed and I was unable to make the rush of mixed emotions come together to form real words.

"I've lived every day since his death with regret and sorrow," he continued, his voice now in my ear. "I would do anything to undo it, to not have killed him." His finger curled mine into his palm.

My lids fluttered open and I swiveled my head, so we

lay nose to nose.

A hurt so real and deep hid behind Reid's eyes. I was familiar with that kind of pain. "He was my friend," he whispered. "And I'd *never* do anything to hurt you."

Nick dying was the start of the end of our family. I missed him, my best friend for so long, but I understood he wasn't Nick anymore. And I'd realized as I'd eaten and played games with Mom and Eli tonight that our family wasn't ending—it was just restarting.

Part of me wanted to hate Reid for killing my brother, and part of me wanted to not be afraid to care for him as much as I did despite my brother's death. Because I did care for Reid. I always had. And what was happening between the two of us was moving past *caring for each other* into a different territory.

I stared out to the stars, where everything seemed much simpler. I had a simpler life before and I'd been fine. Lonely, but fine. Being homeschooled, constantly moving and not staying in a place long enough to make friends, I'd always longed for something more. *Something more* and *simple* seemed like opposites, yet they could simultaneously exist. And Reid was definitely something more. He was acceptance and inspiration and compassion. He made me a better version of myself.

His hand wrapped around mine as I watched the sky and my chest suddenly seemed full. Reid was like quicksand—all consuming, sifting into parts of me I didn't even know needed filling. I was tired of fighting the quicksand.

I turned my head, meeting his gaze. "I forgive you."

His eyes squeezed tight and reopened. "You have no idea how much those words mean to me."

I did know. I'd needed to say the words. Forgiving him, and my mom, wouldn't take away the storm of sadness and anger inside me, but maybe it could be the start of understanding and healing.

But to really make things better, to make *us* right, I also needed to ask for forgiveness. "Can you forgive me? I killed Santos. I killed your best friend."

"My best friend deceived me. He betrayed the Resistance. He was trying to kill you, the girl I—" Reid cleared his throat. "He knew how I felt about you. That makes what he did all the more painful. All the more personal."

"Still. I robbed you of a relationship. I ended it before you got an explanation, or closure, or—" Santos's horrified face flickered behind my eyelids as I blinked.

Reid touched my cheek. "I forgive you, Josie."

The back of my throat ached, and I wanted to say more, but I kept a hold on my emotions.

I don't know how long we stared at each other, lying there, memorizing each other's faces. It was like a veil had been lifted between us. I saw him before, but now he was clearer. He'd shown me the vulnerable side of him, a true, selfless part that was beautiful.

"I lied earlier," Reid finally said. "I've shown this place to one person."

Jealousy itched through my chest. I wasn't sure I wanted to know about another girl he'd brought here. "Oh?"

"I discovered this place when I was nine years old. I

finally showed it to my mom about a year later. She said it should stay my secret place, that I needed something to call my own, since I shared my life and home with so many others. Mom thought I should only share this with someone who was as special as the place itself." His dark lashes fanned down as his eyes closed for a moment. Then his gaze met mine again and his thumb drew circles on the back of my hand. "You're the only one who has ever been special enough."

Before we entered the Hub, Reid said he couldn't wait for the next time he could show me how he felt about me. I thought he meant make out with me, but this was better. Honest. Real.

I struggled to find the appropriate words. "I'm not sure I'm worthy of—"

"You're more than worthy, Josie. I want you to be mine. Can I, uh, call you my girlfriend?"

I couldn't comprehend his words. Absolutely astonished and slightly embarrassed, I opened my mouth to speak, but nothing came out.

The last couple of weeks were proof that all we had was the moment in which we lived. The next day wasn't certain. If I wanted to do something, as long as it was reasonable, I needed to do it. I wasn't going to live with disappointment, not when I could do something about it. So I shifted toward Reid and he began to get up, but I placed my hand in the center of his chest and shoved him back down. His eyes widened in confusion or maybe surprise.

Bracing myself on all fours, I looked down at him. No

smart-ass comment, no sly smile. His gaze traveled over my face, then he licked his lips. *For the love of Kahn.* How did I, the sci-fi nerd, end up with a person with a heart of gold who looked like a movie star? I finally answered him. "Yes."

I lowered my mouth to his, his eyes closing before mine, which did something silly to my insides. He wanted me to kiss him. The feeling of being wanted and needed melted my mind. The softness of his lips surprised me every time. I pulled away from the sweet and tender kiss, allowing only a breath between our mouths. "Thank you for this. Thank you for setting up my chat with Hannah. Thank you—"

He cut my *thank you* off with his lips.

Reid

Josie opened her door and I closed it behind us. She walked backward slowly, her eyes locked with mine.

I glanced to my sleeping bag on the living room floor then to her.

Josie tilted her head and smiled, her hair sliding over her shoulder, exposing her neck. "Will you help me fall asleep?"

Help my girlfriend fall asleep? Adrenaline spiked my blood, slamming my pulse into overdrive. A wide smile commandeered my face.

Josie turned into her bedroom. I rounded the corner and Josie was frozen beside her bed. "Josie?"

She didn't answer or move. I reached her side in three long strides. By the lamp, a tiny round metal piece lay on the white nightstand. My guts twisted.

The happiness that had lighted Josie's face only moments earlier had been replaced with pallid fear. "How long has that been here?" she asked.

I shook my head and knelt next to the bedside table, twisting to get a view of what was directly above the standard bug. A tiny dark spot stood out on the metal lampshade frame. I pressed my finger to the spot. It was tacky. Glue. The bug had lost its hold and fallen, and it was impossible to know how long it had been there—sometime after my second bug sweep. I grabbed the transmitting microphone, dropped it, and stepped on it. With silence as the backdrop, the crunch seemed louder than it should have been. I picked it up to examine it, to make sure it was destroyed. It had busted into four pieces.

Josie hadn't moved, she just stared at me, nibbling on her lip. I said, "We need to search, to make sure there aren't any other microphones or cameras. And to make sure no one is in here. It's safer to stay in the same room as we search."

Her shoulders pulled up toward her ears as she sucked in a deep breath. "Okay," she whispered.

We checked every inch of her place, Josie staying within two feet of me at all times. The disgust and resentment I had for the mole, or whomever they had do this, increased tenfold. To get this close. This act, her finding a tap in her place, was psychological terror, whether they meant for her to find this or not.

All rooms, appliances, cupboards, everything, were clear. Josie had grown unusually quiet and I knew that smart brain of hers was thinking, working out ways the mole could have done this.

"I'll stay awake all night to guard. Why don't you get ready for bed? I'll text Cohen to update him on the situation and ask if he can take over early morning so I can snooze a little."

She jetted to the bathroom and was out before I was even done getting the whole story texted to Coe. Josie crawled into bed while I finished my text and emptied my pockets onto her bedside table.

I tugged my shirt over my head and simultaneously Retracted my jeans and Pushed sweats. I slipped under the covers, raising my arm to wrap around Josie, and she was already tucked in by my side. She held on to me as if I might vanish from underneath her.

She suddenly gasped. I followed her stare to our shadows moving on the wall. "It's just me. You're okay."

Peeking over my shoulder, I Pushed the switch on the lamp and darkness surrounded us. "Try to get some sleep, okay? You need your strength. I've got you."

Josie tossed and turned forever. I changed positions with her, rubbing her back, holding her, playing with her hair—anything that might help her sleep. She finally fell asleep, but even then, she was restless, jerking and mumbling.

Looking over my shoulder, I checked my phone again.

The conversation bubble blinked on the screen, indicating a text. I slowly rolled onto my back to grab and read my phone. It was 6:02 a.m. Cohen returned my text.

Shit. You awake now? If so, let me know. I'll come hang out in J's living room and you can sleep.

I typed: *Yeah, still awake. I'll meet you at her door in 5.* I didn't want to leave her, but I had to get some shut-eye if I was going to be of any use.

I got dressed and let Cohen in. I closed the door and we stood in the small entryway of Josie's place. "Meeting here at eleven," I said.

"Who do you think should be here?"

"Us, Zac, and Kat."

"On it. Go catch some Z's."

I made it out to the living room at eleven after having made a couple of calls to Dad. Everyone sat in the living room, quietly whispering, except Josie, who was guzzling water in the kitchen.

"Did you get in a morning workout?"

She let out an exaggerated laugh. "You could say that. If you consider hurling inanimate objects across the room at varying speeds exercise, then yes. And that was after having tried the Force Push thingy four times with Cohen and once with Zac after he begged me to try. I couldn't control the Push on any of my attempts."

Zac had a bandage on his left arm and a bruise on his forehead. "Geez. Hope your insurance is paid up, VP junior," I said.

He flipped me off.

Josie moved to the couch next to Kat. "I can't control

it. It's either too much force or not nearly enough. I can't practice with these guys anymore; I keep hurting them." The pitch of her voice had elevated.

I pulled two chairs from the kitchenette and placed them across from the girls and Zac. Cohen and I sat. "Well, I take it Cohen and Josie brought you two up to speed on what happened last night." They both nodded. "I checked on a few things this morning. Nothing suspicious happened to Meg or Eli last night or so far today. I had the cameras checked to see who accessed Josie's room, but it shows that literally no one went in or out of her room during the time Josie and I took a walk."

Josie rested her forearms on her knees. "I have some ideas on that. The mole was either in my room earlier and hid for hours or—"

Kat's mouth twisted in disbelief. "There's an *or*? That's creepy enough."

"Well," Josie continued, "they could've accessed my room another way, like Retracting walls to get in from a surrounding area. Or else the person has access to the cameras."

"It can't be someone who hid in the room," I said. "I had the footage of the cameras checked for the last twenty-four hours, and there wasn't anyone we hadn't already known about. So we have to assume it's someone who has access to the cameras or they Pushed and Retracted their way in from a neighboring apartment. You have neighbors on each side. I don't see them being okay with someone coming into their home to break into yours, but maybe they didn't know. I keep coming back to the idea that it has to be someone who has some kind of clout, enough to get to the cameras."

Josie pulled the master list from her coffee table. "The list of possible suspects is just too long, and while the council gave us guards, an official inquiry will take too long."

I crossed my arms. "It could, but I think we need to check out a couple of Council members who are fairly new to their positions. Like Jared, for instance. I can't find much background info on him at all. Red flag."

Cohen popped his knuckles. "Agreed. Better check that shit out."

Josie sat back and crossed her legs. "I still think we need something that will trigger a response faster. We have to set a trap. The mole could have gotten me twice now. It will happen for real if we don't control the situation." She laid it out there with no hesitancy whatsoever. Josie looked around the room, at each of us.

"No," Kat said.

Cohen shook his head. "Too dangerous."

Zac's brows arched high. "No way."

Her green eyes slid to mine. Hell no, I didn't want her to do this. I knew exactly what she meant when she said trap. She was going to be the bait. I didn't want to put her in harm's way, but I knew if she wanted to do it, she'd do it. I had to be truthful, though. "I'd rather not."

Josie stood and gathered her hair into a ponytail. "I understand. But I came here to take down this mole. I know what I'm risking. With the Consortium being one step closer to singling out Anomalies and having one of their own inside the Hub, it's time. We need to do it soon, like tonight."

I stood, reminding myself that the three others were watching. "Man, you're infuriating. I knew you were going to say that."

She shrugged and gave me a sorry-not-sorry look.

I huffed out a fake laugh. "Fine. What's your plan, because I'm sure you've come up with something." I stepped behind my chair, bracing my arms on the back. I was too antsy to sit. My skin was crawling.

Josie loudly inhaled and exhaled, looking between the four of us. "Here's what I've come up with so far. Reid is going to make a show of looking super tired and worn down today. The mole will notice—clearly they've been watching closely."

Cohen smiled. "That won't be too hard."

"Reid and Cohen stage an argument about how Cohen should watch me tonight so Reid can get a full night of sleep, but Reid refuses. Cohen will 'get mad' and leave, then complain to Max about it. Then Reid gets his dad to do a 'surprise evaluation' of the camera surveillance room in the Eye in the Sky, kicking out the normal staff, which he can do, since he's a Founder. No one but Reid's dad will know it's happening, and his dad can watch untampered footage of the halls near my room."

She took a deep breath, glanced down at the floor. Then she squared her shoulders and kept going. "I will pretend to drain myself too much in practice today trying to control the Force Push. I'll talk loudly about it in the Pub at dinner. Cohen will be hiding in the garage as a

safeguard where the only exits are. Reid will be on standby
to follow them out of my room when they come. He and
I can Push and Retract to capture the mole. Kat and Zac
need to be near my mom and Eli's room, in case the mole
tries to use them as insurance or in case he has help. If you
hear Reid yell for you or text you, you may have to assist
us with the mole."

The room had grown warm as we all stared at Josie. "It
could work," I finally said. "We're hoping the mole only
wants to kidnap Josie, not kill her. They could have already
killed her if they wanted to."

My phone buzzed with a text from Dad.

Meet in Meg's room.

I shoved my phone back in my pocket. "Apparently,
Josie and I have a meeting with our parents. Is everyone
good with the plan? If not, say so now."

No one spoke, until Zac stood. "What time are we
meeting for dinner in the Pub tonight?"

"How about seven?" Kat asked as she stood.

No protests. No hesitancy in Kat's eyes.

Cohen stood, too. "Works for me," he said, his deep
voice firm.

We were going to go through with Josie's crazy plan.

"Seriously guys?" I eyed everyone. "You all stood up all
dramatic like. What is this? A freaking superhero movie?"

We all laughed, but I was scared shitless. I think we all
were.

12.

JOSIE

We walked in silence downstairs to my mom's room. Cohen followed us, saying Harrison asked him to care for Eli. If anyone was going to hang with my little brother besides me or Reid, it would've been Cohen.

I couldn't believe I'd gotten everyone to agree to the plan for the trap. Well, they weren't trying to stop me, anyway. Reid clearly wasn't excited about it, but that was because he cared about me. And that turned my insides to goo.

Harrison let us in, and Eli immediately came at me with a hug. I snuggled him in, ruffling his hair. Mom's lips turned the faintest bit upward as she watched us. That was not her norm—not for the last two years, anyway. She didn't approach me with open arms like my little brother had, but I didn't expect her to. The barely there smile was enough for me.

"Eli is going to get a tour from Cohen while we have a little meeting," Mom said, "but he wanted to see you first."

"I want to see you, too, buddy. You doing okay?"

He shrugged, his bangs flopping across his forehead. "Yeah, I guess. It's been really weird. Like, something-from-one-of-my-video-games kind of weird."

I nodded and Mom let out a short laugh.

Cohen leaned out from behind me so Eli could see him better. "Hey, I'm here to show someone a good time. Oh, I mean take you on a tour of this compound." Eli grinned.

After a quick reintroduction, Eli seemed comfortable with Cohen, especially when Cohen mentioned the garage and a secret spring where they went swimming sometimes.

Eli hugged me again on his way to the door. I didn't want him to go. He'd already been impersonated and I didn't want anything else to happen. Movement out of the corner of my eye caught my attention—Cohen beckoning me with a wave. He closed the distance between us and gently laid his giant hand on my shoulder. "Don't worry. I won't take my eyes off him and I'll protect him with my life. Growing up, Reid was like my brother in the Hub, and I always heard about your family. He cares about you guys. I'll treat you like my own family. Promise."

In less than two days, Cohen had proven himself trustworthy and I believed him, that he would take care of my brother. The anxiety building inside me calmed. "Thank you, Cohen."

When Eli and Cohen left, they took the easiness and smiles with them.

"We ordered brunch. Let's eat and get started," my

mom suggested on her way to the table.

We filled our plates with bagels, fruit, and bacon, poured coffee or juice, then sat around the small table. Mom opened her laptop. She wasn't wasting time.

"While she pulls that up," Harrison said, "we've yet to hear from Vice President Brown directly. We don't know his whereabouts, and the Council doesn't seem to be as concerned about this as Meg and I are. We want to make sure both he and the enhancing serum are safe." He glanced to Mom then grabbed his coffee cup. "He's the Resistance's 'in' with the government."

Worry festered in my stomach like an ulcer. The food didn't seem as appetizing, but I forced myself to spear a chunk of strawberry, knowing I needed to eat if I'd be tapping into my energy bank later in the day.

Reid shook his head and mumbled "crap" around a bit of bagel.

"But," he continued, his voice lilting upward, "Meg managed to hack the VP's private email address that he usually uses to correspond with her."

"And?" I asked.

Mom wiped her mouth with a napkin. "He's been extremely careful in what and whom he emails. The only thing I could pick out was a mention of meeting someone soon in Colorado. On a separate note, the history seems to be missing from Jared's private file. He was the last official to be elected to a Council position. The only people with access to such information are the Founders and Council members. Red flag. We'll dig deeper into Jared's background."

Red flag on Jared, a Council member. *Holy shit balls.*

Mom took a bite of bagel and held up a finger as she finished chewing. "I'm going to ask Dee if she's overheard anything from the Council members when I let her know about the missing file. I thought that would be better to do face-to-face. After talking with her the other day, it seems like she's struggling a little."

I swallowed another strawberry. "What do you mean?"

"She's not coping with grief well. Her daughter, Stella, and now the Davises, who were like her parents, are presumed dead. She said she's easily overwhelmed, hasn't been going to meetings unless she has to, suffers from insomnia, stuff like that. I also want to keep her in the loop, engaged in life."

I nodded. Reid and Harrison didn't argue with keeping Dee in the know. All four of us at that table knew grief on a personal level. We knew the trenches too well.

Harrison rotated back to my mom. "I have calls to make. You do, too." He wrapped the rest of his bagel in a napkin and stuffed it in his pocket then grabbed his coffee cup. "Can I escort you to see Dee?"

Mom closed her laptop, pushed her chair away from the table, and grabbed her cane that'd been leaning against the table. "Yes, that would be great." She grabbed the other half of her bagel with her opposite hand and grunted to a standing position. Harrison held a hand out, allowing my mom to the lead the way. She turned to me. "I'll talk to you later. Stay safe."

Reid was going to talk to his dad about our plan for a trap later, but I asked that he not share it in front of my mom. She'd been through enough; she didn't need to worry about this, too. I was keeping it from her for her own benefit, but guilt still burrowed through me.

Reid

We went straight to training room number five for Josie to practice sightless Pushing. If she could even partially figure it out before we put the trap into action, it would be less risk.

I walked backward and watched her hips sway in her spandex workout pants. Damn.

"Are you up to trying something a little unorthodox?" I asked.

She cocked an eyebrow.

I held my empty hand out. I Pushed and a folded red bandana lay diagonally across my palm.

A smile pulled at the corners of her mouth. "A blindfold? What exactly do you have planned?"

I barked a laugh. "I could say a lot of things right now. But I won't." We didn't have time for my mind to be in the gutter. "Let's cover your eyes, and I'll guide you through the steps to Push something into existence."

Her gaze shifted from the bandana to my face, her brilliant green eyes shimmering in the overhead lights. "If you're the only one who's ever done this, what makes you think I'll be able to?"

"Because I saw your brother do it several times. The first time was in this very room." She watched me, unblinking. I hadn't wanted to tell her because I didn't know how she'd react. Now guilt bit at my conscience. "Sorry."

"You don't have to be sorry. That's good to know."

"I'll give you an example, okay?" I closed my eyes but continued to face Josie. Palms up, side by side in front of me. She needed to witness my eyes closed as I Pushed and Retracted. I Pushed one of my favorite books, a leather-bound copy of *The Lord of the Rings*. I opened my eyes. "It took me six months of practice to get it down. Give it a go," I urged, holding out the bandana to her.

Josie folded the cloth another time before placing it over her eyes and turned for me to tie it. I took both ends, my fingers brushing hers. Her hands moved to the front, to keep it in place as I secured the knot. It took all my strength to not run my finger over the soft curve of her collarbone. I let my hands drop. "Can you see?"

"No."

"Good. The trick is to visualize it in your mind's eye. Once you have a mental picture, concentrate on the senses. How does the object or environment smell, taste, feel, sound? You have to let your other senses take over for your eyes."

I didn't watch our surroundings. I watched Josie, whose hands shook at her sides. She let out a sigh, pulled in a deep breath, and widened her stance.

"Relax a little. Don't force it," I said when her whole body trembled.

"Ow," her hand flew to her forehead.

Yeah, the wicked headaches and nausea were a part of it. "Some of this is going to feel like the first few times you Pushed and Retracted. It sucks, but it'll pass."

Josie bent over and braced her hands on her knees. "This is way worse than before."

"It—"

She puked in front of her feet. I didn't remember making the decision to soothe her, but there I was, my hand on her back, Retracting her thrown-up brunch. "You're okay."

"I can't do this." Josie wiped her mouth with the back of her hand then rubbed her hand on her pants. Her opposite hand quaked on her knee as she attempted to stand. "I think the blindfold is the only thing keeping my eyes in my head."

"You can do this. I know you can."

Standing tall, with the blindfold still in place, she held out her hand toward me, giving me the backward Vulcan sign—meaning die and languish.

She couldn't see my smile. "You better watch yourself, smart-ass. You're blindfolded."

"No, you better watch *your*self. I just puked and I can aim if I need to."

I stepped to her side, to watch her face. I didn't want to be in the line of fire if she got sick again. Her hands balled into fists and her jaw clenched. Josie's forehead glistened with perspiration and her teeth bit into her bottom lip. My chest tightened, watching her hurt.

I stepped behind her again, this time placing my hands on her shoulders. She stilled under my touch. I squeezed my fingers into her tense muscles. She was going to give herself an aneurysm if she didn't chill out. "Relax a little. You're always so calculated in your thoughts and stiff in your movements. It's okay to use your instinct, to go with the flow. Let go a little. Let it be organic." My thumbs dug into flesh. Her shoulders were smooth on the surface but knotted underneath.

She sighed and allowed her head to fall to the side, lengthening one side of her neck. My heart bucked like a bronco. She had no idea what she did to me. That innocent stretch made me want to run a finger down her porcelain skin.

A heartbeat later, a small package of some kind appeared on the floor. "What is that?"

Josie yanked the blindfold off. "Dear Loki. I tried Pushing an apple." She picked the small container up and held it out to me. "It's an applesauce cup for lunches."

I chuckled, earning me a dirty look from Josie. "Hey, it was close. It could've been a puddle of apple juice or something. I know most things come naturally to you, but not everyone works like that. Everything takes practice, and a part of practice is failing. It's okay to fail sometimes. It means you're trying something new or trying to better yourself."

She tugged the blindfold down. "Okay. Tell me what to Push. Maybe that will be easier."

"Okay. Uh. Hold out your hands. Push that necklace your mom gave you with the Dragon's Eye symbol."

Josie nodded as she held her hands out, side by side. Her arms trembled.

"Remember, think of the feel of the necklace. Maybe cool, metal. What metal tastes like. The shape of the Dragon's Eye. And—"

"It should be there," she said. "Is it there? I don't feel it."

I'd been watching her hands. "No, sorry. No necklace."

Her arms swung down to her sides dramatically and she grumbled something incoherent. Her right hand went back up to take off the bandana and something dark on her arm caught my eye.

"What's on you?" I asked, as she whipped the bandana from her head.

"Where?"

I grabbed her arm. "Forearm. On the inside."

We both twisted to see the black spot better—to see her new Dragon's Eye tattoo better.

Her eyes bugged out of her head and she covered her mouth. "Holy shit balls!" she said behind her hand. "I just gave myself a tattoo."

I tried not to laugh, and I failed.

Josie inspected her new ink. "Seriously? I suck at this."

"You can Retract it. One of the perks of being an Oculi—permanent tattoos can be temporary." I smiled, trying to make her feel better.

She peeked up to me. "It looks ridiculous on me, doesn't it?"

I took her arm in my hand. "Actually, you wear it well. It's pretty badass, but that's just my opinion."

Her cheeks flushed. "Okay, let's just try again."

"Don't you want to Retract it?"

"I'll keep it for a little while to remind myself about my *badass* failure."

I understood that and even thought it was adorable. "Okay. Let's do it."

Josie tugged the bandana over her eyes, placed her hands at her sides, and set her feet. Her chest rose and fell a few times, and then a red sunset maple manifested out of thin air ten feet in front of us, the leaves bright and ready to drop.

"Look," I whispered.

Instead of messing with the knot of the blindfold, I Retracted it. Josie's head straightened then she turned and her eyes landed on me.

"Is this what you had in mind?" I said.

A sheepish grin danced on her lips. "Yeah. Do I get an A for effort?" she asked, stepping closer to me, but eyeing her tree.

"An A plus."

She jumped up and down, clapping her hands.

"The pretend grade excites you more than Pushing something without sight, doesn't it?"

She cocked an eyebrow.

"Joking, joking. Let's hope you don't need to use it, but you did fantastic."

My mind was eased a little knowing Josie had Oculi skills that few others, if any, possessed. Those skills, the blind Pushing and Force Push, would give her an advantage over the mole.

13.

JOSIE

The small victory of blind Pushing and Reid's pride boosted my spirits. Hope floated inside me, making me smile. I headed toward the door, with Reid close behind.

I tugged the door open, turned, and paused in the threshold. Reid shoved his hands in his pockets and waited for me to speak, his face patient. "Thank you," I said. A slow grin spread across his lips and the hallway lights behind me reflected in his eyes. If we were in a private room, I would've hugged him, but that wasn't a good idea out in the open where we were probably being watched.

Out of the corner of my eye, a figure dashed down the hallway. For whatever reason, the quick movement made me turn my head away from Reid. I craned my neck to get a better view of the male figure. Just as they turned into the doorway to the infirmary and restrooms, the guy looked at me.

Reid.

The guy down the hallway, staring back at me, was Reid.

My breath caught in my lungs and my heart stalled.

Reid was simultaneously down the hallway and in front of me. But that couldn't be. I knew better. One was the mole trying to play mind games. The mole was trying to psych me out. And it was working.

I gulped in air and a strained gasping noise sounded from my throat.

"What?" the Reid in front of me asked.

I turned to him. The guy in front of me. That was Reid. Wasn't it?

My head oscillated back to the hallway, but the other Reid—the mole?—had disappeared.

Unless the guy in front of me was the mole. But I'd been with him since my room.

There were two options. Either I just saw the mole imitate Reid or I was experiencing an Oculi Degradation. Neither option was good.

I stared at the Reid in front of me, his eyes now narrowed in concern as his brows pinched together. He leaned closer. "Josie?"

Without thinking, I backed away abruptly, swinging the door open farther into the hallway.

"What's wrong?" he whispered.

"Nothing." I shook my head. "Nothing."

I could've told him that I just saw him down the

hallway and he probably would've thought it was the mole. But I wasn't so sure myself if it was the mole. It was only a moment, and my head was pounding. What reason would the mole have to show himself to me as Reid for such a brief amount of time? Just to rattle me? Did that make sense?

Instead of saying anything, I shook my head again and mustered a half-hearted smile. "I'm just a little tired after the training I've already done today."

"That's understandable. These training sessions can drain you. Observing reality taps into a different kind of energy. Our bodies and minds can only handle so much."

Yeah, that's kind of my worry. My mind may be at its literal limit.

"I think I need to lie down for a little while. Maybe take a short nap or something."

"Yeah," he nodded.

I stepped backward into the hallway and couldn't help but glance down the hallway again. No second Reid. I turned my head back to Reid, ready to walk in the opposite direction toward the living quarters, but Reid stared at me with a wide stance and a fire in his gaze. He looked like he was prepared to tackle me. Or Push or Retract. Or was he angry?

Was this *my* Reid? I stumbled away from him, my foot catching on the uneven floor.

He grabbed my wrist and tugged me back up before I fell. His brows creased deep. "What is going on? What did you see?"

His words were fast but his voice soft and thick. He was worried.

Dear Loki. Maybe I was losing my grasp on reality. Maybe the Council was right, and I was experiencing the first symptoms of Degradation.

"I need to know this is you," I said.

Reid's eyes widened in realization. His Adam's apple bobbed as he swallowed and his gaze left my face and darted randomly. He released my wrist and inched closer to me, cautiously moving his mouth toward my ear. "I made you fall down a chasm back at the warehouse then you punched me," he whispered. A shiver ran up my spine, remembering those terrifying minutes. No one besides Santos and Reid knew that happened. "A couple of days later," he continued, "we made out on a pool table. It's been a helluva week."

His nose brushed my cheek as he pulled away to peek at my face. He winked and one side of his mouth curled into a mischievous grin.

It was Reid.

As I released a breath, my posture slumped like I'd bottled up the anxiety over the last sixty seconds. Fear was utterly exhausting, and I didn't have time for that.

"Reid." I smiled.

Taking a step away from me, he gestured toward the living quarters. "Let's get you a nap."

"Okay."

He moved his fingers over the screen on his phone and I began walking. He caught up in several long strides.

We walked in silence to my room, but I could still feel his eyes on me. He was worried because I wasn't telling him why I was a spooked. But I couldn't talk about it—not until I figured out my mental state.

As we ascended the stairs, Cohen came into view, standing by my door. "Coe's going to take watch for you."

I nodded but didn't make eye contact with Reid.

"Hey," he whispered, lightly tugging my shoulder back and halting. "You all right?"

I finally looked up. His dark hair was messed to perfection. I'd seen him get ready on our trip up from Florida. He never really tried to look good, yet he did. Maybe it was more the fact that he didn't try so hard that I liked. His face was welcoming, warmer than it was less than two weeks ago when he took me on a motorcycle ride to show me that we were Oculi. Of course, I now knew he was really Cal, but there was more. He let down a wall with me that was still firmly in place for everyone else on this planet.

"I'm okay. Really."

"Swear by, uh, I don't know, the Jedi code of ethics or something equally nerdy?"

A giggle erupted from me. "There really is a Jedi code, you know."

"I didn't know. But, of course, you would know that."

"I'm fine." I smiled despite the lie. I should've been worried about how easy it was to lie, even if it was small fibs.

"Okay. Text when you're awake. Or want to talk. Or need an escort. Or, eh, whatever." He smoothed his hand over his jaw, and his gaze dropped to the floor. I'd not really seen him like this. It was out of character for him. He seemed awkward or something.

"I will." My words rushed out to reassure him. "I'll contact you soon."

I walked to my door and waved at Cohen. "Thanks."

His head tipped to me. "Sweet dreams."

I peeked over my shoulder to Reid. His eyes hung on to mine, almost keeping me from entering my room. I broke away from the spell and tried to smile before I slipped into my apartment and closed the door.

I made myself a peanut butter and jelly sandwich, snarfed it down, drank a glass of water, and flung myself onto my mattress. The bed squeaked under the sudden weight, but I felt heavier than the sound it made. With tired muscles and tangled thoughts, I welcomed the quiet, soft reprieve.

I closed my eyes, knowing I'd probably fall asleep before I resolved any of my issues, and the first thing I thought of was Reid. I replayed the last weird minute with him outside my room.

My eyes snapped open. Reid knew something was wrong, and was hurt that I wasn't sharing it with him. He'd be equally as hurt if he found out I was having a breakdown like my brother, who ended up killing innocent people.

I couldn't do that to Reid, or my mom and Eli. Seeing my mental state deteriorate before their eyes was not something any of them should have to endure. They had all been through enough already.

I pushed myself up and sat crisscross with my back against the headboard. The dim, warm bedside light made it seem like it was evening, but it was only late afternoon. I stared at the lamp shade, drawn to it like a moth.

Life would be easier as a moth. I mean, the Avengers have Ant Man. I could be Moth Girl, his trusty sidekick who could fly him around. And gets easily distracted by lights. I could be just as good as the Wasp. Okay, snap out of it.

I shook my head and pulled my sights away from the lamp. Regardless of the state of my mind, which was highly questionable, there was still a mole who could destroy the Resistance from the inside and hurt others. We had a plan, and I needed to focus in order to execute it.

Throwing my feet over the side of the bed, I stood and paced the length of my bedroom.

Maybe I could take care of the mole by myself then disappear. Reid and my family wouldn't have to watch my Degradation if I left them. I'd keep them safe that way, too. Reid wouldn't put himself in danger—again—on my behalf.

I had to face the fact that I didn't know for sure if I really saw a Reid look-alike or not. I didn't know if it was the mole down the hallway or if my eyes and mind were playing tricks on me. That was significant.

I needed to move up the plan to lure the mole tonight. But I needed to do it solo. That meant convincing Reid to leave me alone in my apartment, if not for the whole night, then maybe not showing up until later.

When I was alone with the mole, I'd kill him, leave him in my room for Reid to find and identify, then vanish. The part I wasn't sure about was being able to leave the three people I cared about most.

I plopped onto my bed and rested my face in my palms. My eyes closed and I envisioned playing video games with Eli. He always beat me, but I didn't care. I loved his laugh and just being with him. Maybe it was because for the last two years he and I were the only active participants in our family. I'd learned differently last week, that my mom and dad were active in their own way on our behalf, but not really with us—not the way we needed.

Though my mom had hurt me and my little brother, I loved her. She was my mother. I couldn't fathom running away from her—not when we were finally both at a place where we wanted to heal and try at a real relationship. But leaving her—leaving them both—would be for their own good.

Tears wetted my palms. I inhaled slowly, willing the cry to stop before it could fully get started. The faint crisp, clean scent of Reid still lived on my hands. My chest swelled, like even the smell of him comforted me, made me fuller.

Reid. How was I going to leave Reid after all he'd done for me? He'd gone into hiding, changed his identity to make sure the Consortium wouldn't track him to my family, and saved my life numerous times in the last two weeks. Besides, he'd been my friend as Cal for as long as I could remember.

But he was more than a friend now. We were older. We'd each admitted our feelings for the other. We could be with each other after this was over, which would actually be better than I'd ever dared to dream. The fact that I cared about him that much was precisely the reason I needed to leave him before my mind became more compromised.

A dull ache burrowed its way through my chest down into my abdomen. The slow thrumming internal pain amped. I wrapped my arms around my center, laid my head on the pillow, and pulled my knees toward my chest.

Now staring at my bedside table, I noticed my phone lying there. My hand swept across my stomach to my back pocket. My phone wasn't there. I'd apparently put it on the table but didn't remember. But maybe I didn't.

Snagging the phone, I examined it. Same case. My fingers worked against the screen. Same *Guardians of the Galaxy* wallpaper. It *looked* like my phone, but I couldn't recall putting it there.

Dear Loki.

I was questioning everything. My nerves were literally being fried, and I was already experiencing increased frequency of symptoms. Not only was my life unstable, but my mind was, too.

I squeezed my eyes tight, trying not to let tears slip between my lids.

I didn't want to leave them, but I had to. And I had to do it tonight.

A whimper escaped from me, and I turned my face into the fluffy pillow to stifle the sound.

Aware I'd fall asleep if I didn't open my eyes that instant, I kept them shut and relaxed my body into the mattress, welcoming the break from the world.

...

Reid

Something was wrong. Josie was keeping something from me. Her demeanor and body language had changed in a matter of seconds. She'd backed away from me like she was scared.

I hustled down the hallway back toward the training room we'd just left. I could've taken a nap like Josie, but I needed to work off tension. The workout room usually provided me some stress relief.

Something Josie saw had gotten to her. Even the way she looked at me changed over the span of minutes. We were our normal selves—or as normal as we could be— then she looked petrified. She wouldn't look at me on the way to her room, which was fine, but she seemed to be going out of her way to avoid my eyes. That wasn't her usual. Right before entering her place, she'd glanced at me. Her face had shifted from dark fear to sorrow. Her eyes pulled up in sympathy, or maybe apology. I wasn't sure. But whatever was wrong, whatever that look was in her eyes, that sadness was enough to make me worry. She didn't have to tell me everything, but it seemed she was suddenly keeping something from me intentionally. My worry teetered on the edge of fear. If we weren't honest with each other, we could nose-dive into a dangerous situation.

I busted through the door to the empty mini gym. With the blink of my eyes and barely a thought, I Pushed and basketball shorts took the place of my clothes. No shirt. Nikes replaced my boots. Black boxing gloves appeared on my hands.

The warm room held standard exercise equipment but wasn't large, since a lot of the Hub's residents got unconventional workouts through practice in the larger training rooms. Just by looking at the room no one could guess that it was housed in the middle of a mountain. Treadmills and stairmills took up one corner. Free weights lined the front mirrored wall. I beelined for the punching bags.

Rotating my arms in circles frontward and backward, I tried to loosen up my shoulders. Like Josie, and many others, my tension settled in my upper body. I glanced at the stereo system in the corner, Pushed, and Linkin Park blasted from the speakers.

My fist slammed into the punching bag, making it jerk slightly. That felt good. I swung the other fist and a tiny thrill wriggled in my back. Dancing on the balls of my feet, I started a sequence of jabs and kicks Santos and I used to use in workouts.

With every punch and kick, I felt better. On my toes, twisting, ducking, hitting. Adrenaline flooded my body, along with endorphins. I was jolted to life by the feel-good natural chemicals, yet it eased my nerves.

I planted my back foot for a series of alternating high roundhouse kicks. I'd be sore the next day, but it was a good hurt. I liked the feeling of muscle fatigue and soreness. The resulting pain was a sign that my muscles were literally healing, growing, getting stronger.

That idea had always fascinated me. Our own bodies were proof that we had to be challenged, we had to work hard, and even torn down to a certain degree sometimes, in order to come back stronger.

After twenty minutes, sweat covered my upper body in a sheen. Drops of perspiration plunged off my brows and trickled into my eyes. Time for a break.

I Retracted my gloves, Pushed a bottle of Gatorade into my hand, and chugged until it was empty. Letting it drop to the floor, the sound of the plastic bottle echoed through the room, barely audible over the heavy beats emitting from the speakers.

I snagged a white hand towel and wiped my face, my breathing still ragged. I rested my hands on my hips to catch my breath before I started another round. Slow inhale, slow exhale.

I pulled my arms overhead, let my hands join, and let them fall toward my back to stretch my triceps. Pivoting, I raised my sights to the mirror at the front of the room and behind the punching bag. Sweat beaded on my red face.

A figure moved in front of the window on the door to the hallway. I waved to make sure they knew they could come in; I didn't need privacy to workout.

I watched as the person stepped closer to the window in the door. A familiar face. Santos. Santos stared back at me. Shock immobilized me and my stomach lurched.

It can't be Santos. He's dead. I have to be hallucinating.

I squeezed my eyes then blinked repeatedly. His lips slowly pulled into a menacing grin. *It's not you.*

As I rushed to the door to face him head-on, he winked,

and walked away. There was no hesitation. I swung the door open, ready to tackle, but I ran into a woman who was passing by at the wrong time. She knocked into a man approaching from the opposite direction and all three of us stumbled into each other.

"Sorry. I'm sorry. Are you okay?" I asked them both.

I tried to help the woman get her footing, but she waved me off. "I'm fine." The man, who I recognized from the garage, held her steady. With hardly a glance at me, she hightailed it down the hall. The guy continued on his path in the opposite direction.

No Santos in sight.

I wiped sweat from my forehead.

I usually trusted my gut and my gut said I was being duped. It wasn't Santos. That was the mole. The mole was playing with me.

My fists balled and white heat snapped up my spine. Why hadn't I done something? I could've done something to capture him, to kill him. I now had a pretty good guess at what happened to Josie earlier. She was probably scared because she saw someone, probably Santos.

I sprinted to Josie's room. Coe was standing in front of her door with his gun drawn, looking my direction.

"It's me, man." I gave him the salute. "I just saw Santos."

"Santos is dead."

"Exactly."

He holstered his firearm. "Well, that's cause for concern. Either we have ghosts, zombies, or a mole."

"Yeah, I need to talk to her."

He opened the door. "I'll stand by until you give me

the go-ahead to leave."

"Thanks, man," I said over my shoulder as I hurried through her apartment. No lights were on but a glow emanated from her room.

Josie lay in bed and twisted around to look at me in the doorway to her room. She rubbed her eyes, rocking major bed head. "What?" Her voice croaked. She had clearly been asleep.

I moved to her bedside. She looked at me, from head to toe. Suddenly, she sat up.

"What's wrong? And where's your shirt?" Her cheeks darkened. "Wait. How do I know this is you?" Her heels dug into the mattress as she scooted closer to the headboard and farther away from me.

We didn't have time for this, but I completely understood why she'd need the reassurance. Especially now, after I'd seen someone who was dead and Eli had been impersonated. "Uh. Okay." I signaled the one index finger to her.

She continued to stare at me, expressionless. I needed something more convincing. "Okay. The first night I met you—or, uh, re-met you as Reid—we took a ride on my motorcycle to a park. You thought I was a creeper until some Consortium jack-ball tried killing you. Then later that night, I crawled through your window because you were, understandably, scared. And you'd Pushed a boulder in your room as big as Mount Rushmore."

She nodded but didn't seem entirely sold. I needed something more specific.

I crouched next to the bed. "Last night I took you to

one of my childhood hiding places. No one had seen it besides you. And my mom."

Josie let out a rush of air. "Reid. Here, sit." She scooted against the headboard to give me room.

I couldn't sit. I was too revved. Shaking my head, I leaned toward her. "You need to tell me what you saw earlier. Was it Santos?" My heartrate was still in the "turbo" range.

Her entire face contorted in confusion. "Santos? Santos is dead."

I straightened up and ran my hand over my sweaty forehead. "Yeah, no shit. But I just saw him."

Josie's eyes nearly bugged out of head. "What?"

"Josie, what did you see? What scared you?" She stiffened. "I could see it in your eyes. I heard it in what you weren't telling me. You're behavior changed in a matter of seconds. You didn't want to tell me."

Josie let her gaze drop. How was I supposed to take that? Was I reading her wrong, the situation wrong?

"Josie?" She didn't look at me, she didn't move a muscle. I squatted next to the bed, placing my hand on her knee, and tried to peek at her face. "Josie, please. Please talk to me."

I waited for her to speak. The warmth from Josie's hand gently enveloping mine spread through me, helping to calm my heart and my brain which were stuck in overdrive.

Finally, her head lifted. Her hand closed tighter around mine, and she tugged me toward her. I answered her silent request by sitting on the bed facing her.

"I saw you earlier."

Of course she did. "Uh, yeah."

Her head shook quickly. "No. I saw two of you at the same time." Her jaw fell open for a few seconds as she tried to find her thoughts and words. She was seriously distraught. "You were in front of me in the training room doorway. And, simultaneously, you were at the end of the hallway, going into the bathroom and infirmary entrance."

"That wasn't me in the hallway. I was with you. You know that, right?"

Josie didn't answer but shrugged.

"That was the mole in the hallway. This is me." I plucked her hand out of her lap and placed in on my chest. "I'm real. Okay?"

"I'm not sure what's real anymore. I think maybe—" Her voice broke. "I'm not even sure if I saw that person, the other you at the end of the hallway. Because of the Force Push, then practicing blindfolded, I think my mental stability is wavering. I, uh, I might be experiencing symptoms. You know, like my brother." Her eyes closed. "I think my brain—"

Nonsense. She wasn't experiencing Oculi Degradation.

I leaned closer, tucked a crazy piece of hair behind her ear, and cradled her cheek. "No. This is not Degradation." Her eyes opened. "This is the mole being disgusting, playing with both of us, taunting us. Trying to make you do exactly what you're doing now—doubting yourself. I was meant to doubt myself, too, when I saw Santos."

"But I—"

"No. Your mental state is on point. So is mine. You

saw what happened this afternoon, right? You shut me out, isolated yourself. I went to the gym and punched shit because I didn't know what was wrong. The mole just played us both and we reacted exactly the way he wanted us to."

"I'm scared to death that I'm losing my mind. This is all... It's just too much."

Leaning closer, I placed a hand on each of her cheeks. She placed her hands on top of mine, maintaining eye contact. "Your brain is magnificent and it's healthy," I whispered. "Do you hear me?" Her chin tipped downward once. "The mole wanted us both to doubt ourselves and each other. He wanted to separate us. We won't let him, though. We're stronger together. And we aren't going to doubt again. Self-doubt is natural, but it steals motivation. We don't have time for that."

Shifting forward, she let her forehead rest against mine. "I was going to—" She cleared her throat. "I was going to take care of the mole myself then leave. I don't want my family and you watching me deteriorate before your eyes. I don't want to be a burden. You've already had to do that with Nick."

My stomach twisted, and I pulled away to clearly see her face, which was now crinkled into a full-out cry. The thought of her leaving, being alone, was enough to make me sick. "You are fine and will never have to be alone. Not as long as I'm alive. And you are a dream, the best thing that's happened to me, not a burden. You never will be. Well, a pain in the ass, yes, but not a burden."

That got me a smile.

I pulled her hands into mine. "I promise you, I'll be by your side until the end. We'll get through this together."

She nodded and her lips tightened into a smile. "Together."

I pressed my lips to her forehead. "Want to sleep more?"

"I think I need it."

"Can I stay and sleep?" I hadn't realized until earlier when she was acting weird toward me, pushing me away, how much I needed her for myself. It wasn't a feeling of rejection and pride being hurt, but more of me really needing her as a partner and as an anchor.

"Please do."

The bedside lamp shined into the side of her eye, making her iris a lighter shade of green and illuminating the scant sprinkling of freckles over the bridge of her nose. Her hair gleamed fiery in this lighting. She reminded me of an illustration, an angel or fairy, glowing from within.

I stared at her for so long she was going to get creeped out. I smiled and stood. I Pushed my phone into my hand and texted Cohen: *We're good. I'm going to catch some sleep with J. Inform Dad of my sighting?*

He responded immediately: *Got it. Rest.*

Josie pulled the blanket down on the bed. "So, um, you never said. Why aren't you wearing a shirt?"

"Oh," I glanced down at my bare torso. "I was working out. I'll shower. Don't worry, though. I know you can't take your eyes off me, so I'll be fast."

She rolled her eyes and was still giggling when I shut the bathroom door. I showered in record time.

When I returned to the room, Josie lay under the covers with her eyes closed. I placed my phone on the nightstand, shut the lamp off, and sat next to her, trying not to jar the bed too much. My feet slipped between the cool sheets and I turned to face Josie.

Her warm hand slid up my stomach to my chest. "Hey," she whispered. "Thank you for staying with me tonight and for being my partner in this."

"You don't have to thank me." I swept my finger along her arm up to her shoulder and down along the outside of her waist. My hand rested perfectly on her waist. "I'm honored you let me."

She pressed her lips to mine, firm and brief, then tucked her head into my chest. "Thank you, too, for not putting on a shirt." Her hand ran over my chest again.

"I knew you couldn't resist this." We both quietly laughed. I kissed the top of her head. "Sleep well. Tomorrow's a big day."

Josie snuggled closer and fell asleep fast, her body moving in rhythm with her deep, slow breaths. I was dead tired but my mind couldn't shut off for quite a while. She was going to put her life on the line, which meant I was, too. That's what someone did when they loved someone.

14.

Reid

Josie and I slept forever. We'd laid down about five thirty in the evening and didn't wake until the next morning.

The day went quickly, since five of us were in the training rooms all morning. We practiced with weapons, used the virtual training system, worked on Josie's Force Push, and she even nailed Pushing a few things with her eyes closed. It wasn't all hunky-dory. We were all tense and Josie got plenty frustrated. After lunch, we had another Force Pushing session, then logged into and practiced on a private messaging group on our phones that Kat had created. For the rest of the day we'd communicate through a secured group chat. The five of us plus my dad were included.

Josie hung with Eli and her mom for a while before she and I took naps, knowing we'd likely not get much, if any, sleep that night.

After we napped, Kat texted asking if someone could keep watch in the hallway so she and Josie could hang a little. She thought it would be nice for Josie to have some "normal" time, which was cool of Kat. Zac said he'd stand guard so I could spend a few minutes with my dad.

Dad and I didn't have time to go into detail about where he'd been undercover, but we got everything ironed out for the trap later that night. The short amount of time with him was still satisfying, though. I mean, he was alive.

It was show time. I turned toward the Pub Hub and was happy to see it was full. More people could hear and possibly spread word to the mole about my and Cohen's fake spat. Weaving through the tables, I headed to the pool room in the back of the restaurant. I saw a flash of red.

Josie's reddish hair was my personal beacon. She was the person who made me feel the most like myself, like I didn't have to meet set expectations and could just be me. She seemed to guide me back to the shore, back to who I really was.

I watched her laugh with Kat, sipping on a drink. Soft curls cascaded down her back, and a tank hugged her curves.

Kat said something to Josie, and she glanced over her shoulder to me. I nonchalantly raised a hand.

"Reid!" Cohen yelled. "You can join in a minute when I'm done schooling Zac." I knocked my fist to his. Taking a seat on a stool, I leaned against the bar.

"Hey, now!" Zac hit the cue ball and it sailed past the five ball, his target. "While you guys did this in your spare time, I was forced into cotillions and country club sports."

Cohen clasped Zac's shoulder as he passed him. "Naw, you're fine."

"For a fifth grader," Chase said from the doorway in a *Call of Duty* shirt. We hadn't seen Chase since he met Josie her first night in the Hub while checking out the virtual training room.

I couldn't help my exaggerated laugh, but it earned me a glare from Zac.

The eight ball clanked into the corner pocket, and Cohen raised his hands in victory. "Get wrecked! Reid, you in?"

Shaking my head, I said, "Chase, go ahead." Chase annoyed the hell out of me, but he was a great guy to have around if we wanted info to spread. No doubt, Josie would be getting to know Chase better if she stayed here much longer. The guy was a social butterfly. Or maybe more like a social mosquito.

Chase strutted toward the cue rack. He tried looking cool, but instead resembled Shaggy from Scooby-Doo. "Thanks, boss." My stomach sank like I'd swallowed a bowling ball. Santos used to call me "boss." I'd been trying to push every thought of Santos to the dark recesses of my mind.

"Did you guys see?" Chase asked, pointing out into the main area of the Pub. "News said the VP announced a nationally broadcast press conference tomorrow from L.A."

Zac craned his neck to see a television screen. "When was that?"

"Earlier today."

"Have you heard from your dad since he went on vacation?" I asked.

Zac didn't make eye contact but shook his head. He settled on a stool, leaving one between us empty. Leaning against the bar, his arms crossed over his chest, he watched Cohen rack the balls. "I've texted my dad three times and tried calling. Nothing." He looked pissed.

My gaze extended past Cohen to Josie laughing with Kat. She deserved to laugh, to enjoy as normal a day as she could before springing our trap later tonight.

Josie turned, her eyes darting between Zac and me, and ambled over. She was probably concerned I'd poke fun at Zac somehow. And she was probably right. Josie hiked up onto the stool between us. "Hey, guys." Her words were light and bubbly.

"You seem happy. Having fun?"

Her face almost glowed. "Yeah. Yeah, I am."

The rigidness in my spine melted away and I relaxed back onto my arms. I never knew someone else's happiness could have such an impact on my own.

"So, Zac," Josie said, trying to include him in our conversation. "We're the newbs. What do you think about the Hub? Did you know about the Oculi world growing up?"

He seemed surprised by her questions. Uncrossing his arms, he rotated toward Josie and planted an elbow on the bar behind us. "Like you, I didn't know anything about the Oculi world until I turned seventeen, when I got a crash course by my father. Instead of being fully immersed and sent here, though, I only had my dad." His eyes skirted mine. "I had to continue what was expected of me. I'd graduated early from a private boarding school, preparing for college. I guess you could say I lived two lives."

Yeah, it wasn't just you, buddy.

Josie crossed one leg over the other. "That's gotta be tough. Are you in college, then?"

Zac shifted on the stool "I went this academic year, first semester. I'm taking a little break this semester while I figure out this Oculi stuff. As far as the press knows, I'm taking this semester off while I figure out what I'm doing with the rest of my life. It's not a lie. I begged my dad to let me train in an environment where I could learn more about Oculi. He finally gave in and I'm here."

"And what do you think?" I asked before Josie could.

His green eyes, a duller shade of Josie's, finally met mine. "You really want to know?"

"Yeah." *Hell yes.* It could give me some insight to his dad or him, or both.

"Schrodinger's Consortium and the Resistance mirror our own government on many levels. One group wants one thing, the other group wants another, but their goal is similar. The opposing sides both want what's best for the people, including safety and their rights respected. Neither are necessarily wrong or right, but they fundamentally don't agree on how to achieve the end goal. They'll continue fighting with nothing ever being resolved. There has to be something we're not thinking of, you know, to strike a balance."

He took a rather neutral stance, but that's what

politicians did. They played to whomever they were persuading at the time.

"I see it a little differently," I said. "The Consortium wants to be a governing body, trying to control and regulate Oculi. They deem Anomalies dangerous because we have too much power. Just because we have these abilities doesn't mean we're going to use them for nefarious reasons, though. They want to be a police state and that's not what most Oculi want. Especially Anomalies like us, whom they want to terminate. Well, unless you're Josie's family—then they want to recruit you to use you."

Amusement danced in Zac's eyes. "Then what does the Resistance want?"

I swiveled my chair toward Zac and Josie watched me with interest. "The Resistance is for every Oculi, the individual people. The people want to govern themselves, not be told what to do and how to do it by a government. They want freedom and to be allowed to live. So, I don't think they do have the same goal—the opposing sides don't want the same thing."

Zac grinned. "Interesting perspective."

I smiled back. His words didn't give me much to go on. I knew he wasn't the mole, but I still didn't know how much trust to give him.

"You were raised deeply rooted in a way of thinking. I have a more objective perspective," Zac said, bracing his hands on his knees. "Again, neither one of us is right or wrong. It is what it is."

No. I was right, but I didn't feel like arguing it further.

"Well." Josie drew both of our attention as she

uncrossed her legs and straightened. "Regardless of who is wrong or right, the way things work now with the differing ideologies means the system we have in place won't sustain. You know, like in thermodynamics? Physics?"

I shrugged. Zac shook his head.

"Chemistry?" she asked. We both just stared at Josie.

Josie rolled her eyes. "In an isolated system, entropy doesn't decrease. Eventually all systems will gradually decline into disorder. When you add human beings with emotions to the mix, the lack of predictability increases. Or, to complicate it further, you add Oculi with superhero abilities, and then entropy is inevitable."

Zac's eyes widened and he glanced to me. "That was deep." He moved his hand an inch over his head and whistled, indicating that it had gone over his head. *Right there with ya, man.*

I stared at Josie and knew I had a stupid-ass grin on my face. Her brain turned me on like no other.

Josie shot me a quick smile. "Well, that killed my sugar high."

A server delivered platters of food, all of us sharing everything, along with a stack of plates. Josie stayed at the bar to eat, the perfect place to be sure that her voice could be heard out in the main dining room, if someone was trying to listen. Zac filled a plate with wings and left the bar to stand, leaving his seat open for Cohen.

Kat stood between me and Josie to snag a plate then carefully dished a couple of wings, a few nachos, and some kind of meatball things. "Josie, you have to be exhausted after working so hard today. You, too, Reid."

"I'm okay. Thanks, Kat."

Chase came around the other side of Josie. I didn't want him to sit in the open seat for Cohen. But just then Cohen slid onto the barstool from the other side. Chase inspected the plates of food. No one officially invited him to join us. It was fine, since he was a gossip—but man, what a mooch.

"Josie, seriously," Kat continued, holding her plate. "You looked like crap earlier after practicing and weren't feeling so good even an hour ago. You should go sleep."

"Look," Josie said, dropping her chicken wing. "I appreciate you being concerned, but I can decide when I want to rest and I'm okay. I'd like to hang out for a little while." She took a big sip of her drink I watched her Push. Probably root beer.

Wow. Josie was better at acting than I expected her to be.

Chase had paused between Josie and Cohen, watching the girls talk. He accidently made eye contact with me and took off for the jukebox.

Kat moved from in between us toward Cohen. "Cohen, help me out. After all she's been through, then the intense practicing, don't you think Josie should get some rest? Exhausting herself could be dangerous."

Cohen, about to nosh on a cheesy nacho, seemed genuinely surprised Kat asked him to chime in. He placed the nacho back on his plate. "I didn't want to get into it, but yeah, Josie should go get some sleep. And so should Reid." He played this well. Really well.

I finished chewing my bite. "What?"

"Josie is spent and you need to sleep, bro. You don't sleep, you start getting sloppy."

"I'm not sloppy. And I'm not tired."

"Damn it, Reid." Cohen stood from his stool. We had an audience now. Most of the people at the dining area tables were watching us. "You don't have to be so stubborn—you're clearly exhausted. You haven't slept a full night in four days!"

Josie looked between me and Cohen. "So when I do go to sleep, who is staying with me tonight?"

"Me," I said.

Simultaneously, Cohen said, "I am."

"I'm staying with her."

"You need to sleep! It's been days since you slept well. I saw you in the training rooms—you were making mistakes."

"I'm staying with her. The end." I yelled the last two words, drawing even more stares.

Cohen waved a hand at me, shook his head, and sat back down. He looked positively pissed. Kat reeled around to join Zac sitting at a pub table.

I thought our little performance seemed convincing. Hopefully, it got to the mole and he thought it was real, too. Or that someone would tell the mole about it, anyway.

I threw cash down on the bar. "Take your time and eat, but I'm ready to leave whenever you are."

Josie glanced around the pool room at our friends. "I think I'm ready." No one would look at us, so there were no good-byes.

We walked back to her room in silence, in case cameras

were watching or listening.

I closed the door behind us and Josie stopped in the entryway, a dim lamp from the living room the only light.

"That sucked. I mean, it was good. But still."

"Yeah, it went well."

Josie tugged me toward her, pulled up my sleeve, and twisted to see my tattoo. Josie's fingertip lightly traced over the lines of the upside-down triangle. The touch was ghost-like, yet the significance of the symbol held a mighty weight.

Her finger rubbed over the three individual triangles inside the large one. "Why have you kept this? We aren't in Florida anymore. You can get rid of it, since I accidentally Pushed it on you."

"No. It's a good reminder. Like yours."

"Of what? To not be around first-day Oculi girls?" she said through a smile.

"Of what it represents. That both individually, and collectively, we have to stay balanced. Wisdom. Power." I paused. "Love."

Love—now even the word meant more to me than it used to.

Josie's tired stare rose from my arm to my eyes. Wrapping one of her hands around my neck and up into my hair, she pulled me down and pressed her soft lips to mine. This nerdy, hot girl had pocketed my heart.

Curls cascaded over her shoulders and her eyes shined bright.

She was beautiful, but she was so much more. She was the whole package. It was her confidence, her mind, her determination.

She leaned back on the wood door, waiting for me to do something. She wasn't leaving, she wasn't warning me—she was waiting. For me. Kissing her would've been the easy thing to do, but I was a masochist. Words were much more difficult. So, naturally, that's what I had to do. Talk.

I pulled in a deep breath as if preparing to dive into the deep end of a pool. "You make me feel. You've made me want to be more, to do more. You've made me look at things—everything—differently. You've made me a better person." I took a step toward Josie, her lips parting as she listened. "I want you. I need you. But I'm scared I don't know how to care for you, that what I give won't be enough." I tried swallowing my fear, but it wouldn't go away. I was afraid of her rejecting me, of her telling me I was crazy for the way I felt, but I had to be honest, even if I scared her away. "I don't know if I can love you the way you deserve, but I want to try."

Her chest rose and fell as she watched me, the seconds ticking away into eternity, then a smile played on her lips.

JOSIE

I could barely breathe. I didn't know how to act, what to do, what to say. My head spun, the words he said swirling inside me, making me dizzy.

He shifted closer, the air between us becoming hot.

We'd been near each other before, we'd kissed before, but this was different. This moment mattered. This moment was all those other kisses, and touches, and years of watching each other rolled into one. He felt it, too.

He made the final move, making me look up into his stunning eyes. I didn't know how to reply. My heart beat against his chest, or maybe his was beating against mine. "Reid, you already know how to love me. At least, that's what I've felt from you."

Reid's gaze dropped to my mouth and his lips collided with mine. There was no softness to this kiss, no gentle teasing. It was all need and desire.

His fingers threaded into my hair as he pressed my mouth open, and all thought processes ceased. The world slipped away. As far as I was concerned, nothing else existed but us.

Reid's opposite hand gripped my waist like I was going to run away. I wasn't going anywhere, though. If we were separated, we wouldn't really be apart because he'd already tethered himself to me. He'd woven himself into the fabric of my heart.

We'd shared tragedy and sacrifice. We'd both given our blood and sweat. Those trials brought us to this moment.

His mouth pulled away from mine, and I was about to protest until he kissed a warm trail along my jawline. My heart fluttered out of control, my breathing erratic. With the softness of a feather, his lips skimmed along my collarbone and a gasp escaped from me.

He pulled away to see my face, his hands paused on my waist and his features drawn in concern. "Is this okay?"

Under his tough guy facade was a sweet guy, asking my permission to kiss me. That made him even more attractive. We were doing something dangerous in a couple of hours, and I wanted to kiss my boyfriend. *My boyfriend.* "Yeah," I breathed.

He smoothed his thumb over my bottom lip then swept me into his arms, lifting me from the ground, and carried me to my room.

15.

Part of me was floating, high on Reid and the two hours we spent talking and making out. Time alone with him was a gift. The other part of me felt as if I was drowning, staring mortality in the face, and terrified. Terrified that maybe the mole did want to kill me after all, and I wouldn't get more time with Reid and my family.

I'd been lying in my bed with my eyes closed, unable to fall asleep. Reid was on the couch, pretending to sleep on the job while guarding me.

My bedroom door squeaked. I tried not to change my breathing pattern or move my eyes under my lids even though my heart thumped so hard I could hear my pulse in my ears.

At least a minute went by with no other sounds. Maybe it was Reid. Or maybe it was just my imag—

A needle pricked my upper arm and I flinched, but I pinched my eyes tight rather than opening them. Why? Why didn't I open my eyes? Someone just injected me with something. We weren't prepared for the possibility of me being drugged.

Something jostled my body and I opened my eyes, but I couldn't see. I struggled to make noise, but nothing came out of my mouth. My voice vibrated in my chest.

My body was being carried. I couldn't command my own appendages to move. I screamed again to alert Reid, but nothing happened besides a whispered grunt in the back of my throat.

No. No, no, no. They'll all think the trap is going as planned. But it's not and I can't tell them.

My body was angled and then turned. Most likely, I was being taken from my room, which we expected.

My body stopped moving, my feet lower than my head, like I was being carried by more than one person. I had to be in the living room. Unable to move or make noise, I couldn't have signaled to Reid that everything was okay even if it was. But that was my only thread of hope—that Reid wouldn't get a signal from me and he'd understand I was not okay.

Just in case, I tried to scream, but, again, nothing happened, besides a dull ache in my throat. Suddenly, something tugged in my shoulder area. My arm swung from my side down toward the floor, weighed down by my hand.

The sensation in my shoulder disappeared and my body moved again. Turn. Straight. Turn. Pause. Straight.

My body tipped, feet elevated above my head. Twelve stairs.

The stairs. That was what I was waiting for. My room was on the second floor. Taking me down the stairs meant I was in the main hall lined with the doors to the living quarters of half the population. My body leveled out as we landed on the floor then the feet transporting me moved quicker.

Miniature holes of light pierced through whatever covered my head. That meant some kind of light was overhead, so I was in the living quarters courtyard.

I Retracted the fabric against my face again. It flickered off and on so fast I almost missed it. Someone was continuously focused on it, Pushing it back on as soon as I Retracted it.

Sheer terror filled me. I was going to suffocate, if not from lack of oxygen, then from the heavy darkness weighing me down. The blackness was like a thick, wet blanket sticking to me.

Something could happen to my body. I could be shot, stabbed, or… I had to do something.

Think, Josie.

What could I feel? Burning in my lungs. Possibly something around my legs, keeping them together.

I couldn't see anything, so I'd have to try sightless Retracting. I concentrated on the feeling of what bound my legs. The kidnappers wouldn't expect me to be loose. It would throw them off more than whatever was on my face coming off. I was having a difficult time figuring out what secured my legs together. Was it plastic? I tried to visualize plastic ties and Retracted. My head throbbed and nausea rolled through me.

It was getting more difficult to concentrate with each passing second. Maybe it wasn't the fact that I didn't know what bound my legs, but I could barely think about one thing for more than three seconds. I wanted to sleep.

NO.

I attempted to thrash my body this way and that, to see what would happen. Nothing. I attempted to Retract whatever bound my limbs. Pain splashed around the inside of my skull, and I held back the need to throw up. I wasn't moving my limbs of my own free will.

The tiny holes of light twisted and leaned and blurred. I felt as if I was perpetually falling. My eyes started closing.

No. Open your eyes. Do something!

Pain gripped my left lung. How could I feel that, but not my arms and legs? No, it wasn't my lung. It was my heart.

My eyes closed. I forced them open. The tiny lights in the fabric over my head blurred and darkened.

Not sure if it would work, I Pushed, attempting to expand my energy beyond my body, not as a shield, but as a force. The energy built, the pressure inside myself mounting, then it shrank, smaller and smaller until there was nothing. I had no energy to expend. I was about to pass out.

Stay awake.

My body tilted. I wasn't sure if that was the mole tipping me, or if it was the drugs. I dropped and landed on my front, my cheek lying on a weird surface. Unless that was the drugs, too. My eyes closed.

No. I have to stay awake.

I tried to listen, to hone in on my other senses but didn't hear anything except my heart jackhammering in my chest. My eyelids were like lead. I continued to blink, trying to keep them open.

Stay. Awake.

Pitch black. I couldn't open my eyes.

Reid.

Reid

Through squinted eyes, I watched two people with masks over their faces carry Josie into the living room area. Another person stood watch, their head oscillating between me, to Josie, to the door. Josie's body was still. Concentrating on her limbs, instead of the people attempting to abduct my girlfriend, I watched for a signal.

We'd agreed that it would be best to give one of two possible signals, either balling her hand into a fist, or three short sounds, to indicate Josie was, for all intents and purposes, fine. We practiced before she went to sleep to see what might work.

Opening my eyes fully, I chanced the mole and his helpers seeing me awake, but I had to be sure of a signal from Josie. One of the kidnappers pulled a hand away from Josie's feet to open the door, before the third person rushed to help, and her arm flung down from her body toward the floor, lifeless.

The dimmed light from the hallway silhouetted the figures in the doorway. For just a few seconds I watched Josie's hand. No fist. Nothing. Her fingers curled in slightly toward her palm. They scooped up her hand, moved into the hallway, and closed the door.

I didn't like it. She was supposed to ball her fist and had the perfect opportunity. I had to follow my gut. I sprang from the couch and called Cohen. It rang endlessly with no answer.

Son of a bitch.

Shoving my phone in my back pocket, I ran out the door and down the stairs. I didn't want to compromise the plan if Josie was okay, but at this point, I had to err on the side of caution. I wasn't taking chances when it came to someone's life—especially Josie's.

I sprinted through the main hallway toward the garage, my steps echoing through the tunnel as if I were an army, not just one guy.

I pumped my arms harder. My thighs burned as I propelled forward faster, not letting up as I approached the training rooms. I couldn't let anything happen to Josie. She'd put herself in danger too many times now.

A blurry memory of me hanging out with Nick, Josie, and Eli on a beach about three years ago rushed through my mind. My family had met hers in San Diego for a little vacation.

Both our families were complete. Besides me having to hide from Nick and Josie that I really lived in the Hub, I was happy. We were all happy.

Then, an onslaught of faded images sifted through my head, one after another. A vacation to the Grand Canyon. Camping. Our families together in the Harper's kitchen or backyard, wherever they were living at the time.

I'd had a relationship with Josie for as long as I could remember. That relationship had evolved into something so much more than I ever thought imaginable. And I'd do anything for the girl I loved. For Josie, I'd fight thousands of Oculi.

Anger propelled me faster down the hall. I was angry with the Consortium and the Council. Hell, I was angry at myself for allowing her to be in trouble.

The hall opened to the cavernous garage, where Cohen should have been in position. As I turned my head, a slit of light disappeared under the hangar door, leaving the massive space dark. I'd just missed them taking Josie.

Shit.

I stopped, braced my hands on my knees, and sucked in a deep breath. "No!"

Footfalls echoed off the walls. Cohen ran to me from the shadows. "What's wrong?"

"Son?" my dad yelled behind me.

I straightened my posture. "She didn't give me a signal. Her hand fell, limp, just as they took her from the room." I whirled around. "I called you both."

Dad ran toward us. "I had company. A masked trooper tried to get me out of the Eye in the Sky. Didn't work out so well for him."

Cohen pulled his phone from his pocket. "It didn't

ring." He touched the screen. "It never came through. The call isn't in my history. Think it was purposely jammed?"

I stepped backward to see both Dad and Cohen. "Maybe. I'm not sure what the mole's intent is. Josie's body was limp. I think unconscious. We need to get to her ASAP. Coe, get Kat and Zac in here. We're going after Josie."

Cohen gave a firm nod.

"Dad, I need vehicles and troops."

Dad pulled his phone from his pocket, ready to deliver my requests.

"We need coverage on both sides of the mountain."

Dad squeezed my shoulder. "We'll find her."

Cohen was already talking to someone on the phone, so I rushed to the key box. I grabbed a set of keys for me and a set for Cohen, then sprinted to the row of vehicles, climbed into a Jeep, and pulled it directly in front of the hangar door.

The lights in the garage came on. That would help. Dad was on the phone while at the light control box.

Cohen jogged toward me from across the garage and I tossed the set of keys to him. He paused a few feet from me. "We'll get Josie. I won't stop looking for her until you do."

He knew how much and how long I had cared for her. "Thanks, man. Means a lot."

Movement caught my eye. Zac and Kat ran across the garage toward us. "Zac, you're with me. Kat, follow Cohen."

I turned the key and the clicks of my and Zac's seat belts seemed louder than they should've been. The hangar door disappeared. Bright white light seared my retinas, temporarily blinding me. Sunrise already.

I turned my hat backward and Pushed Ray Bans on my face, blinking until I could bear to look at the outside world for the first time in days. As soon as we passed through the threshold of the mountain, we took an immediate left down the dirt service road that hugged the mountain.

Checking the rearview mirror, Cohen pulled behind us with Kat in the passenger side, and the hangar door reappeared. There was no indication that some kind of opening had been in the side of the mountain moments before.

"Hold on. This road is pretty bumpy. Keep your eyes open in case we have to Push or Retract quickly. I have the front. Can you watch the back?"

Zac was already turned around. "Yeah."

The sun glowed orange in the east, not yet over the mountains.

We rode in silence down the mountain, on high alert. We wouldn't make up ground between us and the mole until we got off the service road.

I was ready to snap. I had no patience for the road that required attention and careful driving. I just needed to get to Josie.

We rolled onto the pavement and I floored it. Cohen stayed on my tail as we made our way deeper into the valley.

The sky lightened more and the sun peeked over the top of the mountains. Light streaked the highway, making it feel as though we crossed through day and night repeatedly.

I radioed Dad. He'd sent two Jeep patrols around the opposite side of the mountain. "Reid to Harrison. Any luck yet?"

Static filled the emptiness in the Jeep. "Negative. Keep going. I'll dispatch a helicopter."

My left leg bounced uncontrollably. I should've never agreed to this bait plan. She was too valuable. It was her life we were putting on the line. My chest ached, feeling hollow.

We weaved in and around the base of mountains as fast as we could. Following the bend in the road, we turned into another section of the valley. The sun perched above the mountains, pouring light into the valley full of trees and dormant grass starting to grow again.

There were only two actual roads leaving the Hub—this one, and the one Josie and I had used when we first arrived. They had to have used one of them. Most of the terrain was too rough to off-road until they got farther down into the valley. If we had Jeeps searching the only two roads, we'd find her. If they happened to chance off-roading, the chopper would spot it.

She had to be petrified. Unless she was hurt or— *Oh God.* My heart paused. I couldn't allow myself to think of what could happen to Josie.

We took the next curve too fast and Zac braced himself against the side of the Jeep. "I'm not sure what you and Josie, uh, what your relationship is." If he didn't think we weren't just trainer and trainee, then he could tell we were something more. He glanced to me. "But don't worry. We'll find her."

Nice of him to say, but I'd never forgive myself for letting this happen.

16.

JOSIE

My eyes opened and I still couldn't see, but it was lighter than the dark behind my eyes. My head bounced and cracked against whatever was underneath me. Something hard but not concrete. Actually, my cheek was pressed into a material, something like carpet.

My temples ached in rhythm to my heartbeat, but I dared open my eyelids a bit more. A hum lived in the background. My arms were tied behind my back and my legs were bound together. I lay face down, with something over my eyes. The movement made my stomach roll. I stilled, making sure I wasn't going to get sick.

What was happening? Was this a dream?

My eyes shut again, and I was on the edge of consciousness when my body rolled. I had no control over myself. I don't know how long I lay there just trying to keep my eyes open, my body moving without my permission.

I couldn't think. Everything seemed fuzzy and surreal. Was I sick?

All I knew was that I had to stay awake and figure out how to think. Why couldn't I move my hands and legs? Why did I have something over my eyes?

I blinked repeatedly, my lashes brushing against the cloth blindfold.

Eyes. Oculi. I'm an Oculi. My breathing sped. *Reid.*

It all came crashing back to me. The mole. Mom and Eli at the Hub. Being taken from my room. The failed trap. Being drugged.

I listened more closely. I bounced and heard the squeak of the suspension under me. A motor revved and I accelerated forward, my body moving from the force. I was in a vehicle.

My eyes drifted closed and I was almost asleep again when my head bounced. I had to stay awake. I needed to get out of the vehicle.

I was about to try rolling over, using my cheek as leverage. But I stopped struggling. My eyelids closed again of their own accord.

NO. Wake up.

I blinked and kept blinking.

I concentrated on moving my shield outside myself, moving my energy beyond myself. I Pushed. My eyes slid shut. Nothing.

I lay there for a minute, breathing, listening.

Where was I again? Oh, yeah. In a vehicle. Taken by the mole and at least a few others. I turned my face toward the surface under me and slid my face across the itchy material. I needed to get the blindfold off. I moved my face against the surface repeatedly, rubbing my skin raw in the process. Then it happened—the cover on my eyes shifted upward. I continued dragging my face across the surface, trying to ignore the sting on my cheek until the cover inched to my eyebrows.

Exhausted and sweating, I almost couldn't roll myself over. The reward was huge, though; I could see cracks of light. I was in the trunk. There wasn't enough light for me to see what was binding my hands and legs, or to actually see the space around me, but it was something. It was hope, and that hope ratcheted my pulse and woke me up.

I'd have to gather my strength and Push my shield outside of myself to get out, still almost without the use of sight.

Breathing slow and deep, I tried to relax my body as much as possible. I watched the cracks of light above me like they were lifelines.

Electricity snapped on my skin and pulsed through my body. The tips of my fingers tingled and my lips went numb.

One. Two.

I Pushed my shield a few inches from my body. I held it there, steady and sure.

I let the rage I felt toward the mole for using my little brother build inside me. I played the scene over again in my mind, of realizing that the boy I hugged wasn't Eli, that the Reid I saw in the hallway wasn't Reid. Fury burst in the center of me and the current throbbed through my bones.

I let go of my anger and Force Pushed through my shield.

An explosion sounded and my face was against the cracks of light. My head hit something hard and I tucked in toward my chest. Something metal smashed against my spine. No, I smashed against something metal. I ricocheted around the trunk area as the vehicle flipped through the air. Something warm and liquid dripped down my neck. Blood.

I stopped moving, but instead of being face down on the scratchy fabric, I was on my back. My eyes closed.

When I opened them, I screamed for help, first nonverbal sounds, then eventually the word "help" over and over again. My throat was raw, and all I wanted to do was close my eyes and take a nap. I'd used my Force Push against the road under the vehicle, not knowing if it would work. And I still didn't know if it worked.

Maybe I'd died and this was my own version of hell. My eyes shut against my will.

No. I can't take a nap. I'm trapped in a car. I think.

I couldn't pull my eyelids open.

Someone, or something, lifted my body and set me on the ground. Cracking one eye open just a sliver, I had to close it again. I blinked wildly as I attempted to open my eyes in the blinding light. The sun. The light was from the sun, which meant I was outside.

Green. Trees. Trees surrounded me. I was alive.

Suddenly, I could move my arms and legs. I was free. I squinted one eye and closed the other, trying to focus on the face above me. My eyes watered as I blinked.

"Reid."

His face got closer, blocking out the sunlight. "Hey."

Pop. I flinched and tried to look behind me. The sound echoed off the mountains. A gunshot.

Reid helped me sit up, bracing my back. "Go slow. Don't worry. That was Cohen grazing a trooper's leg to take him down. Remember, one of the perks of Oculi. We're almost perfect shots because we can observe where the bullet goes."

I twisted to see behind me. A black sedan lay upside down in the middle of the two-lane highway. Cohen and Zac escorted two troopers, one of which Cohen had just shot. Kat stood guarding Dee, whose limbs were bound. A giant gash in her head was nothing compared to the bloody mess of her leg.

Dee. Handcuffed and hurt. I looked back to Reid. My brain, still fuzzy, couldn't comprehend what I was seeing. *Dee is the mole? Dee is the mole.* She was like an aunt to me. She was one of my mother's dearest friends. Anger scratched my throat and disgust curdled in my stomach. "Dee?"

Reid's lips pressed into a hard line. After a few seconds, he finally opened his mouth. "Yeah." Pain edged the single word he grunted out.

We were all duped. The mole really was a traitor, in the most intimate way, in the most despicable way.

I let my head fall as I tried to think of the signs we'd missed, any hints we'd overlooked. My head throbbed, but a distinct spot in the back stung. I touched my forefinger to the tender, wet area. Blood covered my finger.

I attempted to stand, but I was too wobbly. Reid squatted beside me and wrapped me in his arms. "Hold on." His eyes roamed over my face, then my hand. "Don't move."

He examined the back of my head. I could feel his hands moving against my scalp and in my hair. He was bandaging me. I Retracted the blood from my hand.

Reid examined the rest of me, moving my arms. "Are you hurt anywhere else?"

I shook my head. "I just have a headache. And I want to stand because I was curled in that small space."

He took my hands in one of his and wrapped his other arm around me as he gently pulled me upward. Once I stood to my full height, he let my hands go, cupping my cheek. I'd never seen him with such a concerned look on his face. He tipped his forehead to mine. "I thought maybe I'd lost you and I wouldn't have been able to live with myself."

"It was my fault, not yours." I seemed to be talking slower than usual. "I didn't factor in the possibility that they'd use drugs or—"

He kissed my nose then my mouth. Sweet and gentle. I looked up, and I saw it in his eyes—he was scared. The enormity of what had just happened settled over me, and I allowed myself to feel rather than just think to get through the situation. Tears chased more tears down my cheeks. My closeness to death rattled me, but, simultaneously, the joy and relief of being alive was almost too much to handle. Reid hugged me against him and didn't ask questions, he just let me be.

After a few minutes, I pulled away from Reid, the trails

of tears dried on my face, but the anger inside me still burned. I turned toward Dee, and Reid walked with me, making sure I was steady. Cohen and Zac were getting the troops in a vehicle. Kat waited next to Dee, who was obviously in need of help due to her mangled leg.

I stopped in front of Dee, my head still fuzzy and not fully processing everything around me. My brain seemed to be moving slower than usual, but I could clearly identify my feelings. Staring at Dee, I felt nothing but resentment and loathing. A chair appeared behind me, no doubt from Reid, and I sat, only three feet from my attempted murderer. "Why would you do this?" I spat.

Crimson dripped from the open wound across her forehead and mascara stained her cheeks. Dee leaned against the vehicle, with no color in her face. A tourniquet had been tied around Dee's thigh and Kat applied pressure to a blood-soaked cloth. From the look of her leg and face, Dee's leg was either severely broken or something was severed. "The Consortium has Stella. They gave me missions to complete in order to get her back. The main objective was to get you to them, alive." She lifted her head. Tears pooled in her eyes. "They have my baby. I'm sorry. I didn't want anyone to get hurt. Or die. I just want my Stella. It was me. I impersonated Eli. And Reid. And Santos."

Energy welled inside me, ready to break me apart. I closed my eyes, willing myself to calm down. Inhaling through my nose, I opened my eyes and shoved my shaking hands into my pockets. Reid's hand around my waist tightened.

I cleared my throat, trying to swallow the indignation.

"One life should not cost another. An eye for an eye doesn't work; it's never ended well. Why didn't you take this to the Council for help?"

Dee stared at me, her brown eyes watery and her bottom lip trembling. Why couldn't she go to her own leadership on this? The council should have backed her. Unless maybe she had been tapped or was being watched, like I had been. Which, the more I thought about it, was likely.

She wasn't answering and it just fueled my anger. "Answer me!" I didn't even recognize my own voice. A primal scream, thick with fury. The lock on my temper busted open. "You're disgusting." The words came out violent and raw.

Dee started sobbing. I'd need to address some of these things after we returned to the Hub. Right now, I had to keep a level head.

I stood and turned away from Dee before she could see my own tears forming. Reid's arms closed around me. "Look at me," he whispered.

His eyes sparkled in the morning sun as he wiped my cheek. "It's over. We have the mole. It's okay to be a little happy right now. I know it's not a great situation, but we can celebrate this small victory. Okay?" He pressed his lips to my forehead.

I attempted to smile, but my insides didn't match. It felt wrong to celebrate catching the mole when the circumstances behind it were so grim. If I wasn't handed over, did that mean Stella would be killed? And why wouldn't Dee answer our questions? She had nothing to lose anymore, nothing to hide. Unless maybe she did.

17.

Reid

J osie sat in the passenger seat next to me. I kept looking at her to make sure she was still there. After losing so many others, I couldn't have lost her, too. And there were so many others who couldn't lose her, either.

We hit the dirt road that wound up the back side of the mountain to the garage. I reached my hand across the console to let it rest on Josie's thigh. Zac was in the backseat, so I shouldn't have touched her that way, but I didn't care at the moment. I needed to reassure Josie that she was fine. And I needed to reassure myself of that, too.

We pulled up in front of the mountainside, Cohen and Kat following in the other vehicle, ready to enter the garage as soon as the hangar door disappeared.

I watched the wall of rock, thinking about what Josie had pointed out a couple of days previous—the mountains were layers of history. I'd never thought about rocks that way before. But that's what Josie did; she made me view things differently; she challenged me.

But why wasn't the wall disappearing? Why wasn't anyone opening the door for us? They would've seen us coming. I picked up my cell and dialed the code for the Hub, and then called my dad's number. Nothing. I punched the number for the garage. Nothing.

Josie already had her phone up to her ear. She twisted to me. "I can't reach Mom."

This was shady. Nervousness wriggled its way through my gut.

Josie and I sprang from the Jeep. I approached Cohen in the driver's seat behind us, and she went to Kat. "It won't open. No communication with the garage, my dad, or Josie's mom."

Without saying a word, Cohen typed across the screen of his phone. Nothing. His fingers moved over his screen and we waited. Nothing.

I ran behind my Jeep and stared at the mountainside, making sure to have the entire surface in my sights. I Retracted—or I tried to Retract. Nothing happened. "Josie!"

She and Cohen were at my side in seconds. "I can't Retract the door. Can you give it a go?"

Josie widened her stance, her hands loose at her sides. She began trembling, a tangible heat radiating off her, but nothing was happening to the mountain in front of us.

"Don't hurt yourself."

She huffed and let her head sag. "What's going on?"

"I don't know, but it's not good." I opened the back door of the Jeep. "Dee, do you know why the door won't open? Was anyone in the Hub working with you?"

Dee's brown eyes dragged up to my face, but I wasn't sure if she really saw me. She slumped in the seat, pale and sweaty, her bloody leg across Kat's lap. She had to be in unbearable pain.

Dee slow-blinked. Her lucidity was questionable.

Kat glanced to me. "Let's get some pain meds in her."

"Do you know what to give her?" I asked.

"Yeah, I just went through the training."

Backing out of the vehicle, I turned to Josie and Cohen. "Dee's no help right now."

Josie rubbed the back of her neck. "I, uh. I have a thought. We can't get in and we're assuming they aren't letting us in. Right?"

"Duh," Cohen said.

Josie rolled her eyes. "What if instead of the Hub not letting us in, they are keeping us out? Do you see the difference? Also, who is they? The entire Hub? I don't think so."

My stomach dipped like I was riding a rollercoaster when the realization of what Josie was saying sunk in. "Oh God."

Cohen shook his head, totally lost.

Josie smoothed her ponytail. "They want to keep us out, all of us. Why this particular group?"

"Aw, shit." Cohen rubbed both hands over his face. "We're the youngest group with abilities, therefore the most powerful. We're the strongest."

"You weren't bait. I was," Dee said from the backseat. Her eyes were closed, her head resting on the seat. "I was used, too."

"Used by whom?" Josie asked.

Jared. Parts of his files were missing from the database, parts he didn't want seen.

Dee moaned, her hands in fists.

"Max," Josie said quickly, the word like poison on her lips. "Why did he want us out? What's he doing in there?"

"Not Jared?" I asked.

Josie looked to me and shook her head. "For someone to control Santos, Dee, and Thor knows who else, it has to be someone with authority. Max is logical."

Without evidence, I wasn't as sure as Josie seemed. "I guess we'll see soon enough."

Kat came around the end of the Jeep. "Our families are in there."

"Let's get the two injured troopers in the vehicle with Dee." I waved two of my dad's guys over to us. "Can you handle the three of them until we deal with whatever is going on and get this door opened?"

"Yes, sir."

"Thanks, guys. Okay, everyone else, let's go."

Zac moseyed up to the group, stopping behind Kat. "What are we doing if we're locked out? We can't just blast a hole in the side of the mountain and compromise the infrastructure. It could collapse."

Yeah, I was ahead of him. Forcing our way into the mountain where it wasn't supported wouldn't work. If we were locked out of this side, the mine shaft on the other side would be blocked, too. We had to find a way in that wouldn't potentially hurt the interior structure. A natural entrance would work the best. "I know a way in."

It took us about twenty minutes to trek through the mountain terrain and find the natural hole that peeked into my private crystal cave.

Once inside and past my secret place, I stopped where the path widened, making sure to have everyone's attention. There was yelling and intermittent gunfire coming from inside the Hub. Cohen, Zac, Kat, and Josie watched me, waiting for instructions, but I didn't have any. I wished I did. I wished I was the leader we all needed at that moment.

I ran my hand through my hair. "I don't know what is happening, so I can't exactly give us a game plan, guys. All I know is that we need to find Max and the rest of the Council members. We also need to find Josie's mom, her little brother, and my dad. They are the only Founders of the Resistance left. We'll have to make decisions on the fly once we figure out what we're up against. Hub communications may not be operational. Everyone type number six before phone numbers to reach each other."

"I'll look for my mom and Eli," Josie said, the bluish glow from her phone lighting her face.

"Cohen, you okay to help me with Max and the Council? Not sure how well that will go." He gave a firm nod.

Zac turned to Kat. "Want to help me look for Harrison,

and we'll keep an eye out for your mom?" Kat nodded quickly but didn't speak.

I wasn't sure what we were walking into, but I did know that each of us, save Zac, had people inside that mattered to us in some way. I needed to give them as much inspiration as I could muster. "Listen, they aren't expecting us. Whether it's Max, the entire Council, or whomever. They wanted to keep us out because we're the strongest in the Hub. We have the elements of surprise and power on our side. Just remember to be smart when Pushing and Retracting. We got this."

"We got this, yo," Cohen whooped.

Josie smiled. Her eyes met mine, then she said, "May the Force be with you." Josie's grin was all I needed to give me that extra incentive, that extra nudge of confidence going into the unknown.

Cohen and Zac laughed. "Right on," Kat said. I was probably smiling like one of those goofy heart-eyed emojis.

I led the way down the path from my secret cavern into the main hall of the Hub. It became increasingly louder, along with the pounding of my heart. When we got to the entrance, I turned to the others behind me. The light coming from under the rocky lip shined upward on everyone's faces. Deep contrast and rigid shadows made their faces seem like comic book illustrations. Dramatic and badass. "Let's go." I stepped past Cohen and kissed Josie's forehead. At that point, I didn't give two shits what anyone thought about me being with Josie.

I ducked under the rough rock, straightened, and found myself standing in the center of absolute pandemonium.

Most people were at the far end of the hallway, moving toward the living quarters, but there wasn't an exit that way. Troopers dressed in blue fought with a group of Hub dwellers near the training rooms, the end of the hall closer to the garage. What the hell?

Behind me, the others stepped into the hallway from the cave. "Max," I yelled, pointing toward the garage. Josie pointed in the other direction then took off with Zac and Kat following.

Cohen ran beside me to the small group of Resistance near the training rooms.

"Coe, can you take care of the three in the back when I Retract their guns, and distract them with the big-shot trooper?" He nodded and we separated, both of us hugging our respective sides of the hallway.

A trooper holding an assault rifle pointed at the three Resistance members and yelled, "Your choices are to unite behind Max or burn in the Hub." The guy was only a few years older than me. Three troopers stood behind him, protecting the entrance to the garage.

"Whoa, whoa. Buddy, what's going on? That's not how we do things around here," I shouted as I turned, so his eyes would follow mine. Not always, but sometimes when we look at something, we'll turn our bodies without realizing it. That's what I was hoping for with this punk-ass.

"It is now," he said. "Directed by Max." My stomach dropped. The trooper twisted toward me, his eyes momentarily off the innocent Resistance members.

Dammit. Max.

I Retracted all their guns. Cohen moved quickly,

Retracting the ground under one trooper. Then he Pushed cuffs around the other girl's wrists and ankles, causing her to break the other trooper's fall to the ground with her face. He threw an impressive KO punch to the closest dude trooper. It all happened in a matter of seconds.

I grabbed the clown-stick's head in front of me, yanked down, and slammed it into my rising knee. He was out cold. I let him drop to the floor.

I turned to the oldest of the Hub dwellers, seeing who it really was for the first time—Kat's mom. "Kat?" she asked, her eyes wide with worry.

"Go to the living quarters, there are good soldiers who will get you away from these guys. Kat is at that end."

Kat's mother turned without another word, leading the two other Hub residents down the hallway.

Cohen scooted around the corner into the garage, behind a crate of Hub supplies marked for the Caf, and I followed. Several groups of Oculi were being loaded by gunpoint into the back of army-type utility trucks by troopers.

"We're on schedule." Max's voice came from the stairs of the Eye in the Sky.

I signaled to Cohen that I'd take care of Max and his few guards. He pointed to the door propped open to the Council corridor. Good call. We needed to know where the other Council members were and if they'd attack us.

Max stepped onto the floor from the staircase with his phone to his ear and paused. "Ghost town. I'm leaving now." A couple of troops stood guard around Max. "Consortium soldiers will be there soon to practice, to run a demo for you so we can decide what would be best to present to the President and the Secretary of Defense. It's a remote location, so don't bother to take much security with you. The Consortium will be there—we can be your security."

Adrenaline and horror spiked my blood.

Consortium.

We.

Soldiers.

Max was a part of the Consortium. So who was he talking to? I had to be sure. And I had to stop him.

I blinked and Pushed zip ties around him, binding his arms to his sides, then stepped out from behind the crate. "Looks like you did some reorganization while I was out. Does that mean I'm out of a job?"

One of his cronies came at me, but I stepped out of the way, Pushed a ten-foot-deep pit into the garage floor, and gave her a shove to help her on her trip.

Movement in my periphery pulled my attention to my side where Max stood, no longer bound. I'd never actually seen him use his abilities. I'd assumed he'd used up his bank of energy. Crafty bastard.

I stepped toward him but fell into another deep hole, landing on all fours. Dick move. I Pushed, filling the new hole, and was on ground level before Max was expecting. He'd walked around the hole toward the panicked mass of Resistance being prodded into the back of vehicles like animals.

I grabbed his arm and kicked his feet out from under him. A fury, so deep that I'd never experienced anything like it before, exploded inside me. He fell then scrambled to his feet. I took the three steps to him in two, and my fist crunched against his cheek, whipping his head to the side.

Pain streaked through my hand and his uniformed guards closed around me.

"Kill him," Max shouted, rubbing his face and straightening his clothes. Pulling my hand back over my shoulder, I Pushed a knife into my hand and flung it. The weapon zipped through the air, but some of his uniforms shielded him from my view so I couldn't observe the outcome. The knife stuck out of a trooper's shoulder.

Instead of punching, I should've shot him. I hated thinking like that, but he'd deceived all of us. I should've ended him when I had the chance.

Troopers continued to close around me. I Retracted the ground under two I'd noticed were only Retractors. They'd have a more difficult time thinking their way out of a hole.

I threw a punch and flung another knife at one of the uniformed guy's feet. These guys were just following orders. I didn't want to kill them if I didn't have to, I just needed to get them off my ass.

More blue uniformed troops showed up and made a human shield around Max, leading him toward the chopper in front of the hanger door.

No, he can't leave.

A gargantuan dude stepped in front of me, blocking my view of Max. "You're going to burn in here with the rest of those who won't follow." Okay, he was the second trooper to say that. Not good. I wasn't done with Max, but right now,

I needed to find Josie and get everyone out of the Hub.

I slugged the closest uniform and he went down, which left me with Mr. Muscles. He cracked his neck side to side as he approached me. No weapon besides his mind and muscle. Usually, I'd play along, but I had things to do. I Pushed Josie's gun of choice into my hand, standard-issue Glock, and shot him in the leg. He dropped to his knees, screaming, and I ran.

I ran closer to the helicopter Max was heading for and tried Retracting it, but he had too many people focused on protecting it. The propellers started with a whine and he stepped into the chopper with help from a trooper. I tried Retracting the entire aircraft again. Nothing.

Cohen barreled down the Council corridor toward me. Something was wrong. Pain or sadness or something pulled his features downward as if he was going to cry or maybe get sick.

"Dead," Cohen yelled. "The Council. They're all dead."

Tentacles of fear closed around my chest, making it difficult to breathe or swallow or think.

That's how Max had accomplished this take over. He was a Consortium agent on the inside. What about my dad and Josie's mom? Where were they? We had to make sure they were alive.

I snapped out of my stupor and tried to Retract the helicopter, or even just parts of it, but it lifted from the ground. Max peeked through the door of the helicopter at me then one of the troopers shot at me, hitting the wall and missing me by inches. Had to be a Retractor; Pushers had better aim.

Cohen and I took off down the main hall. I told him what I'd just overheard Max say.

Cohen slowed and cursed under his breath. "What do we do first?"

"We need to get all these people out of the Hub, or we'll all be burned alive." Yeah, we needed to stop Max. Correction: we needed to kill Max. But we also needed to piece this all together. I needed Dad and Josie.

18.

JOSIE

I ran through the crevice in the rock, shining the light from my phone on the uneven ground beneath my feet. Something long and slender lay across the path up ahead. I knew it was Mom's cane without using the light.

I'd searched for Mom and Eli in all the obvious places with no luck. If Mom was not in the open, then she was hiding, and if she were hiding, it wouldn't be in an obvious place. That's how I ended up at the spring. The one Cohen showed Eli on his own special tour of the Hub.

I needed her to be in here and okay. Then, when this was all over, we had to get Dad out of the Consortium headquarters. We needed to put our family back together. That wasn't my thinking two weeks ago, but it was now. I didn't have all the information before. Eli needed a family. *I* needed a family. We needed one another—maybe in a

different capacity than we did even a few months ago—
but still.

I rounded the corner where the rock opened into the
cavernous room housing the secret pool, my eyes skipping
over everything that made the place beautiful, searching,
instead, for anything out of place. My breath caught in
my throat. Two feet—my mom's shoes—stuck out from
behind a large boulder.

My legs moved faster than I thought possible. The
adrenaline spike helped me move past the last lingering
fogginess of the drug in my system. Mom lay on the ground,
her head in Eli's lap, and her eyes closed. Tears streaked
Eli's pink cheeks and his sweaty blond hair matted to his
face. Blood soaked the side of Mom's shirt. I crumpled to
the ground and crawled to her side.

"Mom. No, Mom." I licked my lips, the saltiness
surprising me. I hadn't realized I was crying. I glanced to
Eli. "You hurt?" His head shook, his hair exaggerating the
motion.

Leaning down, I studied my mom's chest then laid my
ear gently against her. Her heart thudded but her breaths
seemed shallow. Sitting back on my feet, I watched her
face. Quiet and calm.

This scene, my mother lying there in crimson, was
at odds with the breathtaking environment—like one of
those pictures where something didn't belong. If I had a
big red marker, I would've circle the three of us.

I texted Reid to let him know where we were and that
Mom was hurt and immobile.

I Pushed a first aid kit and a stack of clean cloths.

Tugging my mom's shirt up as gently as possible, I looked at her wound. I had no idea what I was looking at, though, because I only saw the blood. Not really knowing what I was doing, I poured hydrogen peroxide over the wound. Mom moaned, still not opening her eyes. "I have to, Mom. I'm sorry." I carefully placed a clean cloth over the area and applied pressure.

I knew it would be a miracle if my mom made it out of this cave alive. Two weeks ago I didn't believe in miracles. I would've said there was no plausible way for my mother to survive. But now, a miracle was all I had, and I would've happily accepted one.

Our differences, what I'd said, what Mom had said, none of it mattered if she didn't live through this. So did those things matter if she did live? The thing that trumped any of this—my relationship with my mother, the ways I felt slighted or disadvantaged, my broken family, this messed up Oculi world—was love. My mother wasn't perfect, but neither was I. It shouldn't have taken her being on the brink of death for me to realize that I loved her and that in order for us to heal and grow, I would have to forgive her. And I did.

I slipped my fingers into her cold hand. "You need to hold on, Mom. We're going to get you out of here." I slowly pulled my glance up to my brother. "What happened?" My words came out raspy.

"We went to the garage like everybody else. Mom stood up to Max, and he told one of the soldiers to kill her. We ran, but she can't run very fast." He wiped his cheeks with the palm of his hand. "She was hit on the side and fell.

The soldier thought she was dead and went back to the garage. Mom told me to help her stand and she made us come in here."

Poor kid. I couldn't imagine being in his shoes. His world had been turned upside down, and then this. He deserved more. I shifted to wrap my arms around him, and he let his tired head rest on my shoulder. "It's going to be okay, buddy. We're going to get out of here."

An explosion made us both flinch and the earth around us quaked.

Reid

Cohen and I bobbed and weaved through bodies. Kat called saying my dad was in the Open. I needed to get to him ASAP. Everyone needed to get out of the Hub.

As we turned at the intersection of halls, my phone vibrated in my pocket. Josie.

She and her family were at the spring. Her mom severely injured. *Shit.*

I spotted Dad across the Open, pointing him out to Cohen. It was no use yelling over the chaos.

Beelining toward my dad, we were halted by a group of five people dressed in army-green jackets holding guns. People I didn't recognize. But I did recognize the patch on the left breast pocket—the Dragon's Eye symbol. They formed a circle in the middle of the Open, keeping people out of the middle.

A boom resonated through the Hub. The system of small holes and mirrored windows crashed to the center of the green-jacketed troopers' circle, replaced by a gaping hole, exposing the blue sky above. Dark forms fell from the place that was once our only source of natural light. They landed on the rubble of rock and shattered glass and mirrors.

After assessing the area, the soldiers climbed down the mound of debris as more followed them, coming down through the former skylight. Several of them pulled off their safety goggles and approached the Hub residents with their hands up. "We're with the Resistance. We'd like to get you to safety. Please come with us."

They wore the same jackets as the others. The Dragon's Eye symbol adorned their left side.

What the hell?

"Hey!" I yelled, making my way to Dad.

One of the soldiers jogged my way, but instead of answering me, he looked to my dad. "Sir. We already got several truckloads of Hub residents out via the new exit."

Dad nodded. "Continue." He pivoted to me.

My heart beat in my throat. "Who…" I could barely choke out the words. "What are you doing? Tell me what's going on."

"Just a second. I'll explain," Dad waved me to follow. He ran to the back of the Caf to the intercom system.

I jogged after him. "No, we don't have a second. Max is planning on killing every Oculi left in here because we didn't follow him."

"And he killed the Council," Cohen yelled from behind me.

"I know, son."

The ear-splitting sound of the intercom system turning on rang through the empty cafeteria and echoed in the Open.

Dad watched me as he held his mouth to the wall com. "Attention Hub residents: This is Harrison Ross. The men and woman in green uniforms are here to help you evacuate. Please follow these soldiers to safety, and we'll get you into temporary housing. The Council as a whole is no longer a governing force. Avoid Max and the Council troopers assisting him." My jaw fell open. What was going on? Who was on whose side?

Dad continued speaking into the wall. "Don't bring personal items. Again, do not engage Max or the troopers assisting him. We will get you to safe transportation from the garage or the far end of the living quarters. End message." His finger slid off the red button. "I'm sorry you had to find out this way. I kept it from you for your own good."

I grasped the edge of the counter. The air pressed in on me from every direction, threatening to suffocate me and squash me all at once. Everything seemed off kilter—in my head, inside my body, around me. It was like I was sliding and couldn't grip anything to hold on to.

My world was literally falling apart around me. My home wasn't really home. The one place I thought was safe and certain, wasn't. Identifying and neutralizing the mole should have made this place safe again, but it was quite the opposite. And my dad—I thought he was dead, but really he was some kind of double agent himself, or something. I gulped in air.

Get your shit together. What matters? Save people. Josie.

"I need to get Josie and her family to safety. Meg's hurt." I turned for the Open and was surprised Dad ran by my side.

"Where is Meg?"

"The spring."

Dad stopped, his phone to his ear already. Plugging his opposite ear, he shouted into the phone. "Emergency injury extraction. Spring."

Cohen stepped up to me, watching Dad with astonishment. "He's like James Bond."

Dad continued yelling into his phone. "Meg Harper, co-founder of the Resistance and Eli Harper, her son. Josie Harper, Resistance operative, present. Out." Pulling the phone away from his ear, his finger moved over his screen, and his mouth hardened into a line.

Dad started jogging again toward the main hallway, movement now easier since the crowd was thinning. "Phones are up again. Dial six first. I just got the message that Max got out of the garage, but he left two truckloads of scared Oculi here. It was only him and two troopers."

Just the mention of Max made me want to punch something, mostly his face. Cohen and I ran next to my dad down the long hallway to the garage. "Yeah, I saw him leave. Why didn't you tell me any of this?"

"The less you knew, the safer you were. The Council

got out of control. After your mom died, the Harpers and I wanted to undo what we'd done. We had to make sure other people were on the same page. Some were, some weren't. The underground Resistance covers North America and now spans to Great Britain. Those showing allegiance to the Council, well, Max, are no longer considered a part of the Resistance."

"Dad, I heard him on the phone. He's a Consortium agent. That means he's been planted here for years, just waiting for the right time. He's going to help demonstrate Consortium soldiers to the President and the Secretary of Defense. He told the person on the phone not to bring much security."

"Anything else? Location?"

"Carlock or Garlock or something like that."

Dad's thumbs moved over his phone screen. "Okay." A mixture of fear and fury flooded my bloodstream, first cold then hot.

We passed the training rooms. "Sir," Cohen said. "Do you know where Kat and Zac are?"

"They were escorted out of one of the new exits with Kat's mom and will meet us in the garage, as will Josie and her family."

We entered the garage and it was a different scene than it had been just ten minutes before. The hangar door was open to the outside.

The Oculi who'd been prodded into trucks like cattle were now being driven out of the mountain by soldiers in green. Medics got Dee onto a stretcher. Kat and Zac were escorted through the hangar door by two soldiers in green.

We all moved toward the stretcher.

"Dee." Dad's voice echoed through the Garage. "I need to know what you know. Your deal with the Consortium is already broken."

Dee's eyes focused on my father, but she showed no indication that she'd heard anything he'd said.

Josie ran up and wedged herself between me and Cohen, staring at Dee.

"Fine." Dad glanced to the medic behind Dee. "Take her."

Dee fisted the sheet on the gurney. "Max is working with Vice President Brown." Dee's voice was just above a whisper.

My heart pole-vaulted into my throat. No.

There were so many possible catastrophic outcomes of the Consortium and the government working together.

All eyes turned to Zac. His eyes flittered around the room, and a deep crease had formed in his forehead. This was news to him, news he didn't seem too happy to hear.

"If Brown militarizes the Consortium, with Max as his right-hand man, they could work together to destroy Anomalies." Dee winced, squeezing her eyes shut.

"Ah, yes," Dad said. "If the VP saves the Planck world, he'd have an easy in to the presidency. Hell, Brown would be the savior of all mankind, and Max would be by his side. If he commanded Oculi soldiers, he'd have incomparable power. He could manipulate humanity as he wanted."

Kat shook her head. "It could end up a global cataclysm."

I wanted to make sure I understood, but also that Zac

understood, too. "So." I crossed my arms, and blew a puff of air out of my lungs. "On the phone he said the President and the Secretary of Defense would be there to see a demonstration of the Consortium soldiers. Then he said something about having time before. For what exactly, I'm not sure."

Kat sighed. "We have to stop them. We have to cut off the two heads of the snake."

Zac pulled his focus from his shoes to me. "My dad doesn't have the guts to out Oculi on his own. If we take out Max and whatever other Consortium officials are there, maybe…I don't know."

I wasn't the only one staring at Zac in disbelief.

I weaved my fingers into Josie's and leaned down to her ear. "Your mom? Eli?"

Josie nodded. "They think she'll make it. They lifted her out of a big hole in the Open ceiling."

I squeezed her fingers and reiterated everything we'd learned.

"We have to stop this demonstration from happening," Zac said.

Josie nodded. "Yeah, you're right, Zac. Plus, your dad has or had the enhancing serum that will amplify anyone's abilities. It could possibly give regular Plancks the ability to Push or Retract. If that was the case, they could essentially make any Planck soldier a Pusher or Retractor. Who knows how he plans on using it, or if he already has."

Everyone in our little huddle broke into discussion. Dad silenced us. "A chunk of the Consortium population will all be at this one place. We should take advantage of that."

He was right—this was an opportunity. "Guys, we need to stop this demonstration from happening. But in order to do that, to ensure that a similar threat doesn't arise again, we need to kill Max and as many of the Consortium as possible." I looked to Dad. "Do we even have enough people who could fight against the Consortium with us, that would give us any chance of success?"

"Not here, but yes. There are more of us than you think," Dad announced. "I have two choppers ready to leave immediately for an abandoned town on the west side of the Rockies. Smart play on their part, a remote location. Reid, take your team, we'll hash out details in transit. I'll be right behind you with another team. Backup will meet us there. If anyone does not feel they can participate—" His eyes lingered on Zac. "Please do not feel obligated to complete this mission. Go."

Everyone ran for the helicopters besides me. I turned to my dad, unsure of what to say.

The creases in Dad's face smoothed. "I'm sorry about, well, you know, keeping this from you. It was all to keep you safe. After your mom died, I thought I owed you, and everyone in the Resistance, that. We mistakenly let the Council turn into something it wasn't intended to become and I needed to try to right that mistake. I needed to get back to the root of what the Resistance was—it was for us, the people—the Anomalies and our Oculi friends—who just wanted to be free. I'm proud of you, Cal." He shook his head. "Reid."

I hugged him. His arms closed around me and his chin rested on my shoulder. I was used to taking chances, of putting myself in danger, especially the last two years, but I was about to walk away from my father and seeing him again wasn't a certainty. I needed to say something. "I'm sorry, about a lot of things, Dad."

One of the helicopter's engines started with a high-pitched wail and the blades sliced through the air. *Womp, womp.*

Dad paused with his hand on my shoulder. "I'll be there soon. Don't underestimate Max or Brown."

"You taught me better than that," I said. The weighty truth of his warning wasn't lost on me. With the Consortium, their latest chemical weapons, and possessing the enhancing serum, Brown and Max were the deadliest force the world had encountered in decades, possibly ever. Losing to them wasn't an option.

19.

JOSIE

Cohen leaned out of the helicopter to extend a hand to Reid. Bracing himself against the inside of the chopper, Cohen tugged Reid aboard the second we lifted from the ground. Zac spotted both of them, helping them not fall, and closed the door.

The chopper cleared the hangar then picked up speed as it swooped over the crest of the mountain. The rocky terrain of the mountaintop quickly disappeared under the blanket of evergreens. I wanted to see the beautiful area again someday, but we flew toward a potentially fatal battle. Nothing was certain at this point.

Reid slapped Cohen on the shoulder and turned to me. In one swift motion, he wrenched me against him, his arms squeezing me in a hug so tight I could barely breathe. Burying my head in his chest, he nestled his face against my neck. His grip loosened, but his arms stayed coiled around me.

Mom hadn't opened her eyes before she was lifted out of the Hub through the skylight, but I promised her all the same that I'd try to fix things as much as I could. I asked that Eli be given a phone so he could correspond with me. I didn't want him to feel alone, and that little phone was the thing that could maybe give him hope. I wanted to stay with them, but I was one of the few people in the world who had a chance at stopping Max and Vice President Brown.

I wanted to tell Eli that I'd see him tomorrow, but I couldn't bring myself to say the words. I didn't know if our plan would work or if I'd even be alive the next day. This wasn't an equation with a finite answer. It was a leap of faith with the hardest part yet to come.

The helicopter ride was quick and loud. Transportation waited for us when we touched down, thanks to Harrison. We didn't want to land too close to the abandoned town and give away our arrival. Our pilot stayed with the helicopter, waiting for further instructions from Harrison, but he gave Reid a way to reach him if something went south fast.

We barreled down a dirt road in a bulletproof Infiniti QX56 to the site in the middle of the desert. Cohen drove, Reid rode shotgun, me and Kat sat in the second row, and Zac in the third.

I watched out the window, the sun still high in the blue sky. Warm and bright. The landscape wasn't as cheerful as the sky, though. There was little to nothing on the horizon besides mountains, dirt, and dust. Sparse, random grasses littered the roadside, along with a few trees. It was seriously the Old West.

We stopped in the middle of nowhere. Reid pulled out a tablet with a map. "See this little ridge right here on the map? That's right up there in front of us." He pointed out the windshield. "The ghost town is on the other side of the ridge. It would be best to wait a few minutes for Dad to catch up with his team from the Hub. In the meantime, we need to prepare."

We got out of the vehicle, stepping onto dry, cracked dirt. Dust covered my boots. The warmth felt good, but I knew it wasn't going to help any of us in the long run.

Reid grabbed my hand as he guided me to the back of the SUV. There was something comforting about the sensation of his fingers enveloping mine.

He paused and stared at me, something behind his eyes. I wasn't sure exactly what Reid saw when he looked at me, but I knew he saw beyond the sci-fi nerd, my weirdness, and my defense mechanisms. He recognized my vulnerabilities and flaws. And still, he liked me. He cared for me. Despite all that, he wanted me.

He let go of my hand and leaned to my ear. "Stay safe. Please." His voice was soft, but he didn't whisper.

That one little moment was enough to make my heart explode like the Death Star—a happy blast.

Tipping his head toward the open tailgate that revealed organized tiers of weapons, he indicated our little moment was up. Time to get to work.

Reid

If we weren't about to go start some serious shit, I would've told Josie so much. But now wasn't the time. I had a feeling she understood, though.

Cohen was already handing equipment out among the five of us. "If a good wind comes up, we might want to cover our mouths and noses." He pointed to a stack of bandanas. "Otherwise, dress yourselves with the safety gear and weapons you want. Don't forget a water pack. There are various kinds to choose from."

Kat was the first with grabby hands, pulling a safety vest from the bottom of the SUV. Josie snatched a dagger and slid it into the side of her boot.

We all chose the weapons and equipment that suited each of us best. As we got our safety gear in place, most of us going for the bulletproof vests, and weapons stashed, I thought I should say something. Like, give a pep talk of sorts.

"Guys," I yelled, waving everyone closer. "We are about to lead a group of Resistance Oculi to fight against the Consortium, the very people who want to exterminate Anomalies." That was, besides Josie's family who had unprecedented abilities or the knowledge to create tools to aid Oculi abilities. "Our first priority is to take out Max and as many Consortium soldiers as possible before the President and Secretary of Defense arrive for the demonstration. We have to do this before they get here. Our safety and freedom as Oculi is preserved by being kept secret."

"Agreed," Josie said, slinging a crossbow over her shoulder.

Cohen smiled. "Now who's going all Captain America on us, all inspirational."

"Hey," I said, "Some chicks dig Captain America." Josie's cheeks flushed pink.

Coe hit my shoulder then pulled the binoculars up to his face. "Just giving you shit, man."

Zac shook his head and tucked a HK45C piston, the gun Santos preferred, into the waistband of his jeans. "I'm going to get the enhancing serum from my dad. By force if I have to."

Cohen, looking through binoculars over the ridge into the abandoned village, whistled over his shoulder to us. "I don't see soldiers anywhere. I only see two Secret Service guys outside of one of the shacks. That has to be where the VP is, but no VP."

He handed the binoculars to Zac. "Yep. One of them is my dad's closest security—wait! There's my dad," Zac said. "I don't see the troops anywhere, either." He passed the binoculars back to Cohen. He turned around as his eyes flittered sporadically like a hummingbird. He looked nervous. Or maybe he was thinking. "Think I can go try to reason with him?" he finally asked.

The five of us exchanged looks. I pulled my phone out and texted Zac's question to Dad. My phone rang immediately. Dad.

Everyone stared at me as I listened to my father. "Got it. Thank you," I said, then shoved my phone back in my pocket. Turning to Zac, I said, "If anyone will be able to appeal to him before this situation elevates, that'd be you. Dad said they'll be here in under five, but if you think you can connect to him, or appeal to him in a different way, it's worth a try."

Nobody argued with me and we trekked in silence toward the shack where they saw the VP. The quietness was almost eerie. The only sounds were our feet shuffling through low brush and dirt and the wind whistling.

Josie scrunched low beside me, her determined eyes squinting. Peeking over the ridge, the abandoned town lay before us, if it could even be considered a town. Five or so skeletons of buildings were tossed alongside the paved two-lane road. Three of them were close in proximity to each other, with an ancient water tower looming behind them.

In the distance, several twentieth-century buildings were clumped together away from the older ones. I Pushed binoculars into my hands to check for movement. The newer buildings were surrounded by a fence that was adorned with NO TRESPASSING signs. It appeared abandoned, too.

Scurrying low to the ground and behind the closest dilapidated building, we watched the shack where Brown had to be. Only one man, dressed like Secret Service, stood guard.

Zac, the first in the row of us pressed against the building, waved to the three of us to get our attention. "I want to approach my dad by myself first," he whispered.

I understood that. And right now, it only seemed to be his dad and low security, though I was hoping the element of surprise would be on our side.

I nodded and he ran across to the old building. The door, barely hanging on at the hinges, squeaked open. "Thank you for meeting," Vice President Brown said to someone inside the building. He stepped out of the doorway, into the sun. "I imagine things—" Brown froze, his eyes wide in disbelief. "Zac!" I chanced a peek. He moved to greet his son, revealing his visitor—Max.

Max, standing in the doorway of the shack, glared at Zac, his mouth in a tight line. The rigid stance, the raised chin. He was a cobra, poised to spit venom.

My heart rocketed into my head, the erratic beat thumping inside my skull.

Josie, standing behind me, slowly twisted her body away from the Vice President and Max. She whispered to Cohen and Kat.

"Dad," Zac said, standing sure with his head high and shoulders back. "I need to talk to you in private. Now. It's critical." If the words weren't enough to persuade his father, the urgency in his unwavering voice had to be.

I interlocked my pinky with Josie's. She curled her finger around mine, pulling it into her hand. We listened, not looking at one another.

The Vice President's plan to militarize the Consortium would end badly—badly meaning genocide of Anomalies, when inevitably the Oculi were deemed too powerful. If Oculi or even just Anomalies were outed to the public, things would go south fast. I would have liked to give humans the benefit of the doubt, but people often didn't like what they didn't understand. Those who preached acceptance did so until it was something they didn't agree with. Hypocrisy was just another human condition.

The VP stepped toward Zac with a pointed finger. "You had instructions to follow Max's orders, Zac. To say I'm disappointed in your choices is an understatement. How'd you get here? How'd you know where to find me?" Brown's gaze pinballed around the collection of buildings in ruins as he stepped to the ground from the step.

Zac, unflinching, closed the space between him and his dad. He was a good two inches taller than the Vice President. "What are you really doing, Dad? Using the Consortium in the military isn't safe for anyone, especially for Anomalies like me, like your own son."

"It's more complicated than that," the VP shot back. "Max was going to keep you safe. I've had special arrangements made for you."

Zac shook his head. "No, it's not complicated at all. You and Max want power, and this is the biggest power play there is. You don't care who you hurt along the way, including me." Max glared at Zac, crossing his arms and still standing in the doorway.

The Vice President let out a hefty, fake laugh. "That is an oversimplistic view of the situation."

Another Secret Service officer rounded the corner and reached for his firearms. The VP held his hand up to them. "It's just Zac. We're fine. Please leave us." The security retreated with no questions asked.

Josie and I glanced at each other. This wasn't going

in the best direction. With Max here and Zac's emotions running high, we needed to actually see, be able to view, what was going on to Push and Retract if need be.

Zac's eyes narrowed as he took a step away from his father. "I don't believe the situation is complicated; it's pretty straightforward."

Brown stepped again toward Zac. "You weren't supposed to be a part of it, Zac. You were supposed to stay at the Hub, then go with Max to safety."

Max hadn't moved. He simply watched Zac.

"And leave every other Oculi to fend for themselves," Zac said, not shrinking away from his dad. "How kind, you self-righteous bastard. Who are you to make that decision?"

The VP's eyes widened as if he were surprised. "How dare you talk to me like that."

"Do you hear yourself?" Zac asked. "How dare I *talk* to you a certain way when you are knowingly putting an entire community in danger?"

VP Brown's face softened. "You're young, Zac. You don't fully understand the way of the world yet."

"Stop. I understand more than you think. Don't insult me."

Max stepped forward. "How'd you get here, Zac?"

Zac could've leveled Max with his glare. "I don't speak to murderers. Nothing personal." Brown's collected demeanor fell away, the corners of his mouth curling down into a scowl. "Go. Now. I don't have time for this."

Brown tried to walk past Zac, but Zac blocked his way. "Give me the vial of serum, Dad."

Brown let out an exaggerated laugh in his son's face. The next second, thick, braided rope appeared around the Vice President, holding his arms to his sides. "Give me the vial," Zac yelled, as he went for his dad's jacket pocket.

Kat walked up behind Zac from the other side of the building where we were hiding.

Shit. I hadn't seen her sneak away. I glanced back to Josie and Cohen, who both shrugged and shook their heads. Neither of them apparently had seen her leave us, either. This wasn't part of the plan. I knew she was just trying to help, giving the VP more incentive to cooperate, but she didn't know how dangerous Max was. He still hadn't used up his reserve of Oculi powers. We had no idea what he had left in him. Anxiety prickled up my spine.

I glanced over my shoulder to Josie and Cohen, who stared at me in confusion.

"Don't make him say it again," Kat said, stepping closer to Zac.

Max shook his head. "Silly girl."

The ropes disappeared from around Brown. It had to have been Max who Retracted them, unless Brown had abilities we didn't know about.

Not wanting to give away our location, I held a hand up to Josie and Cohen, indicating to stay put.

The Vice President grabbed one of Zac's arms. Zac threw a punch at his dad's jaw with the opposite fist.

Behind me, Josie gasped. "He just punched his dad!"

Brown stumbled back a step, stunned. Zac pulled his dad's suit coat open, still looking for the enhancing serum. This wasn't going as I'd hoped.

Max, now out of the doorway, had worked his way to the opposite side of Zac and his dad. He was fixated on the family fighting, like the rest of us. Neither he nor Brown fit the scene with their business attire and shiny shoes—not that any of us probably really looked like we belonged in the middle of a ghost town.

The VP bent forward, clutched one knee to stabilize himself, and rubbed his jaw. We couldn't see his face. Zac stood at the ready, his stance wide, hands loose, and focused on his father.

Max squinted as the wind swirled dust between the buildings. He took off toward Kat, maybe twenty feet between them. Kat Pushed a stone wall, at least ten feet tall and just as wide, inches in front of Max. The wall appeared so quickly he didn't have time stop or even slow. He ran into the wall and fell backward onto his backside.

Without warning, Josie sprinted past me toward Kat. She was out of arm's reach before I realized what was happening. I didn't think when I shoved away from the splintered wood siding and ran after Josie. I forced my legs to work harder than they ever had. Two more steps to Josie, ten to Kat.

The wall Kat had Pushed vanished and Max moved. As if in slow motion, Josie decelerated.

Max raised his hand and something metal reflected the afternoon sun. Panic flashed through me and my heart faltered. It could've been a gun or a knife. Regardless, I couldn't take any chances. I jumped in front of Josie, simultaneously Retracting the reflective object in Max's hand.

My body hit the hard ground, but I tucked my head, trying to prevent injury. My eyes still on Max, I Retracted the dirt from under his feet and his body fell below my line of vision.

That was close.

As far as we knew, Max was a Retractor, and that six-foot-deep pit wouldn't keep him contained for too long. I shoved off the ground, tiny bits of rock and dirt sticking to my palms. Nausea rolled through me as a vicious pain streaked down my leg.

I'd been hit. *Crap.* I didn't have time for that.

Josie's face appeared over me. "Oh. Oh, Reid. No. You shouldn't have done that."

"It'll be okay. Just a graze. Guess he got that shot off." I hadn't even heard it. "Where are Brown and Zac? The others?"

Josie's head swiveled around, worry etched into her features. "They took off behind the shed, Zac chasing his dad. Kat's with him."

"Max?" I grunted.

"Cohen just disappeared around the opposite side of the building. I think he's going after him." She looked the other direction. "Your dad is running this way with Resistance soldiers. Thank Thor."

Dad's face appeared over me. "Looks like a graze. We'll get you fixed up." He waved someone over. "We have to act now if we want to take Max and the Consortium before the POTUS and Secretary of Defense get here." Someone ripped my jeans to expose my wound.

"The rest of the underground Resistance fighters are

on their way, but we can't wait for them," Dad said. "It's now or never. We're going to have to make do with who we have here."

Josie and I both nodded. A cool liquid hit my leg, then a tormenting sting radiated through my thigh. I sucked in a deep breath, balled a fist, and dug my fingernails into my palm.

I heard Cohen's voice near. He must've circled back.

"Josie," Dad whispered. She met his stare. "You don't have to do this. You understand this is severely dangerous and the consequences are—"

"Yes. I know I'm risking my life. But I have the greatest probability of killing Max and the Consortium Oculi." She stumbled over the word *killing*, like it stuck in her throat. "I can do this."

The thought of Josie putting her life on the line split me into pieces. Part of me, the part that respected her decision to do this and knew she was capable of making her own decisions, ballooned with pride. But the other part of me, the part that wanted a future with her, the selfish part of me, ached from the terror of possibly losing her.

20.

JOSIE

Whatever that medic guy did to fix Reid's leg did the trick, because Reid ran beside me like he hadn't just been grazed by a bullet. That or Reid was freaking Wolverine and had healed already.

Harrison and Cohen jogged ten feet behind us, leading about twenty men and women ready to fight.

"They ran behind that building," Cohen yelled, pointing to the largest structure in the abandoned town. Half of the rectangular building's roof no longer existed. Parts of the collapsing walls had been patched with scrap metal, which made a low, hollow shuttering sound in the desert wind. An entire corner of the building had crumbled into the ground like a trampled sandcastle.

We approached the structure and sweat trickled down the middle of my back as the sun fried me. The hair on my neck stuck to my skin.

We approached the building, but there were no signs of Brown, Max, Zac, or Kat. Rounding the corner, Reid peeked into the structure. "Empty."

Shading my eyes with my hand, I scanned the horizon. Mountains, desert, a few shells of buildings. The waves from the heat swayed above the ground, almost hypnotizing me. "Maybe they went over there," I said. "That's a large building, isn't it? Or is it an optical illusion?" I gestured to the dark mass on the other side of a ridge.

Reid squinted in the direction I pointed. Cohen pulled binoculars up to his eyes. "We have a problem," Cohen whispered. "That's not a building."

Reid leaned close to Cohen to look through the binoculars. "Shit. Dad, army of Consortium approaching."

"Sir," someone from behind us yelled. "Advise shelter."

Something detonated about twenty feet in front of us before Harrison had a chance to reply or give an order. The blast reverberated in my chest. Soil and rocks flew everywhere, showering us. I turned away, squeezed my eyes closed, and covered my head, Pushing my personal shield over me, Reid, Cohen, and Harrison.

I glanced to Reid, who was already looking at me. A low hum rang in my ears. Reid's mouth moved, but I couldn't make out the words. I shook my head and pointed to my ears.

Reid pulled me up and leaned to my ear. "The ringing will pass. I said that we're lucky the Consortium is made up of mostly Pushers and Retractors. Very few Anomalies. We have better aim." He winked then twisted to his dad, motioning to the approaching Consortium horde.

I smiled. I wasn't sure what it said about either one of us, but I appreciated the wink while facing a possible bloodbath.

Dust floated through the air, diffusing the sun. It looked as if a gauzy curtain hung between us and our enemies. I tugged my bandana up over my mouth and nose.

The muted colors and muffled noises made the world seem like a warped reality. Or at least like I had sunglasses and headphones on.

As our soldiers reorganized behind the cluster of ancient buildings, the Consortium troops approached from the foothills, an open, arid expanse separating us. They moved uphill toward us.

Cohen had his binoculars up to his face again. "Brown, Max, Zac, and Kat leading in an UTV." The veins in his neck stuck out as he shouted.

Harrison pivoted, shouting orders to the Resistance members behind us. I only caught "Don't injure" and "Resistance." Probably warning everyone that two of our own where being held.

For the first time, I really looked at the people behind us, the Resistance. There were at least twenty people in green jackets, underground Resistance soldiers, all armed as I would've expected an Army solider to be. They were all ages, genders, and ethnicities. A few had to be about my age. The rest of the people, maybe thirty of them, were dressed in regular clothing, just ordinary Oculi, most likely from the Hub. Some of us weren't extensively trained for battle. They were simply fighting to keep us, the Resistance, many of whom were Anomalies like myself, alive.

The soldiers stood at attention, listening to Harrison with sober expressions. Most of the other Resistance faces looked focused and ready. I was new to this battle, stepping in only at the last minute. Some of these people had stood against the Consortium for more than half of their lives, like my and Reid's parents. Some of them, like the Davises who disappeared, had silently fought the Consortium their entire lives, before the Resistance was ever formed. This war had been building for decades and decades, and now finally came to a head. Here and now.

Reid stepped to my side. "Don't forget to watch what each person does. Most of them will only be able to Push or Retract. A lot of them will rely on weapons and physical contact. They obviously outnumber us and they'll be ready to kill."

I was ready to fight, but that didn't mean I wasn't scared. A terror, real and deep, thrived inside me. I whirled around to face Reid. His brows furrowed and his mouth pressed into a hard line.

I had so much to say. But what could I say when we were about to test our mortality and we were out of time? "If something happens to me, can you check on Eli every once in a while?"

Reid pulled me closer and his eyes softened. "Nothing will happen. We're going to fight for the Resistance and for humanity and for us. You and me."

My heart stuttered and I nodded. He was right. We were fighting for others but also for us, for a chance to be together. "It's just the beginning for us."

It was a romantic sentiment and I was being positive, but I knew the real stakes. Reid and I both knew our lives, and thus our relationship, was at risk.

Everyone around us yelled in unison, responding to whatever Harrison was saying. Cohen appeared next to us, clasping Reid on the shoulder. His eyes met mine first, then moved to Reid. "It's time."

The next thing I knew, Reid tugged me against him, his lips collided with mine, and he pressed my mouth open. I wrapped my hands around his neck. With his arms still around me, he pulled his face away to take in my reaction. He just kissed me, like, really kissed me, in front of everyone.

We didn't have stupid trainer-trainee rules to follow anymore. Dear Loki, not hiding our feelings felt good. I couldn't not smile. I just wished we could've experienced this, being a normal-ish couple, a little sooner.

Resistance members had started moving in the direction of the Consortium. Reid slid his hands off my waist and one corner of his mouth curved upward. "Time to kick ass."

I nodded. Reid tipped his head in the direction of the Consortium. Shoving my fear to the side, Reid and I fell in step with the Resistance, running toward our enemy. With him beside me, I felt invincible.

Guns fired even though we were still a good distance out. But the distance gave me an idea. "Missile launchers will work from here," I yelled to Reid.

Reid halted those behind us. "Soldiers with experience in midrange missile launchers." Most of our people continued running, but five people stayed behind. Four of them were male, one female, all dressed in green. Which meant they most likely had "real" training. "We're going to make it rain down on them," Reid yelled.

We couldn't see where the missiles were landing from where we stood. It would give us some advantage, since they couldn't see us, but our effectiveness would be low. So I blinked, Pushed, and the seven of us stood on a twelve-foot-high metal ballistic deck. Only one guy seemed fazed by instantaneously standing on a different surface in the air.

"Can you Push the weapons?" I asked Reid. He knew the weapons better than I. He nodded.

Facing the five volunteers, I cupped my hands around my mouth. "Consortium will see us easier when we're elevated," I yelled.

Surface-to-surface missile launches appeared along the deck behind what I guessed was a ballistic shield.

I yelled over the gunfire getting increasingly closer and louder, "Get off as many shots as you can before someone sets their sights on us."

"And," Reid yelled, "these are not infrared guided. You aim and shoot. They're preloaded with the first rocket. Go!" He gave a thumbs up then sat behind a mounted launcher.

The seven of us blasted as many shots off as we were able. Since the weapons were mounted, they were easy to use. The missiles took out groups of random Consortium soldiers dressed in blue uniforms. We were leaving giant holes in their army.

With the bird's-eye view, though, we could see that even with a handful of rocket launchers, our impact was minimal. We could see over the ridge and another wave of Consortium soldiers followed what we faced now. From this perspective, it wasn't difficult to assess how much we were outnumbered. Like, big time. A bolus of adrenaline hit my bloodstream, pulling me out of my momentarily paused freak-out.

"Reid!" I screamed. He followed my shaking, pointing finger and pulled his phone out of his pocket.

I only heard a few complete words. "Enormous." "Divide." "Send backup behind them."

Reid's launcher changed before my eyes—it was larger. He shot the weapon and it flew farther, detonating deeper into the Consortium army. We got several more rounds off before our front line got too close to Consortium troops. At this point, we could end up taking out too many of our own.

"Let's move out," Reid yelled down the line of volunteers.

An explosion rocked our ballistic deck from behind. As the seven of us stood, we were hit again, the structure shaking under us. Two of the volunteers had already made it to the ground. *Tink, tink.* Reid and I were looking at each other. We both heard the sound but neither of us saw what was thrown or where. If we didn't see it, or know what was thrown, we couldn't Retract it. We had to get the hell out of our temporary perch. "Jump! Jump!" Reid screamed, at those helping man the launchers.

I jumped to the ground moments before something

exploded, turning parts of our deck into flying shards, potentially lethal. I Pushed a huge trampoline before I struck the ground, and tucked and rolled, trying to take the pressure off my shins. Bouncing to the side, I jumped off the backyard toy and Retracted it.

I stood, wiping my hands on my pants, and took in the utter chaos around me. The platform where I'd stood moments before was obliterated. In front of me, Oculi fought with guns, knives, and various other weapons. I'd never witnessed such mayhem as the Pushing and Retracting happening before me. People all around me were falling to the ground. Dead.

"Josie," Reid said, grabbing my arm. He tugged and we ran toward the Consortium, bringing up the back of the Resistance.

We moved past people fighting and weaved around fallen and bloody bodies on the ground. Some in black Consortium uniforms, some Resistance. I ran past a young woman not much older than me, face up with her eyes open, lying in a pool of blood that looked black on the soil. Beads of sweat dotted her forehead—proof of her being alive just moments earlier. My stomach heaved, forcing me to gag.

Something caught me from behind and yanked my arm nearly out of the socket. I whirled around and a beautiful brunette smiled. Her hand went for the gun tucked into her side. I pointed my empty right hand at her, Pushed my Glock in my hand, and pulled the trigger. I hit her shoulder and she pressed her hand to it. Red covered her fingers quickly and she collapsed to the ground. I ran, leaving her behind and not knowing if she was going to live or not. Guilt chomped at my conscience. I might've killed another person, face-to-face. As I tried to thrust the overwhelming emotions of possibly taking a stranger's life to the dark corners of my mind, I ran. I pumped my arms and propelled forward, trying not to look too closely at the random bodies lying on the ground. At the same time, I had to pay close attention to the swinging appendages of those fighting.

Womp, womp. A chopper approached from behind the Consortium and it was blue. It wasn't the Resistance backup. And it was armed.

I'd lost Reid and didn't have a real direction. I ducked, dove, and jumped to avoid being hurt by ground soldiers. And now, I had to be cognizant of the flying weapon.

Dust floated in the air, sticking to the layer of sweat covering me. Everyone around me fought individual battles for their lives. I wasn't stopping for just anyone, though. I didn't want to fight some random Consortium jerk, I wanted one person. Max.

After sidestepping several people and shooting a man running toward me, who had to be part ogre, I spotted Max and Brown on their little four-wheeled ride. Zac and Kat stood next to Brown, handcuffed. Four Consortium soldiers guarded them, automatic weapons ready.

The sound of the Consortium helicopter blades stopped and was replaced by a high-pitched whine. All eyes turned to the chopper as it fell out of the sky.

I focused on Max and his entourage. I Retracted the ground under the UTV, the guns from the soldiers, and the handcuffs from Zac and Kat. The VP and Max were in a hole ten feet deep. I blinked and both pairs of soldiers stood handcuffed in quicksand. "Get out of there," I yelled to Zac and Kat.

Zac and Kat ran together, but the UTV was back on solid ground already, having driven up a ramp out of the hole. Reid told me Max could still Retract. One set of soldiers in the quicksand had sunk to their shoulders. The other pair of soldiers ran toward me, but one fell after a gun sounded. Kat had shot him. Zac barreled the other soldier down to the ground and pummeled him.

I chased after Max and Brown, who drove toward a deteriorated building. I Pushed a giant boulder in front of their UTV. The UTV flipped and both bodies flew through the air.

I sprinted to Max and Brown, dirt spitting from under my boots. Reid approached them from the other direction. I slid across the dirt to Max as he shoved himself up to a seated position. Blood trickled down the side of his face. I Pushed my Glock into my hand and pressed the barrel to his forehead. My hand shook, anger almost taking on a life of its own inside me.

Max casually looked to me and smiled. Reid jogged to my side and pulled a gun to cover me. To my left, Zac and Cohen had guns pointed at Vice President Brown.

Max faced both of his palms to me. "Josie, I believe we need to talk."

"We have nothing to talk about."

"Quite the contrary, my dear." Dust, blood, and sweat mixed on his face. "I have eyes and ears everywhere. I have the means to get to your mom and brother. Right now. I will kill them both unless you give yourself up."

My heart stalled. "Your empty threats mean nothing."

"Oh, not true. I have a little plastic bag in my inner pocket just for you. It proves that I mean what I say. If you kill me, I've already given the orders for Meg and Eli. I die, they die."

Reid moved closer and Harrison approached behind Reid, his gun drawn as well.

I placed my gun in my waistband and pulled his coat open, his cheap cologne assaulting me as I snagged the bag sticking out of the top of the pocket. I turned the clear, plastic bag over, something metal stuck in one of the corners. Bringing the bag closer to my face, I could tell the metal was a ring, as in a piece of jewelry. Was this a trick?

With his hands still raised, Max twisted to look at my face. "Take a closer look. It won't hurt you."

I opened the bag and pulled the ring out to look closer. Then I saw the inside of the silver band. My mom and dad's initials. It was my dad's wedding ring.

The world faded away in a blurry mess then tilted. My stomach pitched and mouth watered. I tried not to puke.

"Guess who I finally found this week at Science Industries, the Consortium headquarters, in Los Angeles?" He turned to Harrison. "I found Harrison's secret informant, the Resistance inside man. But I don't have to worry about him anymore." Max pulled his focus back to me. "I had him executed."

I withered to the ground like one of the parched plants that was barely alive out here in the desert. My arms and head were heavy, drooping to the dry soil. I opened my mouth to let out a cry, but nothing happened, no sound left me.

Max hadn't pulled the trigger, but he murdered my father. And now he was threatening to do the same to my remaining family.

A part of my heart blackened and a deep ache ripped through the center of me.

Max pulled a phone out, touched the screen, and said, "Now."

Consortium soldiers surrounded us, their weapons raised. They formed a full circle, moving other Resistance members toward us.

"I do believe this is all that's left of your sweet little Resistance group. Harrison, nice try. It was admirable."

There were maybe fifteen of us, tops. Cohen, Zac, Kat, Harrison, Reid, and me were part of that group.

"Josie, you need to join me now. Demonstrate what you can do for the President." A solider approached Max and helped him stand. Max brushed off his pants and looked down his nose at me. "If you come with no hostility, you'll save your mom and brother's lives. If not, you'll all die and I'll take your body for experimentation, so I'm offering you a good deal."

A good deal.

Why didn't I kill him right away? Why did I listen to him? This is my fault. I could've ended it, but I didn't pull the trigger.

This was it. We'd lost. *I* had lost. I let down my family. And Reid. The Resistance. I let down my entire race.

Anomalies like Reid, and maybe in a few years Eli, would be extinct soon. I'd never see Reid again. Rage and hatred fused in my gut.

I really didn't have a choice, but if I willingly went with Max and he had me close, I could kill him when the time presented itself. It wouldn't solve the immediate problem of Anomalies being murdered, but at least in the end I could take him down.

I looked to Reid. He held his hands up and sweat dripped down the bridge of his nose. "Go," he whispered.

My eyes filled with tears, but not from sadness—from unbridled fury. I shook my head.

He nodded.

I stood facing Max. "I get to tell him goo-bye, then I'll come."

Max rolled his eyes. "Fast."

I stepped into Reid and wrapped my arms around him, trying to hold back the tears, but it wasn't working. They came anyway. His mouth was by my ear. "Kill him later."

I nodded against his shoulder. "I'm sorry," I whispered.

"Enough," Max yelled. Reid squeezed me and a soldier wrenched me out of his arms.

I was led to Max's side, now a good distance from the UTV on higher terrain. The Vice President stood next to Max. My tears had already dried in the heat. I watched Max's soldiers all move in front of the remaining Resistance members and organize them into two lines.

Kat cried against Zac's shoulder. The Vice President was going to allow his own son to be killed. This was disgusting.

Reid nodded to Cohen then reached for his dad's

hand. Harrison interlocked his hand with Reid's and said something to his son. I was almost certain of those words. Something along the lines of *I love you*.

My hands trembled at my sides. Until that moment, I hadn't realized how much I had been keeping my anger in check. It was as if I'd told myself it wasn't okay, or justifiable, to be furious about what Max had done.

He killed my dad. He tried to kill me. He was about to kill my boyfriend and friends.

Pressure mounted in my head. Gutted sorrow and dark wrath erupted inside my brain. My arms and legs quaked as primal sobs wracked my body.

Electricity nipped my skin, leaving my feet, hands, and lips numb.

I wasn't going to be able to wait until later. I had to do something about this mass murderer, this vile excuse of a human being next to me. I didn't want to kill anyone, but this man was an embodiment of evil.

The guard in front of Max talked into an ear piece and the soldiers aimed their weapons at the Resistance members. At good people. At my friends. At the guy I loved.

A deafening noise came from behind the ridge. Everyone turned.

Four helicopters flew overhead and opened fire on the Consortium troops. Reid Pushed weapons in his and the other prisoners' hands.

Resistance troops in green jackets poured over the ridge and two military trucks of Resistance members approached from the opposite direction.

Max's face flamed red. His lead military officer turned to him, waiting for instructions. "End this," Max hissed. His words were as sharp as his tongue and wicked mind.

Electricity sparked in my nervous system. Voltage ran over my skin and my body temperature rose as I unleased the rage within me.

With barely a thought, I Force Pushed Vice President Brown backward, out of my way. I wanted this to be between me and Max. Max's eyes followed the trajectory of the VP. Then his head whipped upward toward the sky because the sun had suddenly been blocked out by fast approaching storm clouds.

He was about to step forward when I blinked and Pushed a stone in front of his foot. He tripped, falling to the ground. I Pushed a metal cage around him. It disappeared.

Max sneered. "I may only be a Retractor, but you'll have to do better than that."

"Oh, I will." I let my energy flow and it crackled as I Force Pushed Max. His body tore through the dusty air, smashing against a large rock formation, and plummeted to the ground. He lay in a lump at the base of the rock.

It wasn't until I was hovering above him, crouching by his side, that one of his eyes cracked open. I'd never gotten close enough to see that the roots of his hair shined gray. A finite line existed between the dark, dyed hair and his natural hair color.

Blood smeared down the rocky surface behind him, from the back of his head. "I almost had your older brother." He coughed. "And I was so close to having you, too."

The energy within my body made my legs tremble under me. I bent forward, grabbed both his wrists, stood, and pulled him away from the rock formation. Using all my strength, I dragged him through the dirt and brush. His body made a print on the ground like a snake, the heels of his shoes digging into the soil and leaving a wavy trail in his wake.

I dropped him in an open area, away from the rocks. Max let out a low groan when his head hit the ground. Neither of his eyes were open.

Electricity bit my skin and flared inside me with each heartbeat. I glanced up to the dark clouds gathering above us. In that moment, I knew I was more powerful than even I had thought. But something was different. I could feel it. I could feel the intensity and amount of energy flowing through me. And I could control it.

I Pushed the growing storm above us, building the heat and cold and electricity. The wind whipped through my hair and dust swirled around us. The energy inside me correlated with the changing environment, mounting with speed and a tangible tension.

I gave my energy some slack, loosening my grip just enough. Lightning flashed so bright it was as if the sky burst open. I didn't flinch, though, I anticipated the lightning. Less than a second later, thunder shook the earth under me.

I walked backward from Max about twenty feet. He lay on his back, both eyes still closed. Dust flew into the air as I dragged my boots backward.

Max was almost dead, but I didn't want to kill another

living being. I knew what that felt like.

Another rumble of thunder reminded me of Reid and Santos's motorcycles. Santos. Max used Santos as a puppet and put his life on the line. Max did the same to Dee. He used her child as leverage. Max contributed to the death of my brother. He ordered the murder of my dad.

He'd played so many people and destroyed so many lives. And that was just the beginning of a long list.

A fury, deep in the center of me, surged. I released my hold on the energy, on the rage, on the fear. Electricity tore through me, heating my flesh and tingling every nerve ending. I felt like an unleased animal. Wild and free.

I gave a final Push. A silver-white streak ripped a jagged line in the black clouds down to Max's body. I Pushed harder and the lightning blazed brighter.

I relaxed and no more lightning. The wind immediately calmed and I let my posture sag, my body tired.

Where Max lay was now a lump of smoking flesh and bone. Max was no more. He couldn't control Oculi or kill innocent people any longer.

I wasn't happy. How could I be happy about ending someone's life? One murder didn't justify another. Max murdering my dad didn't justify me murdering him. I did, however, welcome the relief of knowing he couldn't hurt anyone else. I took one last look at his body. I barely Pushed and the Earth crumbled under Max's remains, like a sink hole. His body was gone, the ground swallowed it.

I inhaled, the smell of rain in the air, and gave one last Push and blinked. The ground was solid and a large boulder sat in the place where Max was buried.

I pivoted and ran back to everyone else. I shifted my thoughts to finding Reid and eventually getting out of here to Mom and Eli. The clouds dispersed, first scattering so the blue sky peeked through between them, then fizzling into nothingness. The sun shined bright again, no indication of an electrical storm.

People ran in all directions. Bodies lay in unnatural positions.

Reid ran up a staircase that manifested one step at a time to fight a Consortium guy. I headed for Kat, two Consortium soldiers circling her. I sprinted, about to pass right by the crashed UTV, and I fell, my cheek striking a rock.

Holy shit balls, that hurts.

I rolled over and Vice President Brown crawled on top of me, a gun in his hand. "No!" I screamed. I Retracted the gun, but it reappeared.

The VP sat across my chest and a blindfold manifested over my eyes. "You shouldn't have this much power, Josie. This disabling serum will rid you of your Oculi abilities." Something pinched my arm, but the weight of Brown suddenly vanished. A headache banged in my forehead and temples, almost debilitating me completely. Nausea swept through me and I scrambled to get the blindfold off.

It was like everything was happening in fast forward. Zac wrestled his dad to the ground, dust billowing into the air. Brown tried to buck Zac off, but Zac punched his dad in the face. Blood spurted from Brown's nose. Zac managed to grab his dad's hand armed with the disabling serum syringe and stabbed the needle into his dad's leg.

Brown lay in the dirt, unmoving. Zac staggered as he tried to stand, watching his father.

I picked myself up and walked to Zac, shielding my eyes from the sun. The brightness didn't seem to be helping my sudden headache. "Thank you."

Dirt caked in the crevices of Zac's face. "He still got some serum in you. I'm sorry." He shook his head, his gaze leaping between his dad and the empty syringe in his hand.

"He could've killed me, though, so it could've been worse. Much worse."

My head still drumming, I perched one hand on my hip and held the other one in front of me. I needed water. I tried to Push a bottle of water into my hand. Nothing.

21.

Reid

There were a few Consortium soldiers who scattered into the desert. We weren't going to go after them. Anyone of rank within the Consortium was dead. My dad called to let me know that Josie had killed Max. I hadn't seen her since the Resistance backup finally showed up. Maybe twenty minutes. It wasn't long, I knew that, but it felt like a lifetime not seeing her for myself, not knowing she was safe.

I stood on the lip of the ridge and spotted Josie's red hair. I jogged down the ledge and sought her out again. This time she was already looking at me. She started running and so did I.

I was exhausted, but I forced my body to move faster. I needed her like I needed air.

She was ten feet from me.

Josie jumped into me, swinging her arms around my

neck, and I picked her up. Our lips crashed and I could finally breathe.

She slid down me to stand and stared up at me, smiling. Her eyes sparkled in the late afternoon sun, reflecting everything we'd been through—sadness and joy twisted together. "You okay? God, Josie. I almost lost you." I pressed my lips to hers and I didn't hold back. Though there was nowhere to go, I pulled her closer. I wanted to breathe her in, soak her up. Finally, she was mine and I was hers.

I moved my lips to her ear. "I'm in love with you, Josie Harper." I wasn't sure why I said it; all I knew was that I had to. Maybe it was because she was the reason I felt again after years of trying to shut everyone out. Maybe it was because I realized that "tomorrow" was never a certainty. Either way, it didn't matter if she reciprocated the feeling. I just needed her to know.

I didn't wait for a response. I dipped my head to kiss her again.

With our bodies still smashed together, she tugged her mouth away from mine. "I love you," she whispered, tickling my lips. Her lips collided to mine. I never knew three words could undo me and stitch me back together in the same breath.

I laced my fingers through hers. A mixture of sweat, dirt, and makeup painted her face. Loose hair no longer held in her ponytail fluttered in the breeze or stuck to her pink cheeks. With the bandana around her neck, boots, and covered in dirt, she resembled one of the characters from one of those post-apocalyptical games, like *Fallout*.

"We need to get out of here before the President arrives."

She nodded. Dead bodies littered the ghost town. Most of them were Consortium soldiers, but enough were Resistance. Too many.

Zac had been sitting with his father nearby. "I'm going now, Dad."

Vice President Brown looked around. "What do you mean? You're taking me with you."

Zac shook his head. "No, I'm not. This is your mess."

Brown tried standing but wobbled back to the tuft of grass he'd been sitting in. With his office attire, he stuck out, completely out of place. "You can't leave me. I don't know what I'll say. How will I explain this? I don't even— uh, wait. Where will you stay? You'll need money."

The VP's gaze bounced around and he mumbled *no* repeatedly. He was on the cusp of delirium. "You need me, Zac," he yelled, his face red.

The disheveled clothes and dirty face surprisingly worked on Zac. He rested his hands on his hips, exhaustion evident in his stance. Kat stepped to Zac's side, then Cohen. Josie and I moved closer to Zac.

Zac's gaze lifted to mine. I gave him a slow, deep nod, hoping he'd understand that I meant we stood with him. We had his back. He was one of us.

Zac stared at his dad for a moment, the wind whistling around us. "I'll be fine and so will you, especially for someone who was approving and aiding murder. You should be in prison."

Lines formed in Brown's forehead. He seemed confused or shocked by what was happening.

"Good-bye, Dad," Zac said.

Clearly upset, Zac started toward us and handed Josie a vial. "It's the enhancing serum that you handed off to my dad. I was right. He had it on him. It's yours again."

He walked toward the chopper waiting on the dirt road. Kat joined Zac, looping her arm through his.

Harrison gestured and the remaining Resistance ran up the ridge to a different helicopter or one of the military cargo trucks waiting. Cohen and Harrison walked to me and Reid, staring at the vial in my hand.

"Is that the enhancing serum?" Cohen asked.

"Yeah," I said. "Dangerous stuff."

Josie held it between her forefinger and thumb so we could all see it.

Dad patted Josie on the shoulder. "You should probably talk to your mom about whether or not you need to do anything to that before you take it."

"What?" Josie and I said in unison.

Dad turned to me. A gaping cut bled at a diagonal across his dirty cheek. "Brown injected Josie. She can't Push or Retract. The enhancing serum is dangerous, but if anyone is going to take advantage of it, it should be Josie, under the supervision of the scientist who recreated it— her mother."

I wasn't sure how to feel about Josie not having abilities. In a way, I feared for her, since a lot of Oculi now knew who she was. But part of me was relieved. Maybe she could have some normalcy.

Without another word, Dad walked to the chopper where Zac and Kat waited. Cohen followed Josie and me into the chopper. Once we were seated, the other helicopter perched atop the ridge, full of Resistance members, took off.

Resistance trucks rolled out. We lifted into the air and we all watched the scene below, knowing the President and Secretary of Defense would be there any minute. Dead bodies lay around the ghost town, in the middle of nowhere, with the Vice President the only survivor.

Kat held Zac's hand, both sets of their eyes fixated on the only living body below. His dad. I felt for him. That had to be difficult. He'd need support, and he had it in us.

My dad slapped Cohen's back in an approving way as he moved to talk to the pilot. Cohen, holding a cold compress to his swollen eye, gave me a half-ass smile.

Josie watched the ghost town disappear from our sight. I couldn't imagine what she was feeling right now. I didn't know what to say about her killing Max or how to console her about her dad. I did know that she was one of the bravest people I'd ever met, though. I closed my hand around Josie's.

Without looking at me, she flipped her hand over and weaved her fingers through mine, our palms pressed together.

The ground was no longer in my sights. All I saw was the blue of the sky, cloudless. Clear. Safe.

I scanned the bodies around me. I had a dad again. I had my best friend back and got to know a friend better. I even made a new friend in Zac. And I had the girl I'd always loved. I had a lot to be thankful for. We all did.

This battle was over. For now, anyway. But I wasn't done with the important people sitting with me in the helicopter. This was just a new beginning.

JOSIE

I walked Hannah to my front door. She lugged her oversize pink duffle bag behind her. Her fingernail polish bag stuck out of the zipper that wouldn't close all the way. I glanced down at my manicure. Hannah was a talented artist, nail art included.

It had been two weeks since the battle in the ghost town. Hannah had stayed with me at home in Florida for the last two days.

She opened the front door, walked onto the porch, and dropped her bag. Her frayed shorts showed off her long brown legs, and her cover-girl hair blew in the breeze. She looked different to me now. She hadn't changed in appearance since I'd seen her—we were only apart for three weeks. It was me who had changed. It was the way I saw her. I'd always been a little envious of her looks and even her perpetually optimistic attitude. She was just as beautiful as she was two weeks ago on our video chat from the Hub, but now I appreciated her model-like features and characteristics more. And it wasn't like she was less pretty or sweet. I think it was more the fact that

I'd become more confident in myself, in my uniqueness.

Without warning, she nearly tackled me with a hug. I stumbled back a step. "Call if you need anything."

I squeezed her tight and reveled in the idea that I was with my best friend again. Two weeks prior, I wasn't sure if I was going to live to see another day, let alone see her again.

She'd been a huge comfort the last couple of days. We talked for hours upon hours about the Oculi world, what happened at the Hub, and the battle. And she cried with me as I talked about Dad's funeral.

We let go of each other. "I promise," I said. My hand gravitated to the Dragon's Eye necklace mom gave me. "But I think since Mom is officially retired now and she has a ton more time, we'll be okay." Mom was recovering physically from her injury, but was having a difficult time with Dad's death and Dee's betrayal. But she was making efforts to connect with me on an emotional level. Hannah and I talked about that at some great length, too.

She swept her hair over her shoulder and smiled. "I know, I know. But still. See you tomorrow."

"Okay."

She strained to see around me with a smile that reached her eyes. "Bye, Reeeeeid. I want to meet this Cohen guy soon." I'd shown Hannah a pic of Cohen, and she'd nearly drooled on my phone.

Reid came out from the kitchen into the living room. "Bye, Hannah. We'll get that set up. I'm sure he'd be happy to meet you." He leaned against a wall and crossed his arms. "Oh, and thanks for taking care of my girl the last couple of days." His gaze shifted to me and he winked.

Hannah waved to Reid then leaned to my ear. "He called you 'my girl.' Ahhh!"

I grinned as big as The Joker and bit my bottom lip in an attempt to hide my giddiness. "I know," I squealed through my teeth.

She blew me a kiss then slung her bag over her shoulder. "Tomorrow!" Hannah skipped down the stairs to her car parked out front in the afternoon sun.

"Tomorrow!" I waved.

Same ol' happy Hannah. Her positive disposition and infectious smile was like a hug for my brain. I needed that, her, more than I'd realized. She was simply comforting after all that had happened, after my world was flipped upside down.

Leaning against one of the columns holding up the porch, I watched Hannah drive away. The bushes rustled in the breeze and the palm across the street swayed. The shadows danced on the driveway and front lawn.

I couldn't seem to get enough of the sun after spending time underground in the Hub. Maybe the light helped me combat all the darkness I'd experienced in the last several weeks.

The day after the ghost town battle, I told Reid about my anxiety symptoms, the chest pains and all that. I started seeing a therapist right away. Well, I Skyped with a therapist in the Resistance specifically for Oculi. I was still having nightmares about Santos every once in a while, but the anxiety attacks had lessened.

I was still randomly breaking down in tears when I thought about Dad. But it was more the fact that I didn't get to say good-bye or be closer with him. I wanted to tell him that it was okay and I understood now what he and Mom were fighting for, and what I'd continue to fight for.

The sunlight appeared and disappeared repeatedly on my body through the leaves. I inhaled the warm, humid air, promising myself to not take it for granted again. After the dry air in the Hub and the cold air in Maine, where my father's funeral was, I looked forward to Florida weather.

Mom held a small funeral service in my Dad's small hometown in Maine. Stella was found alive in the Schrodinger's Consortium headquarters in Los Angeles, but Dad's body was not recovered. We decided it would be best for our family's sake to hold a funeral for some closure. Reid and Harrison, along with several other Resistance members, were there to honor my father. Immediately after, they had to travel for a several days to figure out some Resistance logistical stuff, since the Hub was destroyed.

I closed my hand around a ray of sunshine, as if trying to capture it. Mom and Eli were at the beach, catching rays, too. Eli was understandably having a hard time with Dad's death, but we were all trying to make life better for him. Mom signed him up for summer day camps, Reid planned on teaching him how to play basketball over the summer, and I scheduled day trips he and I could take together. Hannah even played video games with him, and me, the last couple of days—and she was *not* a gamer.

Eli, though the youngest and smallest of the Harper family, was the giant elephant in the room. Mom hadn't brought up the fact that Eli would be like me, or possibly more powerful. We all knew it, though. It was a logical deduction. Still, no one wanted to say it aloud. I think the others knew it was too much for a nine-year-old to handle, but it was also too much for my mom to handle now.

The door creaked behind me, bringing my thoughts back to the present. Reid wound his arms around my middle, from behind. His palms rested against my stomach, the coolness from his touch penetrated my shirt. He rested his chin on my shoulder, next to my ear.

"You okay?" he asked, his voice velvety.

I nodded. "Yeah." It wasn't a lie this time. Right now, I was okay. I wasn't naive enough to think it was going to stay that way. But that was all right—I wasn't always supposed to be okay.

In the last several weeks, I'd been tested in ways I never thought possible. It was hard. It was devastating, yet amazing. The last few weeks had been full of lies and sorrow but also truth and joy. Even if I wasn't a part of the Oculi world, that was life. Messy, crazy, beautiful, and scary life.

His arms tightened around me for a second. "You ready?" he asked.

I grinned like someone had just awarded me Mjolnir, Thor's hammer. "Hell yes. You have no idea how long I've been wanting to do this."

Without another word, he disappeared from behind me. I turned in time to see him bound into the living room.

He sat on the edge of the couch, his knee bouncing. His eyes followed me until I stood at his side, making him look up at me. Taking my hand, he pulled me down to sit next to him.

The words "Star Wars" stretched across the television screen. He'd promised to finally watch the original *Star Wars* movies with me and already had it queued and ready to go. It was our first time watching it as a "couple."

Pulling a throw pillow into my lap, I snuggled closer to him.

"Alone at last," he sighed. Drawing both my hands into his, he tilted his head to look in my eyes. "We've only had a few hours here and there. How are you doing with everything?"

"I'm good. Really." I smiled. "But I'm better than good, now that you're here."

A smirk slid across his lips. "I know you're going to have a hard time keeping your hands off this." He admired his biceps. "But try to contain yourself." He seemed more relaxed since the Consortium had collapsed. Or was dismantled. For now, anyway.

I rolled my eyes almost out of my head. "Pft." Though, he was right. I could hardly stop checking him out, but it wasn't only because of his arms. Reid amazed me. There was more to him than I would've guessed in the first couple of days of training with him. With heart and integrity, he was way more than a good-looking guy. Never mind the fact that I kind of wanted to throw him into a Sarlacc pit the first day I met him. Or, re-met him as Reid, that is. I smoothed my hand over his arm and pretended to ogle it.

I pushed the edge of his T-shirt up and traced the

outline of his Dragon's Eye tattoo. "It kind of sucks not being able to Push and Retract anymore."

Reid pulled my arm toward him to look at my Dragon's Eye tattoo. I could've asked him to Retract it, but after all we'd been through, I'd kind of grown attached to it. His finger feathered over my skin, tracing the lines. "It will get easier. Besides, your mom said it could take a while with her serum. Give it time. And remember, you only got a small portion of the injection."

"I know. At first I felt being an Oculi gave me a place and a purpose. I fit in. I had an identity. The last couple of days I've realized that I don't need to *be* anything to have a purpose. I'm the same person as an Oculi as I am now, with the same purpose."

His hands gently covered mine as he nodded. "You're handling everything better than I would."

I wished that were the case. "Not really. I keep trying to Push ice cream or a salted caramel mocha and end up almost in tears due to the lack of convenience."

Reid tried not to smile.

I shoved his shoulder. "Yeah, it's frustrating."

"Speaking of purposes, that meeting with Dad yesterday? There was talk of starting a Resistance team that traveled the country to investigate suspected pockets of Consortium activity, as well as disturbances that could expose us to Plancks. They also still need teams to train young Oculi. You'd be great at that. Dad suggested a team that he had witnessed and already worked well together." His finger traced my tattoo.

"Cohen, Zac, Kat, you, and me?"

His eyes widened, pretending to be surprised. "How'd you guess? It's just talk right now."

I laughed. "Man, things have been kind of overwhelming the last month, since you pulled up on your motorcycle during lunch, huh?"

His fingers stilled. "Yeah."

Neither of us spoke and the smiles faded. I don't know how long we sat there staring into each other's eyes. Eventually, I said, "Uh, should we start the movie, or…"

"Oh, yeah. Uh, I'm going to get some popcorn." Reid shoved off the couch, but I caught his hand, not letting him go. He turned back to me, probably with some smart-ass comment at the ready, but he saw the bowl of popcorn.

He cocked his head. "Did you?"

I shrugged and smiled. My abilities were coming back slowly, and I'd been waiting to tell Reid until I was sure it wasn't a fluke. "If you dig into the popcorn, you might find M&M's. I know you can't resist them, especially with popcorn. Salty and sweet."

Ignoring the popcorn, he grabbed my hand and yanked so I'd stand. "Yeah, I do have a thing for the combo of salty and sweet, but I already have my eye on a treat. I like Nerds." Arching one of his brows. "Hot sci-fi nerds."

I flashed him the backward Vulcan sign and ran, my socked feet slipping on the carpet. He caught me before I even got to the kitchen. Okay, so maybe I let him catch me.

His hands found my waist and pulled me into him. He rested his forehead against mine before kissing me.

A month ago, I didn't think I had the luxury of choice, but an entire future of choices lay ahead of me. The choices I made would define my reality. I understood now that I couldn't control others or my circumstances, but I could control me, my actions, and reactions, Oculi abilities or not.

It was up to me, every day, to choose fighting for the balance of wisdom, power, and love.

AUTHOR'S NOTE

Dear teen readers,

In *Enigma*, Josie experiences common symptoms of anxiety. More specifically, in chapter one, she has an anxiety attack, oftentimes called a panic attack. Not all anxiety attacks will present in the same way. Anxiety attacks look different from one person to the next, and the cause of an episode differs. Some anxiety attacks are associated with anxiety disorders, while others are not. People experience anxiety attacks as isolated events and some deal with chronic anxiety issues. Anxiety attacks are not fatal, though they can feel like it at times due to certain symptoms.

Here's the thing—anyone can have an anxiety attack, and having one does not make you weak or "less than." There is no shame in having an anxiety attack or any other mental health issue. An anxiety attack is an overactivity of the body's natural fear response. I know firsthand about anxiety because I live with it. I also know that the best thing to do about any mental health issue is to acknowledge symptoms and seek medical attention. I've done this and it helps.

If you, or someone you know, experience a combination of any of the listed symptoms, please talk to a family member or trusted adult to help you consult a physician and/or mental health specialist.

Possible anxiety attack symptoms:

Chest pain; difficulty breathing or hyperventilation; sweating; trembling/shaking; feeling of choking; nausea or abdominal distress; palpitations, increased heart rate, or pounding heart; dizziness; tingling feeling; fear of losing control or dying; overwhelmed with feelings of hopelessness or worry.

Visit the Anxiety and Depression Association of America online, **www.adaa.org**, for more information. For specific strategies to help cope with and manage anxiety and stress, go to www.adaa.org/tips-manage-anxiety-and-stress.

If you experience or have experienced anxiety, know that you are not alone. Please, get help and stay strong. You've got this.

Love, Tonya

Emergency numbers for severe anxiety and depression and/or circumstances:

If you are dealing with a crisis and need a safe adult to talk to anonymously, or have thoughts of self-harm, homicide, or suicide, call: Boys Town National Hotline 1-800-448-3000.

OR

If you are having suicidal thoughts, call: The National Suicide Prevention Lifeline

1-800-273-8255.

Both organizations are open 24 hours, 365 days per year, are accredited, and staffed with trained professionals.

Acknowledgments

Thank you, first and always, to God for the opportunities presented to me.

Secondly, I'm eternally grateful for my readers, my fans, my FRANS, bloggers, vloggers, and my fellow nerds for your support of *Anomaly* and *Enigma*. Thank you for loving Josie—a sci-fi nerd girl who can simultaneously be nerdy, feminine, and fierce—and for understanding that the term "nerd" is synonymous with "passionate."

Kate Brauning, my editor and friend, your insight and guidance have been nothing short of brilliant. A thank-you the size of the moon for challenging me, helping me become a better writer, and believing in me. This wouldn't be a book without you and, for that, I'm forever beholden. For real.

To everyone else at Entangled TEEN who've played a part in the making of *Enigma*—Liz Pelletier, Stacy Abrams, Melissa Montovani, Meredith Johnson, Bethany Robinson, L.J. Anderson, Kari Olson, Christine Chhun, Heather Riccio, Erin Dameron-Hill, and all other production/copy editors/proofreaders—thank you.

Big Wookie hugs to some of my biggest fans and book bloggers and vloggers who saw something in *Anomaly* and helped make this series successful. Ben Alderson (Benjamin of Tomes), Glitter Magazine, Lea at USA

Today Happy Ever After, A Leisure Moment blog, Fallon and Morgan at Seeing Double in Neverland blog, Sarah at Aphonic Sarah blog, Ana at Ana Loves Blog, Ivey Waters at The Hopeless Reader, Danielle Pitter, Ayah Assem, Bibliojunkies, Tanya at T&G Book Boutique, Michele Luker, Sara Santana, Valerie Tejeda, Royal Social Media, Alexandra, Sylvia, and Cassie, and many more I'm sure I'm forgetting.

Heaps of gratitude to the teachers, book clubs, librarians, and booksellers who helped make *Anomaly* successful. A special thanks especially to the Omaha Public Libraries, OPS librarian Angie Ralph, The Bookworm in Omaha, and Stone Alley Books and Collectibles in Galesburg. The fantastic Marcia Jussel at the Oakview Barnes and Noble — you've always treated me like a rock star, and I am sincerely thankful.

Thank you to my writing friends — Lynne Matson, Lydia Kang, Bethany Crandell, Mary Weber, and Jeff Koterba — who've held me steady. I wouldn't have survived the last year and a half without you. Your encouragement and friendship have meant the world to me.

Kitty Burton, Claudia Lokamas, Courtney Suarez, and Debi Auch Moedy: thank you for being incredibly supportive of your weird writer friend and loving me. Mandy Mortensen and Melody Wentz, you cheered me on years ago when I started writing, and, for that, I owe you a lifetime supply of Monday Night Margaritas.

To Laura Hill, Susie Jarvis, Jill Henson, Kristen Trukova, Jenny Robbins, and Jennifer McGuire: thank you for your friendship, even after all these years.

All you nerds out there—the sci-fi nerds, book nerds, writing nerds, pop culture nerds, comic nerds, math nerds, art nerds, music nerds, stats nerds, gaming nerds, sport nerds, theater nerds—keep on being you. Keep on being passionate enough about something that you, or someone else, considers you a nerd. Being passionate about something means you care, and oftentimes passion leads to action. That means it's likely you will do something for or with your passion, and our world needs that. No matter what kind of nerd you are, we need that. Be a nerd and be proud. Get your nerd on.

To some of the many musicians who've influenced *Anomaly* and *Enigma*—30 Seconds to Mars, Linkin Park, Muse, Imagine Dragons, Mumford and Sons, Bastille, Cold War Kids, Halsey, BANNERS, Sia, MGMT, Ruelle, Ellie Goulding—your art has inspired mine. Snow Patrol and Kings of Leon: Without your lyrics and chords in the summer of 2009, I'm not sure I would be an author now. Thank you.

Zachary Levi: Thank you for being a champion for all nerds. Your efforts to make the word "nerd" a positive term have made an impact on so many, including me. Zac in *Enigma* is named after you.

Kat McNamara: You were initially the inspiration for Josie based on your physical traits and intelligence, but you've become more. Your kindness, graciousness, positivity, and hard work make you an amazing example, especially for the teens who look up to you. Thank you for your friendship. Kat in *Enigma* is named after you.

Mom and Dad: thank you for always cheering me on,

for listening, and for loving me as I am, flaws and all. My appreciation and love to my family: Deanna, Brian, Toby, and Cheyenne Trout; Kupe, Brenda, and Ty Kuper; Jackie Kuper; Chuck and Susan Smith; Gary and Roberta Davis; Rich and Pam Kuper. Grandma and Grandpa Davis, if you were here, I hope you'd say I "done good."

Fletcher and Sullivan, your hearts and humor inspire me daily. Thank you. Remember: Own who you are, make smart choices, and create your own reality. Also, never forget that you must fail before you succeed, and compassion does not equate weakness. I love you beyond words.

Chaz, through this journey into publication you've given me patience, grace, and time—all gifts in their own rights. Thank you for believing in me, soothing my soul, and standing by my side. This series wouldn't exist without you and your support. I love you more than I'm able to express.

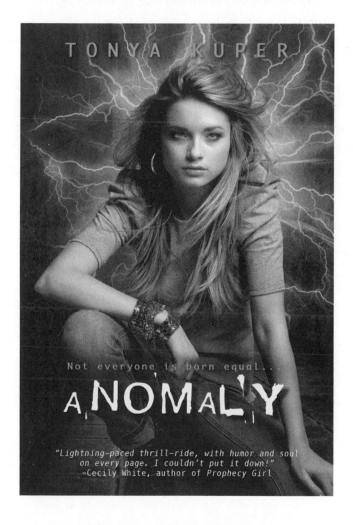

GRAB THE ENTANGLED TEEN RELEASES READERS ARE TALKING ABOUT!

VIOLET GRENADE
BY VICTORIA SCOTT

DOMINO (def.): A girl with blue hair and a demon in her mind.
CAIN (def.): A stone giant on the brink of exploding.
MADAM KARINA (def.): A woman who demands obedience.
WILSON (def.): The one who will destroy them all.

When Madam Karina discovers Domino in an alleyway, she offers her a position inside her home for entertainers in secluded West Texas. Left with few alternatives and an agenda of her own, Domino accepts. It isn't long before she is fighting her way up the ranks to gain the madam's approval. But after suffering weeks of bullying and unearthing the madam's secrets, Domino decides to leave. It'll be harder than she thinks, though, because the madam doesn't like to lose inventory. But then, Madam Karina doesn't know about the person living inside Domino's mind. Madam Karina doesn't know about Wilson.

Project Pandora
by Aden Polydoros

Olympus is rising…

Tyler hasn't been feeling like himself lately, his dreams are full of violence and death, and there are days where he can't remember where he's been.

Miles away, Shannon finds herself haunted by similar nightmares. She is afraid that she has done something terrible.

As the daughter of a state senator, Elizabeth has everything she could ever hope for. But when an uninvited guest interrupts a fundraising gala and stirs up painful memories, everything goes downhill fast.

Murder is what Hades is good at. So when two of his comrades go AWOL, he is rewarded with the most exhilarating hunt of his lifetime. For him, the game has just begun.

Omega
by Jus Accardo

One mistake can change everything. Ashlyn Calvert finds that out the hard way when a bad decision leads to the death of her best friend, Noah Anderson.

Only Noah isn't really gone. Thanks to his parents' company, the Infinity Division, there is a version of him skipping from one dimension to another, set on revenge for the death of his sister, Kori. When a chance encounter brings him face-to-face with Ash, he's determined to resist the magnetic pull he's felt for her time and time again. Because falling for Ash puts his mission — and their lives — in danger.

ALL THE STARS LEFT BEHIND
BY ASHLEY GRAHAM

Relocating to Arctic Norway would put a freeze on anyone's social life. For Leda Lindgren, with her crutches and a chip on her shoulder the size of her former Manhattan home, the frozen tundra is just as boring as it sounds. Until she meets her uncle's gorgeous employee.

Unfortunately, no matter how smoking hot the guy is, Roar comes with secrets as unnerving as his moving tattoos. And Leda doesn't trust him.

Roar shouldn't be drawn to the moody human girl with eyes that leave him weak in the knees. But when Leda gets shot by one of his enemies and survives, Roar finally understands why he's drawn to her: Leda is exactly what he was sent to Earth to find. A weapon of immense power capable of saving his planet.

She just doesn't know it yet.

TRUE NORTH
BY L.E. STERLING

Abandoned by her family in Plague-ridden Dominion City, eighteen-year-old Lucy Fox has no choice but to rely upon the kindness of the True Borns, a renegade group of genetically enhanced humans, to save her twin sister, Margot. But Nolan Storm, their mysterious leader, has his own agenda. When Storm backtracks on his promise to rescue Margot, Lucy takes her fate into her own hands and sets off for Russia with her True Born bodyguard and maybe-something-more, the lethal yet beautiful Jared Price. In Russia, there's been whispered rumors of Plague Cure.

While Lucy fights her magnetic attraction to Jared, anxious that his loyalty to Storm will hurt her chances of finding her sister, they quickly discover that not all is as it appears...and discovering the secrets contained in the Fox sisters' blood before they wind up dead is just the beginning.

As they say in Dominion, sometimes it's not you...it's your DNA.